WINTER KEPT US WARM

ALSO BY ANNE RAEFF

The Jungle Around Us: Stories
Clara Mondschein's Melancholia: A Novel

Anne Raeff

WINTER KEPT US WARM

a novel

COUNTERPOINT
BERKELEY, CALIFORNIA

WINTER KEPT US WARM

Library of Congress Cataloging-in-Publication Data
Names: Raeff, Anne, 1959– author.
Title: Winter kept us warm : a novel / Anne Raeff.
Description: Berkeley, CA : Counterpoint Press, [2017]
Identifiers: LCCN 2017035929 | ISBN 9781619028173
Subjects: LCSH: Domestic fiction.
Classification: LCC PS3618.A36 W56 2017 | DDC 813/.6—dc23
LC record available at https://lccn.loc.gov/2017035929

Jacket designed by Andy Allen
Book designed by Olenka Burgess

COUNTERPOINT
2560 Ninth Street, Suite 318
Berkeley, CA 94710
www.counterpointpress.com

Printed in the United States of America
Distributed by Publishers Group West

10 9 8 7 6 5 4 3 2 1

In memory of my father, Marc Raeff,
who showed me the strength of
kindness and reason

Winter kept us warm, covering
Earth in forgetful snow, feeding
A little life with dried tubers.

—T. S. ELIOT, from *The Waste Land*

I

The Arrival

THE JOURNEY FROM Rabat was not easy. On the long train ride Isaac stood in the crowded aisle outside the compartments, leaning his head out the window to save himself from the cigarette smoke. After the first stop, about thirty minutes in, a young man forcibly dragged him to a nearby compartment. "*Asseyez-vous, monsieur,*" the young man screamed, as if he were telling him to go to hell rather than trying to help him. Isaac explained about his asthma. He would die if he inhaled so much smoke in a closed-in compartment. He phrased it that way so his meaning would not be mistaken for politeness, but the young man had ignored him, pulling him into the compartment as he spoke, yelling at the other passengers to move over. *Make room for the old man*, Isaac imagined he was saying, and he laughed as he fell into the seat they had cleared for him.

As soon as he was seated, Isaac could feel his throat and lungs clamping up. His laughter turned into coughing. The man sitting next to him offered him water, but it was air he needed, so he gathered his strength, pulled himself up, and ran back to the corridor, to his space at the window. He reached for his inhaler, but he didn't need it. The sea air was enough.

After that, they left him alone.

The train stopped frequently and lingered at each station. He did not allow himself to look at his watch, knowing that would only make the journey seem longer. And then, finally, they were in Meknes. One minute longer, he told himself as he stepped off the train, and he would have slumped to the floor right there in the aisle.

At the station in Meknes, he engaged a taxi. The driver asked him whether he had a reservation. "The Hotel Atlas is always full," he said.

"There will be room," Isaac assured him.

"But you do not have a reservation," the driver insisted.

Why, Isaac thought, had he not simply said that he had a reservation? Why had he never learned to lie even when it made things easier?

The taxi smelled of smoke, though the driver wasn't smoking. Still, Isaac rolled the window down just in case. This upset the driver, who explained that the air-conditioning was on, despite the fact that it was hotter in the cab than outside, where, Isaac was sure, it was already near one hundred degrees.

"Ah," Isaac said, making sure there was not even a hint of sarcasm in his tone. The last thing he wanted was an argument with a taxi driver.

His parents had been in a taxi accident in New York shortly after arriving in the United States from France in 1942, where they had been living in exile. His parents and the driver had been arguing, the driver insisting that the West Side Highway was faster, but his parents wanted him to take Amsterdam Avenue. "The lights on Amsterdam are timed," they explained.

"I know, I know. Do you think I'm some kind of idiot?" the taxi driver said, turning around to face Isaac's parents and losing control, driving into the divider. Somehow none of them had been seriously injured, but after that, Isaac's parents lost their interest in the outside world. They retreated to the Russian classics and the safety of their dark apartment. Sometimes Isaac caught them speaking Yiddish, which he had never heard them speak before, though as soon as he walked into the room, they reverted quickly to Russian.

After the accident, Isaac's parents rarely went out, and they never got into a car again or left the city, not even to visit their oldest friends in Connecticut. His parents, who had not allowed themselves to be vanquished by Stalin or Hitler, had, in the end, been defeated by an ornery taxi driver. It was as if their brush with death had given them the license to admit defeat, to accept that their exile was now permanent.

But Isaac had been happy to be in New York, far from the old battles of Europe. Still, he had planned to enlist in the army as soon as his parents were settled. He wanted to be part of the fight against fascism. Though he was not particularly optimistic about the world's future, or even sure that war was the best solution, now that it was on, he wanted to do something. But then his parents had been so shaken by the accident, so derailed, that he did not feel he could leave them. He knew it was just a matter of time until he was drafted, so he relaxed for the first time since the war began. He got a job at Florsheim's, fetching shoes from the storeroom for the salesmen, and when he was not working, he explored the city.

His favorite activity was walking from their apartment on 106th Street to Brooklyn, across the Brooklyn Bridge. Once, before he gave up on trying to get his parents to embrace their new home, he took them to see the bridge. His father was an engineer, a builder of bridges. Perhaps, Isaac thought, standing in the wind, looking up at the sky, they would be comforted. They went to see the bridge on a Sunday in spring. His mother had thought there was something not quite right about walking on a bridge just for the sake of walking. "It is not a park," she said.

"No, it is not a park," Isaac had agreed. "But that is what is so wonderful. Only in America would people take a leisurely Sunday walk on a bridge."

"And why is that wonderful?" his mother asked.

But Isaac could not explain. His father walked slowly, his hands deep in his pockets. They walked from the Manhattan end to the Brooklyn end, and then they turned around and walked back. Isaac pointed out the elaborate spiderweb mesh of the cables and various buildings of the Manhattan skyline. Then the three of them took the subway back to their dark apartment on 106th Street.

"What did you think?" Isaac asked his father on their way home.

His father had shrugged. "It's just a bridge," he said.

But it was not just a bridge, Isaac thought. It was a bridge about which poems had been written, a bridge that made history. Perhaps he had never dreamed of changing the course of history, but he still wanted to be part of it, to see what would happen, to live. He opened the window wide, breathed in the dry, hot air of Meknes. The driver accelerated and turned on the radio, loud. "*C'est merveilleux, cette musique,*" Isaac said, but the driver did not respond.

When they arrived at the Hotel Atlas, the driver wanted to go in himself to make sure there was a room available.

"There will be a room," Isaac said again.

"But you don't have a reservation."

"How much do I owe you?" Isaac asked, opening the door as he spoke.

"Calm down, monsieur. There is no rush."

"I will pay you now or not at all," Isaac said, getting out of the car with his bag. He walked around to the driver's side, and the driver rolled the window down halfway.

"Here," Isaac said, holding out the money.

"As you like," the driver said, grabbing the money and speeding off.

Isaac approached the hotel. He took several deep puffs from the inhaler and concentrated on breathing, making sure that the air was flowing smoothly to his lungs so that he would not be gasping for breath as he stepped inside. That was not the entrance he had imagined.

She was at the reception desk. "Ulli," he said, and when he reached the desk, he was out of breath.

"Isaac," Ulli said. "Come, sit down." She led him to a sofa in the lobby. His breathing was deep and phlegmy.

"I'm fine," he insisted. "It sounds worse than it is. Asthma."

"It's back?"

"Yes, for about twelve years. It happened right after I retired, but the medications are much better now. I hardly notice it, really."

"It's good to see you, Isaac," she said, sitting down beside him and putting her hand on his shoulder, letting it rest there, asserting the gravity of the moment. "Welcome to the Hotel Atlas."

He smiled, remained very still. Her hand felt as if it were touching his skin directly. He wanted to reach up and take her hand, but that would have been too much. After all, he had just shown up, and she had had no time to prepare for his arrival. Yet she seemed calm. He realized then that he had hoped she would not be. Had he expected her to cry, to embrace him—not just lay her hand on his shoulder as if she were comforting him, though he had not asked her for comfort? But he had not come all this way to be angry. He smiled, and she smiled back.

"The girls?" Ulli asked.

"Simone and Juliet are well," he said without further elaboration.

"They are well," Ulli repeated. She took a deep breath and let go of Isaac's shoulder. "And to what, then, do I owe this honor?" she asked. He could still feel her hand on his shoulder, though he knew she had removed it. Like a phantom limb, he thought.

"It's been almost forty years. It's just too long," Isaac said, turning toward Ulli. "You look the same," he said, though this was neither true nor what he had wanted to say. She looked like Ulli, but she was old now. Her eyes were still that same husky blue, but they seemed as if they were covered with gauze. He wondered whether that was how the world looked to her now, as if she were seeing it through a fine curtain.

"Yes," she agreed. "It's been too long. Did you fly into Rabat?" she continued.

"Yes, and I took the train."

"I could have sent a car, you know," she said.

"But then it would not have been a surprise," Isaac said. "And anyway, I like trains, especially now that flying is so unpleasant. Even now, two years after nine-eleven, it's always code red."

"The first few months after the attacks, people just stopped coming to Morocco. I thought I might have to close the hotel, but I guess people can't live in fear forever, so now things are finally getting back to normal. Before the attacks, at this time of year I wouldn't have had a room for you."

"I'm sorry. I should have called, let you know I was coming. It was presumptuous of me to think there would be a room," Isaac said.

"Nonsense. We would have figured something out. But you must be tired, exhausted." She was in hospitality mode now, the hotelier, the keeper of clean rooms and comfortable beds.

"It would be nice to wash up."

"Let me take you to your room, then. You can shower, rest. Would you prefer a room facing the courtyard or the street?" Ulli said this all in one breath, as if she were afraid he would disappear, walk out, find another hotel before she could finish.

He wanted a room looking out onto the street, facing the morning sun. He wanted to watch people come and go. He wanted the sun to burst in through the window in the morning.

"In the morning the sun is encouraging. By the afternoon we wish we could shoot it out of the sky," Ulli said.

She showed Isaac to his quarters.

"I could never have imagined a more perfect room," he said, pulling the curtains aside.

"All the rooms are painted a different color—tangerine, light blue, ochre, watermelon, avocado, terra-cotta," she explained. "When you open the curtains and the sun floods in, it's quite impressive."

"The tile work is magnificent." He pointed at the rug. "And this is beautiful."

"It's a Berber rug. I don't know why they're not more appreciated in the rest of the world. Do you know that some of the fancy hotels here have wall-to-wall carpeting in the rooms? Anyone who prefers that to tiles and rugs shouldn't bother coming to Morocco."

"I've never liked fancy hotels—all those columns and fountains and obsequious staff. This is so much better."

"Thank you, Isaac," Ulli said.

"It must be a lot of work, running such an establishment," Isaac said.

"Yes, but it keeps me active. I have found in my dotage that I am not good at relaxing. Even when I first started the hotel, I pictured myself dozing off in my chair in the afternoon sun, but there is really no time for dozing here. There's always something to be done: windows to wash, floors to scrub, carrots to peel, figures to add. So I work just as hard as my employees. I know they find me a little odd. In Morocco, the boss doesn't clean toilets and iron. But I would rather make beds or scrub bathtubs than sip sugary tea and stare out at the street."

"I would make a good bellhop, you know. I could wear a fez. I always wanted to wear a fez."

Ulli laughed. "I thought you don't approve of obsequiousness."

"Does wearing a fez make one obsequious?" Isaac asked.

Ulli laughed again. "Come to think of it, you wouldn't look bad in a fez." She went to the window and pulled it wide open. "Come," she said. "If you lean way out, you can see a patch of the medieval wall."

"I see it," Isaac said. "Remember that time we ate snow from the windowsill?"

"With spoons," Ulli said.

"That was Leo's idea," Isaac said, regretting it immediately. He had not wanted to bring Leo up so soon, before she even had a chance to get used to his presence.

"Yes," Ulli said, pulling her head back into the room, but he kept his out for a few more moments, letting the hot, dry air fill his lungs.

The Medina

ISAAC LINGERED IN his room. He needed to catch his breath, steel himself for the next step. He took his time hanging his clothes in the closet, washing his hands, setting out his toiletries. He wanted to be prepared for their first real conversation. There would be tea waiting for him when he went downstairs. He would try to explain himself, why he had come. He took a shower. In the shower, he thought of climbing out the window, jumping to the street. Fleeing. How absurd. On the plane, he had not allowed himself to think of their meeting.

Ulli had not seemed disappointed to see him.

"Isaac," she had said. "Isaac," he said out loud in the shower. He emerged from his room invigorated and confident. "Isaac," he whispered as he descended the stairs, stepping slowly, as if he were a dignitary, a Latin American general with a sash of medals.

"Ah, monsieur." A middle-aged man with thick, graying hair and bad teeth approached him. "Madame would like you to wait in the dining room," he said, taking Isaac's arm and leading him across the lobby to the dining room. After a few moments Ulli appeared, carrying a plateful of oranges. "I thought you would like something fresh," she said. She sat down, took up a knife, and began to cut carefully; the peel came off in one piece. She separated the sections, arranging them on the plate. "Take some, please."

Isaac put a section of the orange into his mouth. Only when the orange had burst open did he realize how thirsty he was. He took another piece and another. "Aren't you going to have any?" he asked.

"They are not good for my stomach," Ulli said.

"But I cannot possibly eat six oranges myself."

"Of course you can't." Ulli laughed. "But it would not be hospitable to offer only one orange."

"But six?"

"I will not be offended if you do not eat them all," Ulli said, smiling. Isaac ended up eating three oranges.

"In some strange way, I don't think I was surprised to see you," Ulli said.

"Don't tell me you have turned into a psychic," Isaac said.

"You know I have no use for such things," Ulli said, and they left it at that. They were good at that, at leaving things.

"I thought the air here would do me good. The humidity is hard for me," he said, knowing how ridiculous this sounded, for his decision to come had nothing to do with something as mundane as the climate. But he had to ease into things, give Ulli a chance to get used to his presence.

"The mountains are nearby, and so is the ancient site of Volubilis," she said, following his lead. "I have not been on an excursion for a while. Perhaps we could go."

"I would like that, but don't feel you have to entertain me."

"Of course not," Ulli said, squeezing his hand. Had it really been almost forty years since he'd seen her?

"And now you must excuse me. I have to attend to my duties," Ulli said.

"Can I help?" Isaac asked.

"Absolutely not. You are my guest."

"Then I will explore the medina," he said, for wasn't exploring what one did when one arrived in a new place?

"I will ask Abdoul to accompany you."

"Thank you, but I prefer to be on my own," he said, resting his hand briefly on her arm.

"You are not too tired?"

"No, Ulli, I am not too tired."

"You must take a card, then, in case you get lost, though you can't, really. Eventually, no matter which direction you take, you will find your way out of the medina. And when you do, it will be like emerging from the Middle Ages."

"And what if I just keep retracing my steps, only to find myself on the same street?" he asked.

"You have to have faith, Isaac."

"Since when have you had faith?" he asked.

"Only in this. We are all allowed our occasional irrationalities, don't you think?"

"I suppose," Isaac said.

"The merchants can be quite aggressive, but it's all an act, part of the charm," she continued. "You cannot get angry. You must laugh or pretend that you're hard of hearing. Or you can speak to them in Russian. That usually keeps them at a distance. I have found Russian to be very useful in that way."

A young couple, looking as if they had not bathed in a while and were exhausted by the heat, entered the lobby and walked tentatively in the direction of the reception desk, so tentatively, Isaac thought, that if Ulli had not quickly moved to the desk, they would have turned around and walked out.

"Thank you," he called to her, waving as he headed for the door, and she smiled, a smile both for him and for the couple, who had set down their backpacks and were taking out their passports.

Of course, she needs time, Isaac thought as he pushed open the door into the afternoon sun. What had he expected? For her to drop everything just for him? A hotel did not run itself. And he was perfectly capable of exploring on his own.

When Isaac was a child, he had wanted more than anything to visit Egypt. When Simone and Juliet were young, he thought of taking them to Europe, but he had wanted to put Europe behind him and he liked the efficiency of American highways and motel rooms in the middle of nowhere. It was important for the girls to know their own country before setting forth to explore the world, he told himself, so every summer they traveled up and down the East Coast, visiting national monuments and parks and Civil War battlefields. He could have taken them somewhere far away, but as an adult, he no longer felt the pull of exotic places. His trips to the Soviet Union were enough.

The sun burned his scalp through his thin hair. He wended his way past men younger than he but more bent, weighed down by woolen djellabas and hoods, shuffling in backless slippers. He felt young among them, lifting his feet up, standing straight, breathing in dust and summer smells—garbage and exhaust. He supposed he would have to eat eventually, but for now he liked feeling hungry. The hunger and the heat combined to make him light-headed, as if he were slightly drugged. Noises seemed to come from a distance: car horns, hawkers, music, steps.

Isaac laughed as he walked in the early-afternoon heat, thinking that it had taken him his entire life, more than eighty years, to get even this close to Egypt. Perhaps this was close enough, even though there were no pyramids here, and they had always been the attraction, that and the ostrich egg. If he had the ostrich egg still, he would have buried it here in Morocco, out in the desert maybe, because he would not get to Egypt. One must be realistic. But he did not have it, had not even thought about it since his daughters were young and he had told them about it, about how his father had brought the egg back from Egypt, where he had been building a bridge.

Isaac was ten years old when his father returned with the ostrich egg. It was before he understood that his father didn't actually build bridges, but merely designed them. At the time he still thought of his father as a real bridge builder, swinging high up over the water, strapped onto a girder or tightroping across a cable. Isaac had wanted to be like his father, and he dreamed about building a bridge across the Atlantic Ocean. He imagined ostriches running round and round the pyramids, with men in white robes and long beards running after them, trying to catch them.

He brought the egg to school and showed it to his class. "This is an ostrich egg from Egypt," he said, holding it up in the palms of his hands for the class to see.

"There are no ostriches in Egypt," his teacher said, and the class laughed, but he just smiled, thinking they were stupid and knew nothing about the world because they didn't have fathers who went to Egypt to build bridges. He did not try to argue with them; he already knew there were some things one could not argue about. So he put the egg back into its blue velvet bag and returned to his seat.

At dinner that night he told his father what his teacher had said. "He is right," his father said. "I bought the egg from an African trader in the bazaar in Cairo. He was unusually tall, and he had a box of ostrich eggs. He wanted me to buy them all, but I told him I only had room for one. We haggled for almost an hour over the price," his father said proudly.

After that, the egg fell out of favor. Isaac moved it from its position of honor on his desk to a dresser drawer, but every few weeks or so, he checked on it, just to see that it was still intact, and slowly he realized that it was childish to blame the egg for not being Egyptian. Neither the egg nor the ostrich had done anything to mislead him, so he stopped being angry. When he was bored or having difficulty with math or an especially convoluted passage from Virgil, he would stroke the egg and talk to it in his head.

He was disappointed in his father, who had proudly announced upon his return that he had not bothered to see the pyramids, had built the bridge and then returned to Paris, glad to be done with *that country*. Isaac could not understand his father's lack of interest in one of civilization's greatest achievements, for he naturally favored the past, which seemed so much more tangible than the future that so interested his parents. "The past is only important because it is what creates the future" was one of his father's favorite phrases, and though Isaac never argued with his father, he disagreed with him about this.

While Isaac read about Spartans and Turks, Napoleon's victories and defeats, the Hapsburgs, the Moguls, Genghis Khan, and Catherine the Great, his parents and their small circle of Russian exiles—Mensheviks who were allowed to live in France as stateless, passportless refugees with no right to work—concentrated on the future. They stayed up until all hours of the night even when they were tired from working the menial, under-the-table jobs that they could find. They typed away furiously on crippled typewriters to keep alive the free Russian press and the "soft" revolutionary principles of the Menshevik cause—what they referred to as *the humane path to socialism*—to prove to the world that though they had fled from Stalin's madness (their deaths would have accomplished nothing), though they lived in dingy apartments in the outer arrondissements of Paris and were forced to build bridges in Egypt, they had not given up, would not give up until all the betrayers of socialism had fallen.

Yet Isaac did not take the ostrich egg with him when they left Europe. As he contemplated it for the last time in his room at the *pensão* in Lisbon, where they had spent eight long months waiting for the visas to America, he thought that bringing the egg would be a weakness on his part, a cowardly clinging to the past and to Europe, which had so obviously betrayed them. However, once he and the other refugees had all boarded the ship in Lisbon, he understood that the opposite was true: the ostrich egg was the one thing he should have taken with him, for it contained in its fragile shell more certainty than any future.

If they had been on an ordinary voyage, he might very well have walked right off the ship and returned to the *pensão* to save the ostrich egg. But he was certainly not the only one who had left behind the wrong things. On deck, after realizing his mistake, he had tried to calm himself by touching the soft leather of his shoes, which was a trick his mother had taught him on his first day of school. "Pretend your shoelace is untied and just let your fingers rest on the soft leather of your shoes. You will see. Everything will be all right." And although at the time he'd been skeptical about his mother's advice, he found himself trying it out that first day during recess while the other boys ran around the playground. He knelt down and found that his mother was right. On the day they left Europe, the leather felt dry and cold. He realized then that he should have destroyed the egg instead of leaving it exposed and naked on the *pensão's* rickety dressing table. There was a moment, brief, for that is what a moment is, when he almost decided to go back, not *for* it—they were too close to departure to even hope there was a possibility of retrieving the egg and bringing it safely back to the ship in time—but rather to return *to* the ostrich egg, to save it. It was then, after that brief moment of indecision, that he knew he would be a historian. He would not make the mistake his parents had made of trying to change history. He would stick with what was known.

At the mouth of the medina, Isaac hesitated, unsure whether he was strong enough to tackle the cramped chaos, the shrillness of commerce, but he could not turn back now, could not return to the hotel with nothing to report, with no accomplishments. He took a deep breath and plunged in. I will end up where I end up, he thought, letting himself sink into the shadows of the covered streets. He laughed and pushed onward. "I am in Morocco in the medina," he said out loud. "Imagine that."

He stopped at a nut stand and bought a bag of cashews, his favorite snack, and another of dried figs, which he devoured as he walked. He had not been that hungry in a long time, for since his retirement, he'd been in the habit of eating as soon as he detected the slightest presence of hunger. He stopped at a food stand and ate a kebab at a crude wooden table with several other men. He ate fast, as if he were in a hurry, as if he had to be back at his shop to meet an important customer. He was proud of himself for watching first to see how much the other men paid, surprised that no one approached him promising the most beautiful rugs in the world, the shiniest brass, the highest quality leather, as Ulli had said would happen.

Isaac continued on after his lunch, past shops that smelled of cheap, recently cured leather. He sensed vaguely that men were calling to him, but they did not pull at his sleeve or run after him. Then there were the tailor shops, each hardly large enough to hold the tailor and his scissors and threads. Isaac came to the section devoted to slippers, where the salesmen held them over their hands as if they were puppets or mittens. In every shop they sold the same kind of yellow slippers. He had never owned yellow shoes and thought it would be nice to buy a pair, but he had no idea how much he should pay for them.

Isaac knew about shoes and, though it was more than sixty years since his job at Florsheim's, he still felt at home in shoe stores. He loved the smell of shoe polish, and his shoe-shining kit was always well stocked with brushes and cloths and black, brown, and neutral polish. He wanted to ask the merchants whether they held the slippers to their noses when no one else was around, let the leather come alive so that the animal from which it was taken was reborn—just as Isaac had been reborn in New York when he was finally far away from danger and the old arguments of Europe.

Isaac picked up a pair of the yellow slippers without realizing what he was doing. He noted that the leather was not of a good quality. It was stiff and hard, smelled of curing. "Very beautiful, very strong, and very cheap," the merchant said, taking the slippers from him and clapping them together like cymbals.

"Yes," Isaac said. "I am just looking."

"Looking? Looking is no good. Sit down." He pushed Isaac onto a little stool and began removing his shoes.

"Thank you. I do not need slippers."

"Yes, yes," the merchant said, pushing them onto Isaac's feet. "Stand," he said. "You will see how comfortable."

Isaac took a few steps in the slippers.

"Perfect," the merchant said, though they were obviously too big. If he had been a serious salesman, he would have been able to tell by the way Isaac walked.

"Too small," Isaac said.

"No, perfect," the man insisted. A price was mentioned, and Isaac explained that he did not need them. Another price was mentioned, and again Isaac explained. Once more, he was pushed onto the stool, and the slippers were removed, wrapped in newspaper, and put into a pink plastic bag. "Eighty dirham," the merchant said. Isaac paid dutifully, put on his shoes, took the bag, thanked the slipper merchant, and left.

With the pink plastic bag, he was no longer invisible. The merchants who before had let him go by without a word, without even a nod, beckoned to him from their medieval stalls like prostitutes from murky corners. Not that he had ever been the type of man beckoned by prostitutes. Even when he was stationed in Germany after the war, when there were more prostitutes than teachers, he was usually spared their advances. There was something about his height and the determination of his steps, the way he always looked purposely ahead, that discouraged attempts to rope him in. That is not to say that he avoided prostitutes altogether. He had been a soldier, after all, but each time—how many times was it? Two, maybe three?—he regretted it, as he now did the poorly made yellow slippers. Copper pots, silk rugs, Berber knives, jewelry, European underwear, fine cloth, belts, goldfish, watches. What if I put my hands over my ears and scream? Isaac asked himself, but he dared not do it. He had a feeling they would laugh.

Instead, he put his hands in his pockets and trudged onward. The card Ulli had given him was there, sharp-edged and practical. He clutched it for reassurance, but he was determined not to use it. And so he kept walking, looking straight ahead, ignoring their calls, ignoring the tugging at his sleeve. At one point he felt a crowd gathering around him, but he kept walking, feeling the crowd move with him. He felt as if he were walking through waist-high water, through streets thick with floating garbage—plastic bags and bottles, pineapples, a mattress, newspaper—somewhere he had never been before. It weighed against his chest and flooded his lungs. He had never understood why so many people loved the smell of rain and talked about how it cleansed the air, how they could breathe more freely after it had fallen.

The crowd of merchants drew nearer, encircling him, pulling him this way and that, grabbing at his clothes, hammering him like a summer downpour. He counted slowly, following each breath. His doctor had taught him to do this. He said it was a form of meditation, but Isaac did not think of it as such. It was purely a method to keep breathing, to be conscious of the act of breathing. There was no other goal, no desire to clear the mind, to focus on peace or understanding or nothingness. It was all about breathing. Yet it was the thought of collapsing there in the medina and everyone coming to his aid—carrying him into one of the shops, opening his shirt, listening to his heart—more than the counting that kept him moving forward, kept his lungs sucking in the thick smells of cigarettes and cheap leather and male sweat. And then he found himself catapulted out of the covered lanes of the medina and into the shocking brightness of the plaza. He could feel his pupils contracting from the light, his lungs expanding. He did not dare to look back, but he knew they had not followed him. If they were laughing, it did not matter. He had made it to the safe zone. He had emerged, as Ulli had told him he would, from the Middle Ages.

Isaac arrived back at the Hotel Atlas tired but with no desire to rest. "Isaac," Ulli said, "look at you." And she was right. His shirt was drenched in sweat, his hair disheveled, his shoes covered with dust.

Isaac held up the slippers. "For you," he said.

Ulli opened the bag carefully. She held them up. "Thank you, Isaac," she said.

"They are not of good quality," he apologized.

"No," she said, "but I will wear them with pleasure."

He said he would take a shower, and then they would have a late lunch together in the garden. "Nothing heavy," Ulli promised. Before his retirement, Isaac had not been in the habit of eating lunch at all. He fortified himself with a good breakfast—yogurt, fruit, kasha, or a thick slice of bread—and then he was set for an uninterrupted day in the library or in class. Sometimes he would get light-headed from hunger by three or four, but he always knew it would pass, and then he could sail on until dinner at seven or eight.

He lingered under the hot water of the shower longer than he had planned. He had almost forgotten the pleasure of cleaning up after physical activity. He lay down on the bed. There was an almost imperceptible breeze passing through the room. He would not have noticed it if he had dried off. He did not want to keep Ulli waiting, but he was so tired that he did not have the strength to rise from the bed. He would rest for just a while. Ulli would not mind.

He was awakened by a knock at the door. Ulli's voice. He knew that he was awake, that she was knocking and calling to him, but he could not answer. He tried to get up, but his eyes were closing on him. When he awoke the next time, it was almost dark. Someone had covered him with a light cotton blanket. He was shivering. But it was so hot before in the market. He felt that there was someone in the room, someone sitting next to him on the bed, touching his forehead, his lips, or was that just his imagination?

The next time he awakened, he was alone. He was bothered, briefly, by a flickering light from a sign across the street. He heard people talking, the sound of water. For some reason he was worried about fire. If there's a fire, I won't be able to get up from the bed, he thought. He pondered going to the window to see how high up he was, to see whether jumping was a possibility, but the idea of placing his feet on the floor, of walking to the window, of parting the curtains made him weary. Before he fell asleep again, he wondered if this was what dying felt like.

For the past year or so, he had been worried about not waking up. His doctor told him that this was a fairly common fear for the elderly. His doctor often informed him that what he was feeling— aches in his limbs or itchy eyes or dizziness when he got up from his reading chair—was all "fairly common for the elderly." This did not comfort him. He did not like the term *the elderly*. He did not mind *elderly* as an adjective, but the noun, he felt, was patronizing. He did not tell his doctor any of this. His doctor did not think of language in this way. For him it was a tool, like the light he shined into his patients' eyes or his stethoscope. His doctor had insisted that it was not healthy to harp on the end of life—he never used the word *death*—but here Isaac was, despite the doctor's orders, thinking about it once again.

"It is not a topic I choose to think about," Isaac had explained to the doctor. "It is simply there, waiting for me when I have time to think, which is almost always. I feel as if I am back in my adolescence. There was a period from when I was maybe fourteen until seventeen or eighteen, until we left Europe, during which I would lie awake at night getting myself worked into a state about my eventual nonexistence. One day, I would not know that I had existed or that I no longer existed. My consciousness would simply be deleted from the world."

"I don't think of it that way at all," the doctor told him. "I think of being reunited with the earth, and I feel at peace."

"But I did not come from the earth, so how can it be a reunion?" Isaac asked, and the doctor thought for a moment and then said, "It is a manner of speaking."

He wanted to tell Ulli about the doctor. He knew there was a phone by the bed. He could lift the phone and dial zero for the front desk, but he could not make his arm move. He tried. He grew angry with himself for not being able to pick up a phone. How feeble can one be? he thought. How ridiculous that Ulli must be the one to find me.

Sunstroke

ULLI FELT RESPONSIBLE for Isaac's sunstroke, for letting him go out by himself at the hottest time of the day, especially after such a long and tiring journey. She knew all too well how grueling that train ride was. When she first came to Morocco, before she bought the old Mercedes, she often had to travel to Rabat by train—always with a bagful of cash to pay the hefty bribes to ensure that the necessary paperwork for the hotel was processed and submitted to the proper officials. She should have gone with him to the medina. She had her trusted staff to handle things while she was gone, but she was not ready yet to have him so near. Isaac didn't seem frail. He did not have the stoop of an old man. He was old, of course, as she was, his reddish hair gone thin and gray, yet he stood as he always had—tall, still tall. She did not easily admit to the limitations of age. The older she got, the closer to death (for that was what getting old meant, and tiptoeing around it certainly wouldn't make it come any more slowly), the more she felt like an adolescent. Though it seemed irrational, she could feel, all in the same moment, a tremendous impatience to get things done, along with a conviction that she still had all the time in the world to do them.

Isaac was certainly not the first guest to have succumbed to the powers of the sun. Every summer, despite her warnings, there was at least one. She had learned that a doctor was not necessary, that plenty of fluids and rest were all that was required, which was how she handled Isaac. She stayed by his bed, made sure that he drank water whenever he awoke, kept his face cool with a washcloth soaked in ice water.

But why had he come? Her first thought when he walked through the door was, of course, that something had happened to the girls. As he said their names, her heart had feared the worst, her palms had begun to sweat. Yet what right did she have to worry about their well-being? None. She had a right only to the familiar sadness that surfaced when she thought of them, when a memory of them made its way into her consciousness while she was scrubbing the floor or making beds, or if she paused for a moment while doing the bookkeeping. Lately she had been picturing them at the window of her apartment in New York, not standing against the pane, but keeping back, as if they were afraid the glass would not keep them from falling. She did not try to stop these memories, for she learned that it was best to give them free rein. Otherwise, they became like an oppressed people, inclined to rebellion, and then she was confronted with an army of thoughts that came at her with rocks and placards.

Keeping vigil in the chair next to Isaac's bed, watching him sleep, listening to the distant wheezing in his chest, she imagined him sitting with the girls when they were sick, reading their favorite stories, taking their temperatures, shaking the thermometer down and placing it carefully underneath the tongue. She didn't remember having done this for the girls, didn't remember them ever being sick, though surely they had been. She imagined that the nanny—what was her name, something with a *D*, something Irish—had cared for them when they were sick.

But she would watch over Isaac now, sit with him until the fever broke. That was something she could do, finally. Perhaps she would even sing a song, something cooling to combat this heat. Schubert would be nice, the one about the trout in the stream. She had loved the song as a child, but then Hermann had ruined it. How could she have forgotten that she had tried singing it for Hermann as she sat at his side while he lay on the bed in the Hotel Vienna, refusing to open his eyes or to let her touch even a wisp of his hair. "What a stupid, frivolous song," he had said. This was the first man she had chosen.

She knew Hermann first as Herr Meyer, her mathematics teacher in her last year at the *Realschule*. All the girls were taken with him, smitten even, but Ulli thought she had a more mature appreciation of him. He was not like the other teachers. He did not have his students keep their notebooks neat or much care if they kept notebooks at all, though of course they did. Herr Meyer put up with their need to copy what he had written on the board as he talked them through the problems, speaking quickly, writing just as fast. "Wait," they would call, "not yet," and he would stand by patiently, waiting until they told him it was okay to erase the solutions and begin again with a new set of problems.

In Herr Meyer's class they engaged in what he referred to as speed mathematics, and it was a rare event when someone else in the class beat her to a solution. "Faster, faster," Herr Meyer would call out, holding a stopwatch high above his head, running, despite his pronounced limp (he had lost his leg in the last war) from one student to the other. "Too slow, way too slow."

But there were times, perhaps once a week, when Herr Meyer became the opposite. On these days he would stare at the board, chalk in hand, as if he had forgotten why he was there, and then suddenly he would jump to attention and say, "Let us take a look at question six." The strange thing was that the students did not take advantage of his disorientation. They did not giggle or throw papers or talk among themselves. At the time, Ulli believed it was out of respect, like an orchestra waiting for a conductor to raise his baton; later she understood it was out of discomfort.

Ulli's involvement with Herr Meyer began in October 1937, when she was seventeen. It started off innocently enough. He invited her and a few others to meet with him twice a week after school for lessons in what he referred to as "the beauty of math." She looked forward to these sessions and to working out the problems he gave them, which often took her past midnight to complete. After one such occasion Herr Meyer asked, as they were walking out together, "How about a coffee?" Ulli agreed, and they talked, he more than she, about their childhoods, their aspirations. "When I was young, I wanted to be a poet," he said. "I had the usual romantic notions about the life of poets, but then the war came, and when I returned, I found comfort in the reliability of numbers." That was the only time he ever spoke to her about the war.

They did not talk in private again for a week. In class she continued to be attentive and diligent. They met again by accident; later it became clear to her that it had not been an accident at all. She was in the habit of stopping by a used bookstore on her way home from school, for she had always maintained an interest in reading, and it was here where she ran into Hermann. She should have realized that it was unusual for him to be there so soon after the end of the school day.

"Hello," she said.

"It's a wonderful store, isn't it?" he asked.

"Yes," Ulli said.

He reached over and took the book she was holding, pulling on it gently. "Sophocles—a good choice," he said, flipping through the pages. "The Greeks will never disappoint you."

"No," she said, hoping that she would be like the Greeks, that she would also not disappoint him.

"Perhaps you would like to join me for another cup of coffee?" he asked.

Ulli accepted. The café was crowded, but they found a table in the back. Hermann offered her a cigarette, her first. She took to smoking easily, following his lead, letting the smoke waft slowly out of her mouth, feeling the taste coat her teeth and gums.

Ulli was not a girl particularly interested in romance, and she had not, up to that point, felt anything close to desire. She did not fawn over movie stars or write about boys in her diary. In fact, she did not keep a diary. She found that writing down the events of her life only made her feel bored and ordinary. Yet she knew what was going to happen with Hermann, and she longed for it, felt it in her stomach and her limbs, felt him pulling her away from ordinary life into one full of passion and the beauty of advanced math.

"Will I see you here tomorrow after school?" Hermann asked as they were leaving the café.

"Yes," she said.

The next day, she arrived before he did, so she stood outside in the sun. It was a beautiful day, warm and balmy, and she did not mind waiting. It did not occur to her that he might not show up. He appeared soon enough, walking briskly toward her despite his limp. "I'm sorry," he said.

"I was enjoying the sun," Ulli replied.

Every day for a week, it was like this. She waited, he arrived a little bit late, and she said she was enjoying the sun. Their visits lasted one hour. She had not been aware that there was a time limit until Hermann apologized to her about it on the third or fourth day. "I wish we could spend more than an hour together," he said sadly, looking at his watch, "but I must go. I do not want my wife to worry."

Of course, she knew he was married. They knew such things about their teachers. She wondered now whether he had said it in a last effort to stop himself from doing what he was going to do, whether he thought the mention of his wife would send Ulli running, but it was too late for that.

They arranged to meet at the end of the week at the Hotel Vienna. Ulli put on her most fashionable clothes to meet him there at four o'clock sharp. Her hands were shaking when she presented herself to the desk clerk, as Hermann had instructed her to do, and the desk clerk handed her the key to the room. She did not think, as she took the key, that she was about to commit adultery, that this was her teacher whom she liked and respected and that he had a wife who loved him.

The hotel still had an open elevator that rattled its way up and down the floors without stopping, so that one had to jump on at just the right moment. As a child, Ulli had loved these elevators and would annoy her mother by waiting until the elevator passed the floor before jumping on. On that day, however, she boarded when the elevator was perfectly aligned with the lobby floor. When she arrived at room nineteen, she knocked before unlocking the door. Hermann rose to greet her and led her to the table near the window, where a bottle of brandy and two glasses were already filled. He made a toast. "To you," he said.

He instructed her to go into the bathroom until he called for her. She stood in the bathroom, waiting so long that she grew tired and was about to sit on the edge of the bathtub, when she heard his voice. "You can come now," he said.

She emerged slowly, focusing on keeping her balance, as if she were walking on ice rather than carpet.

"Don't be afraid," he said.

"I'm not," she said, looking right at Hermann, at his nakedness, at the shiny roundness of his stump leg.

He began to instruct her. His voice came to her as if from a great distance, and she followed as if hypnotized. "Take off your clothes, slowly, slowly, put them on the chair, stop, turn around, stop, turn around again, yes, like that, come here now. Touch me, like this," he said, guiding her hands up and down the length of his hairless body, along the stump that was once his leg. "Slowly, gently," he said, and she felt that her hands were burning.

This was her first experience with the erotic.

"Am I hurting you?" she asked him.

"Why would you think such a thing?" he asked.

Hermann lay still on his back, passive, completely immobile, while he instructed her on how to move on top of him. She let herself sink into his flesh. Though he was not fat, there was a softness about him, especially in his belly and arms.

He sometimes said "faster" or "not so fast, slowly," and Ulli did exactly as she was told until she reached orgasm. Shortly afterward, she felt him shrinking inside her.

After that, they met twice a week, on Tuesdays and Thursdays, at the Hotel Vienna. They drank brandy. They made love, sometimes as they had done that first time, sometimes more like the way he taught math, fast, fast, fast, grabbing her, pushing her down on the bed. Afterward he would hold on to her very tightly and make her promise she would not leave him. "I need you," he would say, or "You have saved me." She did not ask what she had saved him from, for she understood that it was not that kind of saving.

In the beginning, he brought her gifts—a Montblanc fountain pen, chocolates. She always ate the chocolates on the way home. The other presents she kept hidden in the closet of her room.

Ulli and Hermann did not talk about grand things, such as the meaning of life or love and pain. They spoke about his work and how difficult it was for some students to understand the simplest mathematical concepts. Often they would prepare his lessons together or she would help him grade tests. After she graduated that spring from the *Realschule* and began working at her father's business, she amused him with tales from the world of commerce, which he scoffed at, though he enjoyed helping her practice her sales pitches. A great deal of their time, when they were not making love, was devoted to mathematics. Hermann gave Ulli difficult problems to solve and then lay naked on the bed, watching her think. He liked that she would not give up. Sometimes she had to take the problems home with her to work on. "The homework," they called it.

There was nothing extraordinary about the time they spent together, but perhaps that is precisely why it was extraordinary. They were simple together. At night before she fell asleep, Ulli would imagine him lying next to his sleeping wife but thinking of her, wishing he could come to her, and she half believed that he would, that one night she would hear pebbles hitting her window.

They continued on like this through the summer and into the next winter. By the summer, Hermann became melancholy. When Ulli asked him what was wrong, he shook his head. "I am just so very, very sad. But I would be dead if it were not for you." She believed that was true. Maybe their time together had kept him, however briefly, from falling into the abyss. Instead of making love, he asked her now only to touch him, to run her hands slowly up and down his body the way he liked it, to kiss him while he lay there softly weeping. It did not occur to her to refuse him or to ask anything in return. Later, Ulli would leave the hotel trembling.

Now he preferred the lights off, the curtains drawn. He wanted the room to be in a permanent state of dusk. "Dusk is the most beautiful time of day," he said. Often he would not even let Ulli take off her clothes. Touching him became a form of meditation, a cutting-off of the will, of the self. She felt neither desire nor disgust, neither fear nor pain.

One day when she arrived, he said that he had thought she would not come.

"Am I late?" Ulli asked, though she knew she was not.

"No. I just had a feeling," he said.

One night at home she took out the gifts Hermann had given her and lay with them on her bed. Eventually she started taking off all her clothes and imagining that he was there, writing on her body with the Montblanc fountain pen, but after a while she could no longer imagine the feel of the pen on her body, so she wrote on herself, drawing circles around her navel and breasts. The next day, she arrived at the hotel convinced that he would find all the carefully drawn swirls too beautiful to reject. She was so excited that she arrived early, which was not allowed, so she walked around the block until it was time.

As soon as she entered the room, she began undressing, slowly, the way he liked, taking time to fold every piece of clothing carefully. She was afraid that he would stop her, but he did not, and he did not look away. When she was completely naked, she traced the circles she had drawn with her fingers, beginning first on her stomach and then moving slowly to her breasts. But he only lay there, watching.

After the Montblanc circles, things got worse, and there were times when he said not one word to her. When she threatened to leave, he would repeat over and over in a monotone, "Please, please do not go."

"How can I help you?" Ulli asked. "Please, tell me."

"No one can help me," Hermann said. She held his hand and stroked his brow, and finally he fell asleep, and she sat at the edge of the bed counting his breaths just to have something to do.

Hermann knew that another war was imminent. "Can't you smell it—the rot, the sweat?" he asked over and over. She could. She could smell it on him, and she was afraid. This, what she had with Hermann, she realized, was not love. She wanted to feel, to run, to walk through the streets, to sing. She had mistaken Hermann's devotion to speed and pain for passion, but she was afraid of what would happen if she left him alone in the hotel room, lying on the bed, thinking of war. She could not, she felt, abandon him.

One Sunday, Hermann's wife came to her parents' door and left a note with their maid, Renate. The message was on a piece of stationery that had been folded and torn in half. Before Hermann, Ulli had been in the habit of doing her homework at the kitchen table while Renate finished the evening's tasks. When Ulli first started coming to work in the kitchen, Renate had tried to be quiet, setting the dishes down without letting them knock against each other, keeping the cutlery from clanging, but after a while she got used to having Ulli there with her, and often, when she finished her work, Renate made tea and they sat together at the table, Ulli working and Renate reading one of her women's magazines. Sometimes Renate would interrupt Ulli to show her a dress or shoes that she particularly liked, and once, Renate had shown Ulli a photograph of the boy from her village whom she loved. Georg was his name. In the photograph he was holding a lamb.

After reading the note, which read, *I must speak to you immediately. I am waiting across the street. If you look out the window, you will see me. Hannah Meyer*, Ulli was annoyed with Renate, rather than with herself, who had brought it on. She was sure that Renate had read the note and understood its implications, so after that day Ulli avoided Renate as much as possible, and Renate accepted Ulli's distance as easily as she had accepted her presence.

Ulli had folded and crumpled the note, clenched her fist around it, and went directly, without looking out the window, to meet Hermann's wife.

"I am Ulli Schlemmer," she said, holding out her hand.

Hermann's wife took her hand and produced a forced smile. "Hello," she said. She moved closer, looking her straight in the eye. She had tiny teeth, like those of a child, which made her look both young and old at the same time. She looked at Ulli for what seemed to be a long time, as if she were trying to memorize her features so that she could paint her face afterward. Ulli did not avert her eyes, but focused her gaze on the woman's lips and tiny teeth until Hermann's wife said softly, "He does not want to see you anymore."

"He would tell me himself if that were true," Ulli said calmly, though her heart was beating furiously. She felt both a terrible relief and all the old longing she had felt when she watched him racing around the classroom with the love of the infinite beauty of numbers.

"He will not be at the hotel on Tuesday," Hannah Meyer said. Ulli did not respond.

Hermann's wife put her hand on Ulli's arm gently, as if she were trying to comfort her. "You are just a child," she said.

After Ulli stopped seeing Hermann, her days were devoted to her father's typewriter business, which was booming as Germany geared up for war. At night, alone in her room, she cried, not because she missed Hermann, but because she did not miss him, and because she understood that what he had seen in her was not joy or strength or life, but weakness. She realized then that Hermann had chosen her because he thought she was like him, and it was this, this desire to prove him wrong, that gave her the strength to leave the Hotel Vienna behind.

Then the bombings began.

At first, while her parents and neighbors crouched trembling and silent in the bomb shelter, Ulli waited for the end, ready to confront the horrible death that awaited her. She believed that her lack of fear was a sign of strength, of bravery even, but with each attack it became more difficult to keep her fists unclenched, especially during that dreadful silence between explosions. She found that the more she gave in to her fear, the more Hermann receded into the background, and she understood then that she was afraid because she refused to give in, because, unlike Hermann, she wanted to live.

Now, all these years later, as she got up from her chair to leave Isaac, his fever finally broken, his breathing even and relaxed, she understood that though Hermann had tried to take her with him

into his despair, he had also saved her. For what if, instead of allowing herself to be pulled into Hermann's soft and unhappy arms, she
had been sucked into the fervor of the *Hitlerjugend*—the mountain
excursions with fresh air and milk and plenty of sun, the facile
camaraderie, the simple passions like hatred and pride and love of
country? If she had allowed herself so easily to fall into Hermann's
arms, would she not also have looked for passion in the mass hyste-
ria offered by National Socialism? Thus, in his strange way, had he
not saved her from the worst of it by keeping her bound to that hotel room, so far removed from the tragedy unfolding around them?
Yet he had pushed her back out into a world where the bombs were
falling and where, in 1945, the bombs would finally stop.

The Apartment

It was terrible, the winter of 1945. If she believed in God, Ulli would have had to believe that God felt they had not been punished enough, that Europe needed more battering, more misery for its uncountable sins. By the end of the war, after hundreds of air raids, almost half the residents of Berlin had abandoned the city, escaped to the countryside, but Ulli and her parents had stayed behind, partly because they had no relatives in the country and partly because the buildings on their block stayed standing to the end, though all around them was shattered glass and rubble heavy with snow. At night the bombed-out structures groaned like dying soldiers, and Ulli lay awake listening to beams and bricks breaking loose and falling. Otherwise, the nights were quiet, some would have said it was a deathly quiet—the bombed-out blocks, the snow, the hunched citizens in frayed coats clutching bags of potatoes and carrots, more snow—but it was this quiet, this absence of sirens and airplanes overhead, the absence of bombs falling, that saved Ulli from despair.

During the day, she walked for hours, from one end of the American Zone to another, avoiding human contact. On one of these walks Ulli found the apartment of a family who had disappeared. It was on a day when she felt that she could not spend another moment with her parents, sitting in their un-bombed home, talking about the future of their typewriter business, which to her seemed not like a future at all, but a return to the terror and drudgery of the past. On her previous walks around the city she had not been moved to wander into any buildings. Her whole purpose was to stay outside in the open, to breathe in the air. Interiors suffocated her. But she found herself climbing the worn wooden stairs, holding on to the banister, listening to her footsteps echoing in the stairway, pushing the door ajar, sitting down on the sofa, just sitting, waiting perhaps for someone to find her, to order her to leave. Outside, the day turned to dusk, the furniture to shadows. She grew hungry but could not bring herself to get up.

At some point she must have lain down, for that is how she found herself in the morning when the sun flooded the room with light, and since she was reluctant to leave the quiet of the apartment, she drew a bath and lowered her body into the hot water until it grew cold and she began to shiver. It was then that Ulli decided that she could not return to her parents' house, could not go on working at her father's typewriter business, even though there was no lack of opportunity there. "An army needs typewriters, and there will, whether we like it or not, always be armies," her father liked to remind her.

Ulli's father had been too old to serve in the war; by its end, he was over sixty. He had not done badly during the war, not well, not great, but he had managed to keep the business going. In fact, at the end, there were no typewriters left in the warehouse, though they had not all been sold. The Nazis had confiscated what was left, melted them down for the final effort. Ulli was the one who supervised the process, writing down all the serial numbers, as her father insisted, so there would be a record. Whether this was because her father expected to be reimbursed at some point, or whether he simply could not give up his meticulous business practices just because bombs were flying and the Soviet Army had reached their borders, she did not know.

Ever since she could remember, her future had been the business. She was her parents' only child, so her father began grooming her for the business from a very young age. When she was six, her father taught her how to type. He wanted her to have an appreciation for their product, to *master* it, was how he put it, almost as if it were a wild beast that had to be tamed. He had developed a special training method and never hired secretaries who already knew how to type. "Once you have gotten used to bad habits, it is difficult to break out of them," he said. Instead, he schooled his secretaries himself, and as a result, they were fast and accurate and graceful. "My pianists," he called them.

Every evening for an hour and on Sunday afternoons for two hours Ulli practiced, so that by age twelve she was a prodigy—one hundred and twenty words a minute without one mistake. Her fingers flew across the keyboard as quickly in French or English as they did in German. Her father was proud of her progress and often brought her to his office, where she showed off her peculiar form of acrobatics and was given sweets and kisses by her father's secretaries. Each time Ulli reached a new personal best, her father rewarded her with a special outing to the racetrack or the zoo or for a drive to the country. She liked going to the racetrack the best, liked the sound of the horses' hooves and the way she could feel people holding their breath, clenching their fists, their hearts beating.

Her father never gambled, but he taught her how to concentrate on one person in the stands, how to watch and let herself feel as if she were that person, feel his joy when he won, his disappointment when he lost. "That way you can have fun without risking anything," he said, and she believed this was possible, because he was her father and because she was still too young to understand that nothing was possible without risk. After a day at the races, her father always took her to dinner at one of his favorite restaurants, where he ordered champagne and let her have a whole glass for herself. During dinner they would go over the day's races, counting up the money they would have won or lost had they bet.

Sometimes one of the secretaries accompanied them on these outings. It was rarely the same secretary, but each one went out of her way to please Ulli, bringing her chocolates and telling her that she was "such a pretty girl." Once, Ulli said that she would rather be smart than pretty, which caused that particular secretary to burst into laughter, as if this were the most absurd desire one could possibly have. Of course, all the secretaries were pretty, and they were all excellent typists, though by the time Ulli was an adolescent, none of them could type more quickly than she could. As far as she could tell, none of them was particularly smart, which didn't seem to bother her father. Perhaps he was simply looking for some lightheartedness to relieve him of her mother's somber presence.

Ulli's mother was much younger than her father. She was British, from a dreary town in northern England, and had met Ulli's father when he was working in London for some kind of shipping company. The family had visited her hometown only once. Ulli's grandparents lived above the dress shop they owned. The apartment was damp and cold even in April, the time of their visit. They went to church on Easter Sunday, and Ulli's grandfather came home drunk late that night. In the morning he didn't get up to open the dress shop, and her grandmother was crying, and Ulli's mother held her hand and her father shook his head. On this visit, her grandparents paid Ulli little attention. She only remembered her grandmother asking whether she liked school. She answered in the affirmative because she could sense that her grandmother was not interested in Ulli's true feelings about the matter. At one point, when they were in the middle of dinner and Ulli asked politely for the salt, her grandmother said that she was very sweet, which made her start crying because she had no aspirations to be sweet. On the contrary, she dreamed of flying across the Atlantic like Amelia Earhart or being a leader of men like Joan of Arc.

"What's wrong, dear?" her grandmother asked, making matters worse, but Ulli had known that it was useless to try to explain why she was crying to someone who thought that sweetness was a desirable quality, so she simply stopped. "There, there," her grandmother said, reaching over and tapping her stiffly on the back, completely unaware that she had been the cause of the tears. "Children are such mysteries," she said sadly, and Ulli wanted to tell her that adults were the strange ones, the ones who equated politeness with kindness, but she knew her grandmother would not understand. Her grandfather was even more aloof. When she looked in his direction, he turned away, as if he believed that by doing so, he would become invisible. Perhaps he did this with everyone, but she was too young to make a study of him.

In 1944 Ulli's maternal grandparents were killed by German

bombs. Upon receiving the telegram, her mother cried for five or ten minutes and then stopped abruptly, dried her eyes, and announced that she was going to take a walk. During the ten minutes that she was crying, Ulli tried to put herself in her mother's shoes, concentrated on feeling her sadness the way her father had taught her to do with people at the races, but it didn't work. Her mother finally returned soon after nightfall with a bag of oranges. Ulli had not seen oranges for months. Where her mother got them, she did not say, and Ulli did not ask. Her mother began setting the table with the white lace tablecloth and the good silver. She arranged the oranges carefully on her best Delft platter. They ate them all—three each—savoring every bite, not speaking. With her mother there were never many words, and Ulli never quite knew how to be with her.

They did have their times together. Sometimes in the evenings after dinner her mother would ask Ulli to read to her. "What would you like me to read?" Ulli would ask, and her mother always said it did not matter, that she felt like listening to Ulli's voice; that was all. Ulli did not know whether her mother even listened to the stories she read from her favorite books, her mother never commented on them, but when Ulli looked up every once in a while to see whether she was paying attention, her mother was always looking right at her, sitting forward a little bit on her chair.

One time when Ulli and her mother were in the middle of ironing, her father swooped in and announced that he was taking Ulli to a concert. She had never been to a concert, so she was excited. She had to get dressed immediately or they would be late, and she ran to her room to do so, abandoning her mother and the ironing. It was only once the lights were dimmed and the concert started that Ulli thought of her mother standing at her ironing board, alone, but she forced the image out of her mind and concentrated on the bows moving up and down, convincing herself that her mother had no interest in going to concerts.

Perhaps she remembered this so vividly, remembered the music—it was Mozart, one of the later symphonies—because this might have been the first time she was aware enough to rationalize, to reinvent the story, create her own version of what in fact was happening, for isn't that what so much of memory, so much of life, is—reinventing a more palatable version of one's own actions? Ulli suspected that her parents didn't know how much she struggled to balance their affections, to make sure that she divided herself equally. She never held it against them.

Ulli was sure that her mother knew about the secretaries, but she did not seem to mind being left at home, or perhaps this was Ulli's hope, her version of what her mother was feeling. She supposed her mother preferred not to know the details. On the rare occasion when her father joined them for dinner, Ulli always felt that her mother was trying too hard to make pleasant conversation, so Ulli tried to entertain them both with stories about school and long summaries of the adventure books she loved to read. Sometimes Ulli talked so much that her father would have to remind her that the purpose of dinner was to eat.

Ulli did not know why her parents got married. There was not even a story about how they met. She liked to think that in the beginning there was something that drew them to each other, but all she knew about them as a couple was the fact of their being married and having her. It was only after Hermann that she understood how quickly passion could turn into unhappiness, but at least this realization gave her hope that her parents had once been happy together, that they could be this unhappy only because they missed something.

Despite the fact that she preferred silence to conversation, her mother insisted on English, and Ulli's father happily complied, as he was quite proud of his linguistic abilities. In fact, he was the one who schooled Ulli in the mysteries of English spelling and the fine points of its grammar and punctuation, even though he had tremendous difficulties with *r*, *th*, and *w*.

In those days English was not the lingua franca, yet it was, perhaps, the one thing that held their family together, not because they used the words to communicate, but because the words, the language, set them apart from everyone else. Children went out of their way to hide such things as the foreign origin of a parent, so Ulli looked upon her parents' decision to flaunt their difference with a certain degree of pride. On the rare occasions when they were in public together, her family would pretend they were wild characters and speak loudly in English about their various exploits. One of their favorite stories was that they were thieves who had just robbed an important jewelry store. Ulli and her father talked about where they would hide the goods and what they would do in Argentina following their successful escape. Even her mother found this amusing and would add embellishments to the story. Of course, after the National Socialists came to power, they no longer amused themselves in this way. In fact, they did not speak English again until the Americans arrived at the end of the war and English became a tool that helped them survive in the world rather than retreat from it.

When Ulli found the apartment, she informed her parents that she would be moving. They were surprised, though they should not have been, especially her mother. She supposed her parents believed that the worst was over, and perhaps it was.

"We're together now," her father said, even when it was clear that she had made up her mind. She knew he would miss her, but perhaps he was also afraid that without her, he and her mother would no longer be able to live in the same house together, that all the silence between them would finally suffocate them. The strange thing was that the opposite happened. Though Ulli rarely saw her parents those first years after the war, it was obvious that something between them had changed. They sat next to each other on the couch instead of on opposite sides of the room. Every evening from eight to nine, unless the weather was extremely inclement, they walked, not arm in arm, not holding hands, but together, with determination. At some point her mother started working at the business with her father, not as a typist, but as a bookkeeper, for she had always preferred numbers to words. Perhaps they had become tired of being unhappy. Ulli hoped they found again what it was that brought them together in the first place, but perhaps they were only pretending—to themselves, to Ulli—because they did not want to burden her anymore with their unhappiness.

Thus, in an effort to keep her parents from worrying too much about her, Ulli told them two lies: that she had found a job as a clerk in a clothing store and that she was sharing a small place with one of her coworkers. It was time, she explained, to be on her own. "But this is entirely unnecessary," her father argued. "You have a job. What about the business?"

"I have no interest in typewriters," she told him. Afterward she felt bad for being so blunt, but it had seemed the only way to extricate herself.

He did not answer. He simply walked out of the room.

"What will he do without you? What will become of the business?" her mother asked, but Ulli didn't reply. Ulli kissed her mother on the forehead as if she were a child. She realized that this was the first time she had kissed her mother since the night the Russians came. Then she left. She did not take anything with her. The apartment had everything she needed.

In the beginning, she was always half waiting for the original tenants to return. For the first few weeks she disturbed as little as possible. She slept on the kitchen floor on a pallet made from extra blankets she had found in the closet. She used only one dish, one fork, one knife, one spoon, one cup. She emptied the ashtray after each cigarette. She dusted the family photographs—the father in uniform, the wedding portrait, the children. There were two boys who, judging from their toys, had a fondness for automobiles. She forced herself to believe that they had gotten out before the Russians arrived, that they were living happily in the countryside with a plump great-aunt, milking cows and churning butter.

But they did not return, and she was relieved.

She started rearranging things to suit her needs. She threw away their toothbrushes. She still slept on the floor in the kitchen next to the radiator, where it was warmest. She found that she liked sleeping on the floor. It made her feel as if she were accomplishing something, as if sleeping on the floor was making her strong, building up her endurance, or training her for a very difficult future. After a while, though, she began to use the previous occupants' things. She slept in their beds, ate at their table, and examined their photos. Ulli came to think of the apartment as her own.

The Meeting

Postwar Germany was rife with opportunities, and Ulli soon found her place in the postwar economy. She stumbled upon her new livelihood in a bar frequented by American soldiers and young German women who were looking for salvation in the arms of a homesick boy from Iowa or Alabama. When she first started going to these bars, she too believed in this possibility, and she often found herself waking up in an overly soft bed in a dingy hotel room next to a pimply boy with sour breath and a hangover who talked about his mother's cooking and cars. It took quite a few such encounters before she realized that it was safer—and more lucrative—to play Cyrano for the lonely soldiers and their hopeful German girlfriends than to play at love herself.

The business started out quite innocently. Because of Ulli's skill with English, soldiers solicited her help with the women they were interested in wooing. A soldier would ask her, for example, to tell a prospective candidate that she had a beautiful smile. The woman would laugh, he would buy her a drink, and she would ask him where he was from. At this point Ulli would ask him to tell her about his hometown, and she would tell the woman about the soldier's sisters and about what sports he had played in high school, and the woman would invariably want to know whether he had been to New York and whether he had seen the Empire State Building. In turn, the woman would tell him about the fresh cheese on her grandparents' farm, for so many of them had come from the countryside to seek their fortunes in the city. And before long they would be thanking her, the soldier pressing a few bills into Ulli's hands before stumbling out of the bar arm in arm with his date. Thus Ulli became well known for her services in a number of the bars the soldiers frequented. With the money she earned, she could buy everything she needed on the black market—real coffee, vodka, stockings. She slept until eleven or twelve and spent the afternoons wandering the city or reading.

It was in one of those bars that Ulli met Leo and Isaac. They were sitting at a table in a back corner, as far away from the dancing as one could get. She noticed them immediately because they paid no attention to the girls. They seemed to be talking about something important, leaning in toward each other, gesticulating. It was a slow night for Ulli, so she sat at her usual table, watching them. They were drinking quite heavily. Every so often Leo called the waitress over and ordered more drinks.

Isaac was tall and thin, yet he did not have the usual slouch that tall, thin people have. He sat straight, and Ulli could see that his fingers were long and thin too, like a pianist's, and when he leaned back in his chair, letting his arms fall to the side, his hands touched the floor. Leo was neither tall nor short, stocky but not fat. She noted his handsome, square face. His lips were thick, almost like a woman's yet not feminine at all.

They seemed so engaged in their conversation that she was taken off guard when the waitress brought her a drink and, pointing to their table, said, "Compliments of the soldiers."

She tried to refuse it. "Thank you," she said, "but I was just leaving."

"It's already paid for," the waitress told her, "so you might as well drink it."

"Thank you, but perhaps you would like it?" Ulli suggested.

"I'm not allowed to accept drinks from the customers," she said, leaving Ulli with the drink.

Instead of taking a sip, Ulli lit a cigarette and looked away from Leo and Isaac. Of course she could have put on her coat and gloves and hat and walked out the door. She was quite sure that neither of them would follow her. She felt, however, that this was a test, though she had no idea about what, so she did not leave, but she did not take a sip of the drink either. She tried to concentrate on the music and the dancers, who were, by this time, stumbling drunkenly around the dance floor. Finally, the stocky soldier stood up and approached her. He picked up the untouched drink and downed it in one gulp. "Thank you," he said, and returned to his seat.

She left soon afterward, giving herself just a few more minutes so it would not seem that she was running away from them. "Good night, madame," the soldiers called out as she made her way to the door, but she did not respond. Usually there were other people out when she went home, but it was a particularly cold night, so the streets were completely deserted. The trees were covered with ice, and the cold seemed to amplify the sound of her steps on the deserted street. She thought for a moment that she should be afraid of walking alone, but she did not feel any fear and was proud of herself for her adventurousness. If she had been the kind of person who whistled, she would have whistled, but instead she unbuttoned the top button of her coat. She did not want to feel constricted.

The next night, Ulli returned to the bar, but the two soldiers were not there. She spent the evening translating for a young man from New Jersey whose father owned a butcher shop where he was planning to work when he got out of the army. "We've got a classy clientele," he kept assuring his plump young girl. Ulli had read somewhere that Frank Sinatra was from New Jersey, so she told the girl that Frank Sinatra used to be their customer, and the girl smiled, saying she adored Frank Sinatra. The soldier was not at all puzzled by the fact that the conversation had suddenly turned from meat to Frank Sinatra, for he too was a great admirer.

Ulli never thought of her inaccuracies as lying but rather as embellishments, little flourishes she added, like the illuminated first letter in medieval manuscripts. She did it not because she wanted to trick the girls, but because she wanted them to find what they were looking for: a way out. Yet sometimes, if she sensed something particularly mean or annoying about one of the soldiers, Ulli would put words in his mouth that any woman, even the most naïve, would not be able to ignore. She told a very pretty and very young girl, whose father and brothers had been killed on the Russian front, that the young man from Indiana she adored had robbed a liquor store at gunpoint. He had been telling Ulli that he preferred a wife who did not understand what he was saying. He worried that she would learn English once they were in the United States, and then he would be at a disadvantage. Ulli asked him why, then, he had enlisted her services, and he said he wanted the girl to feel comfortable. "Women like to talk," he said, "but if I had it my way, we wouldn't say a thing. Then there would never be any disagreements." When the girl left him for another soldier, a fat redhead from Maine, he blamed Ulli. The man was brutish but not entirely stupid.

Interestingly enough, most of the soldiers did not engage Ulli's services. Perhaps, even though they did not put it into words, they too liked not having to talk. It made things simpler, more straight-forward. Ulli's clients were the romantic ones, she supposed, and she liked to think that the brides they took back with them to small towns across the United States were not disappointed when they were finally able to understand their husbands' words. She won-dered whether the woman with the boy whose family owned the butcher shop had ever figured out that Frank Sinatra had not been their customer and, if she had, whether it mattered. Perhaps they shared a laugh about it. Or perhaps there had been so many other letdowns by then that even Frank Sinatra seemed insignificant.

The next time Ulli saw Leo and Isaac, a few nights after their first encounter, they were sitting at the same table. Ulli mingled with the other customers, looking for someone in need of her skills. She never pushed herself on anyone, but if she noticed a couple try-ing to communicate, she would approach politely and explain what she could do to help. Ulli was standing at the bar when the tall sol-dier got up and made his way to her. "My friend and I would like to invite you to our table for a drink," he said, like a butler announcing the arrival of an important guest. He spoke perfect German.

"I'm sorry, but I'm waiting for someone," she replied. He bowed almost imperceptibly and retreated.

Ulli grew tired of standing at the bar, so she found a table. After about an hour the stocky soldier came to her table. "Are you still waiting?" he asked in English.

"Yes," she replied.

"For a client or for personal reasons?"

"It is none of your business," she said.

"True," he said, and sat down without asking for permission. "Cigar?" He took out two cigars from his breast pocket. "My friend can't stand the smell. He used to have asthma."

Ulli took the cigar and watched as he flicked open his lighter in that way men think is so gallant. She leaned toward the flame and breathed in. "Cigarette smoke doesn't bother him?" she asked.

"It bothers him, but cigars he can't tolerate at all." During this exchange Ulli was waiting for Isaac to turn around to see what kind of progress Leo was making, but he had taken out a book and was reading. She wondered how he could read a book in a noisy bar. Perhaps he was only pretending.

"You're a natural," Leo said.

"A natural what?" Ulli asked.

"A natural cigar smoker. Never trust a cigar smoker, you know."

"Why not?" she asked.

"Because they're not trustworthy. It's a known fact."

"Thank you for the advice," she said, which made him laugh. Every time he tried to speak, he would break out into laughter. Finally he said, "My name's Leo."

"Ulli," she said, extending her hand across the table.

"Isaac," he called to his friend. "Isaac, come over here and meet my friend Ulli."

Isaac waved and went back to his book.

"He's always got his nose in a book," Leo explained.

"There's nothing wrong with reading," Ulli said.

"I didn't say there was anything wrong with reading. I was just trying to explain his rudeness."

"Rudeness?"

"You don't think it's rude to sit there reading a book when I've very nicely asked him to make your acquaintance?"

"No."

That made him laugh again. "Would you like to take a walk?" he suggested.

"No, thank you," Ulli replied.

"Well. Then we'll just have to order another drink." He called the waitress over and ordered a round of drinks for them and for Isaac at the other table. "So," he continued, "tell me the truth. Who is this person you're waiting for?"

"I'm not waiting for anyone," Ulli answered.

"But you told Isaac you were waiting for someone."

"Yes, but I'm not. I just said I was in order to be rid of you."

"Well, I'm glad you told me."

"Why?"

"Because I like to know where I stand in situations like this."

"Situations like what?" Ulli asked.

"Complicated ones."

"I don't think this situation is at all complicated," Ulli answered. Now it was her turn to laugh.

"What's so funny?" he asked.

"The situation," she said, and they both laughed, but she didn't really know why she was laughing, only that she wanted to, that it had been a long time since she had done so.

"Excuse me a moment," he said, getting up and returning to the table where Isaac sat. They talked for a while, but Leo kept watching her out of the corner of his eye, as if doing so would keep her from leaving. Ulli had time to smoke a cigarette before he returned to her table with Isaac in tow.

He formally introduced them to each other, and Isaac and Ulli shook hands. Leo pulled his chair up next to Ulli's, and Isaac sat across from them.

"What were you reading?" Ulli asked Isaac.

"Oh, some kind of French poetry," Leo answered for him. "He takes that book everywhere he goes."

"You speak French too?" she asked.

"Yes," Isaac answered.

"I don't know why he needs the book," Leo said. "He knows all the poems by heart."

"Not all of them," Isaac said. "I don't have a photographic memory like you do. All he has to do is look at a page once, and it's in his head."

"I always thought there wasn't really such a thing as a photographic memory," Ulli said.

"Well, there is," Isaac said. "Show her."

"Now come on; it's not really so interesting. Why don't we all go for a walk? I'm getting tired of this place."

"But it is interesting. I'm sure she would be interested, wouldn't you?"

"Her name is Ulli, Isaac."

"I'm sorry. Of course. Ulli. You would be interested, wouldn't you, Ulli?"

"It's not necessary," she said, realizing only then that Isaac was drunk. He had seemed so quiet, so steady, sitting there reading his book, so she had attributed his awkwardness to his height, not to alcohol.

"Nothing is necessary, except for food and shelter," Isaac said.

"And love," Leo said, turning to Ulli. "Don't you think love is necessary?"

"Not in the same way as food and shelter," she replied. Isaac was looking away, watching the dancers.

"But necessary in some way, right?" Leo continued.

"Well," Isaac interrupted. "I thought we were going for a walk."

"Then let's go," Leo said, jumping up and grabbing Ulli's hand, whisking her toward the door. Isaac grabbed their coats and followed.

It had been snowing for quite some time and the snow was accumulating rapidly. Isaac walked ahead, his long legs making faster progress so that he had to stop every so often to let Leo and Ulli catch up. But as soon as they were at his side, off he would go again at his long-legged pace.

"He doesn't usually drink so much," Leo told her. "I'm the one who always ends up not remembering what happened the night before. If it weren't for him, half my life would be a total mystery to me."

"He seems angry with you," Ulli said.

"Angry?" Leo laughed.

"Why is that funny?" she asked.

"I don't know. It just is," he said.

At some point, Isaac started running. Ulli and Leo watched him take off at full speed, his unbuttoned army coat billowing behind him. He fell and picked himself up and started running again, only to fall a few steps later. "Stop!" Leo called after him, but Isaac kept running and falling, running and falling. "Let's just sleep out here," Isaac said. He lay in the snow, out of breath, his arms and legs spread out. He seemed thinner lying in the snow like that, a stick man in a child's painting, and Leo grabbed her hand and twirled her round and round, first in one direction, then the other so that she would not get dizzy and fall. Isaac began clapping faster and faster, so they spun faster and faster. Then they fell to the ground next to Isaac, and the three of them lay there looking up at the sky. "It's always warmer when it's snowing," Isaac said.

"If you fall asleep, you'll still freeze to death," Leo said.

"Like in the siege of Stalingrad," Isaac said. "That's what happened. After a while people couldn't stay awake. As long as you stay awake, you're okay."

Leo got up. "Well. I'm not taking any chances," he said. "Come." He held a hand out to each of them, and he pulled them up out of the snow. They ran then, holding each other up, ran as if something dangerous were following them, or as if they had someplace to go.

Ulli took them to her apartment. Until that night, she had never had a guest. For the first time, she used the living room. Their clothes were wet, and they were cold, so they made a fire and drank. The blue and green velvet sofas and armchairs and the heavy drapes and the dark wood molding that traced the ceiling frightened her, but with Isaac and Leo there, the room seemed almost cozy.

"Nice place," Leo said.

Ulli told them how she had found the apartment and how she waited for the rightful occupants to return, hoping selfishly that they would not.

"You hoped for their deaths, then," Isaac said softly, gently even, as if he were explaining something to a small child. There was nothing judgmental about his tone. He had simply established a fact.

"Yes," she said, for it was true.

"Must you always be so serious, Isaac?" Leo asked, refilling their glasses.

"Not always," Isaac said.

Leo lifted his glass. "To not being so serious, for God's sake," he said, and Isaac and Ulli lifted their glasses and drank, too.

They continued to drink. Leo demonstrated his photographic memory. He left the room with the prewar phone book and committed the first ten pages to memory. While Leo was in the kitchen memorizing the phone book, Isaac and Ulli waited in the living room. Isaac wanted to know where she had learned to speak English so well, and she told him about her mother and then about her father's business and how she had come to despise the relentless staccato clicking of typewriters.

"Actually, I love the sound of typewriters," Isaac said. "When I was stationed in Arizona, I sometimes stayed up all night typing. I would copy the newspaper from cover to cover just so I could hear the sound of the typewriter."

Leo burst in, telephone book in hand. He rattled off the names, insisting that they check every one, though after the first few pages they did not pay very close attention. When he was finished, Ulli and Isaac applauded and they all drank to Leo's photographic memory. Leo wanted to dance, so she turned on the radio and the two of them danced while Isaac watched. Then Isaac took over and Leo watched, but after one song, Leo took over again and the dancing turned intimate, and Isaac sat on the couch watching. Leo pulled her in closer, his arms thick around her, and he moved her toward the door. If Isaac had said something—"good night" or "where are you going?"—she would not have let herself be led to the bedroom, to the bed that was not her bed, but he was just watching, and she did not want someone who watched. She wanted someone who moved, and that was Leo.

The Desert at Night

LEO WOKE UP the next morning feeling stronger than he had felt for the past three months, since the end of the war. It wasn't until everyone was jumping for joy and starting to believe again in the future that the weakness had started. The doctors had told him that something was wrong with his heart, but he had gone through the whole war feeling the same as he always felt—as if there was nothing too heavy for him lift, no one who could pin him down. He felt strong enough for combat, although that, the doctors said, was out of the question. But then the war was over, and suddenly he couldn't sleep. He lay awake at night listening to the murmur in his heart; in the morning he was hardly able to rouse himself and get out of bed. But in Ulli's house that was not her house, in her bed that was not her bed, his heart seemed to be working like one without a murmur, a heart with a valve that would not slowly get more inflamed until one day it ceased to let blood flow through it, a heart that was not, as the doctors had put it, a time bomb. If it hadn't been for the war, he would have gone blithely along, not knowing about his condition until one day he dropped dead, which is what everyone does. He supposed he was no different from all the other young men who had been going along and then they were sent off to war and suddenly they were dead.

Perhaps if he had been in combat he would have allowed himself to be afraid of death, but sitting there in his office, at his goddamn desk job, typing and calculating and organizing files, he did not feel he had the right to worry about his heart, not when there were others lying in the mud facedown, blood pouring out of them, with no one there to help. So he continued on, and he reenlisted just to prove he could keep going. What else could he do? Go home? There was nothing for him there. The world was out there for him to discover. The world was so much more than Johnstown, Pennsylvania. Where was Ulli? That had not been a dream, for he could smell her on the sheets, and he turned over on his belly and breathed it in, the smell of slightly sour milk and, he thought, if salt had an odor, of salt. Now he could hear her voice and Isaac's in the next room. He could smell the coffee too, and it mixed with the smell of Ulli in the sheets and the sound of their voices and the new strength in his thighs that was almost like pain. He would finish this cigarette, and then he would rise and dress, splash some water on his face, and join them in the other room.

It was Isaac who had found her, noticed her in the bar where they sat drinking vodka: "She is not like the others." He had said it not as a compliment, but rather as an observation as one might say, *Look, there's a cardinal, the first one this spring.*

Isaac was right. She wasn't like the desperate women with sultry smiles glued to their faces and that awful clownish lipstick they thought was so alluring.

"She's not wearing lipstick," Isaac continued. "You know that Hitler hated lipstick, didn't allow anyone around him to wear it. The Aryan woman, he believed, is beautiful in her own right and doesn't need adornments."

And then they had had that ridiculous argument about whether she was a Nazi because she was not wearing lipstick, and Isaac had been surprised that Leo had gotten so bent out of shape and insisted on buying her a drink, which she did not touch, which Leo ended up drinking just to embarrass Isaac, who, of course, remained calm and unfazed despite Leo's theatrical gesture. Yet it was Isaac's idea to ask her to join them when they saw her a couple of days later. It was Isaac who said, "Look, there's the woman without lipstick. Should I invite her to join us for a drink?"

It wasn't just her lips that made her different. She was tall, almost as tall as Isaac, and she walked fast. Later, when they were walking back to her apartment in the snow, Leo noticed that he liked watching her walk. Her legs had a sense of purpose. He imagined her running like a horse through a field, her thigh muscles bulging, her belly taut. He thought now that watching her walk had made his own legs feel stronger, had brought them back to their normal selves. Later, in her room, when she'd wrapped her arms and legs around him, he was not sure he would be able to break loose, despite his renewed strength, despite this strange desire, but he hadn't wanted to break loose. He wanted to be there with Ulli.

What time was it—morning, still, or afternoon? Could it already be afternoon? Hard to tell with this weather, this endless gray, the snow, the dreariness of it all, just like Pennsylvania, where he could not return, not ever. But why—it occurred to him as he was just about to leap out of bed, for he felt that he could leap, that he *should* leap—why was Isaac still there? Why was he sitting at a table with Ulli, drinking coffee, as if he were Leo's goddamn conscience? He remembered now that Isaac had also danced with Ulli, and he had watched them waltzing around the living room, stumbling over the furniture but always catching each other before they fell, like Charlie Chaplin in *The Gold Rush*, dancing at the edge of the precipice. Yet now, remembering their dancing, listening to their voices in the other room, Leo felt no jealousy. On the contrary, all was calm. Was this, he thought, finally the beginning of peacetime?

He emerged from the bedroom. Ulli and Isaac looked up from the table. "Would you like some coffee?" Isaac asked, as if it were his apartment, his coffee, his cups and saucers.

"Sure," Leo said.

Isaac brought the coffee, and Ulli lit a cigarette.

"What have you two been talking about?" Leo asked.

"I have been teaching her Russian. She has an uncanny gift for pronunciation. Listen," Isaac said, and Ulli started counting, *adin, dva, tri, chetyre,* all the way to one hundred, and she would have kept on going, but Leo said, "Have you been up long enough to learn all those numbers?"

"She's a brilliant student," Isaac said.

"I guess it's the language to learn now that they are the new enemies," Leo said.

"Maybe someday we will live in a world without enemies," Ulli said, and Leo lifted his cup up in the air and proclaimed, "To a world without enemies, to peace." Ulli and Isaac raised their cups in the air and repeated, "To a world without enemies, to peace." And Leo laughed, not because he thought that peace was funny or improbable, but because he remembered at that moment how he and Ulli had laughed the night before about cigars. No, peace was a serious thing, as serious as war, though it never seemed to last for very long. Still, it was something to strive for, something to help them move out of the past and into the future.

Leo got up and placed his arms around them. This was a beginning, he thought, a new way to look at things. This was the future now, pulling them in closer, as if into the frame for a photo, though there was no photo, no one there to take it, no camera.

Leo had never left Pennsylvania before he enlisted, had hardly left Johnstown, where he was born, as were his parents and his grandparents and great-grandparents, who had lived through the Great Flood of 1889. In Johnstown, there was *before the Flood* and *after the Flood*. The Flood was like a war, and people spoke of those who died as of those who had fallen, though they had not fallen, but been swept away, which is what war does too—sweeps you up and takes you somewhere you have never been before.

When the war came, Leo was one of the first to enlist, not out of a sense of duty or patriotism or because he hated Hitler—for he did not know enough about Hitler to hate him—not because he dreamed of glory or because he had spent his childhood reading about adventures in faraway lands, but simply because he wanted to go where people were not afraid of water, where they didn't sit around waiting for the next time the waters got loose, which, they were all sure, despite the new engineering, despite the vows of politicians, was bound to happen. Even war, he thought, was more hopeful than Johnstown, for after a war things do not go back to exactly how they had been before.

When he enlisted, he had been ready for bullets and bombs,

or so he thought, but he would never find out how he would have acted in the real war, because the army doctors had discovered the murmur in his heart and declared him unfit for combat. Instead, he ended up in the prisoner of war camp in the desert, where there was not really any danger at all and way too much time to think about things he should not have been thinking about.

When he first met Isaac at the camp in Arizona, he thought that Isaac was like him, not like the boys in the locker room who jacked each other off for laughs and because it was so much more trouble to find a girl to do it. Perhaps Leo thought Isaac was like him because he had not known men like Isaac, men who read books and talked about history, men who liked poetry and art and did not talk about tits and cunts. Perhaps it was because Isaac was so thin that Leo confused his thinness with fragility. So Leo spoke to Isaac of things he had never said before, not about the boys in the locker room, not about the sad man in the bathroom at the bus station in Pittsburgh, but about Johnstown and its terrifying past, which hung over the future like death. Though Isaac's English was not quite right and he often lacked the specific words he needed, it was Isaac who put into words what Leo had been feeling—his fear of being swept away, carried off by the tide of history without ever taking part in it.

The world would be different after the war was over, Isaac was always saying, and Leo wanted that. When the war was over, he wasn't going to look back, wasn't going to go home to Johnstown. He was not going to live the way people had lived before. And because he thought that Isaac was like him, he was sure they could find their way together, and he let this belief grow and it became like music welling up inside his head.

Isaac, Leo realized, was the first man he had ever really liked, not loved, not desired, but just plain liked for his decency and intelligence, as a friend. In the beginning, when they were still getting to know each other, Leo tried to feel desire for Isaac, to imagine what it would be like to kiss him, to feel his flesh, but thinking of Isaac in that way made him feel even more alone than he felt when he thought of other men, men with hard stomachs and arms and thighs, men who played football and fought in wars. So Leo settled into having a friend, but he worried that Isaac would make a move, say something irrevocable that would make it impossible for them to be friends, that a proclamation or an attempted kiss would always be between them. But nothing like that happened because it turned out that Isaac was not like Leo.

Though Isaac and Leo had arrived at the camp in Arizona on the same day, they were assigned to different divisions and would probably not have met if it hadn't been for the Uzbeks. The Uzbeks, Bidor and his father, arrived with the first batch of Russians, many of them deserters who had followed Hitler's retreating army out of the Soviet Union. Some, however, were patriots, or so they claimed, though they were not patriotic enough to commit suicide—as the Red Army required them to do—rather than be taken prisoner by the Germans, which is what happened. So they all ended up—the Germans and their Russian prisoners, the Uzbeks—in Arizona. Swept away by history, swept away to safety across the Atlantic, where the Americans treated them well—ice cream every night for dessert, plenty of cigarettes, clean sheets, a warm blanket, a pool table, Ping-Pong, a library.

When the Uzbeks arrived, no one knew what they were, so Isaac, as the camp's chief interpreter, was called to get them settled in and to figure out where they came from. On their first meeting with Isaac, Bidor and his father sat very straight in their chairs in

Isaac's office, their hands flat on the table, as if they were not accustomed to chairs and tables. This, Isaac told Leo later, was his first clue. Isaac took the seat opposite them. He smiled and introduced himself to them in Russian. They looked at each other, but did not answer. He touched his chest and repeated his name. Then he pointed to them and, still in Russian, asked them their names. The younger man understood, and so Isaac learned their names. Then Bidor, the son, spoke the one Russian word he knew—*chai*. Isaac called for tea, which the orderly brought, and they drank it in a few gulps, and when they were finished, they nodded in appreciation. "You're welcome," Isaac said to them in Russian, and they nodded again. Then Isaac sang a song. It was a French song, something silly from his school days about a soldier going to war, and when he came to the end of the song, he held his hands out, palms up toward the Uzbeks, asking them to sing. They understood and sang a long song with many verses, but in them Isaac could feel the galloping of horses on the open steppe. He started naming cities— Tashkent, Samarkand, Kabul—and they smiled, though he did not know whether they smiled because they recognized the names or simply to be polite, but the older man started drawing with his index finger on the table. Isaac asked the orderly to bring paper and pencils, and the Uzbeks drew horses and mountains and a ship on the ocean and trains—many trains and many angry soldiers. In turn, Isaac drew himself on the deck of the ship that had taken him and his parents from Lisbon to New York. He drew New York and the river and all the tall buildings and trains too, trains moving slowly through the desert. They drew for hours, but Isaac still did not know exactly where the two men were from, though he was fairly sure they were Central Asian, which would have been enough information for the army. Still, Isaac was not satisfied.

After dismissing the Uzbeks, Isaac went to the Records Office, where Leo sat typing up the week's purchase orders. Isaac didn't quite barge into the office, because the door was open and no one was keeping him from entering, but he walked in with great determination, on a mission, it would seem, of great importance. "Yes?" Leo said, and Isaac walked right up to his desk, which is when Leo realized how tall he was: in order to look him in the eye, Leo had to tilt his head way back, as one does when sitting in the first row at a movie theater.

Isaac immediately started telling him about the two men, one older, one young, who weren't Russian and didn't know how to sit in chairs, and how he must find out where they were from because it was such a mystery—so interesting, didn't he think, that they had ended up so far away from wherever they were from.

"Hold on there a moment. Have a seat, have a cigarette," Leo said.

"I don't smoke," Isaac said, pulling up a chair and sitting down. "I have asthma. That's why I'm here and not over there."

"I've got something with my heart."

"Is it serious?" Isaac asked, looking Leo straight in the eyes, as if he were a doctor about to impart bad news.

"Yes, but I don't feel a thing."

"I haven't had an asthma attack since I've been here in the desert. I like the desert. Do you?"

"Yes," Leo said, though until that moment he had hardly given the desert any thought. It was out there. That was all. After Isaac had fully explained about the Uzbeks who were not Uzbeks yet, not to Leo and Isaac, and after they had gone through the names of the soldiers stationed at the camp in search of Turks and had found only Armenians, when Leo was lying on his cot smoking the last

cigarette of the night, he thought of Isaac standing in the desert in
the hot sun, just standing there looking around at nothing, and he
wanted to be there with him, not because he wanted to touch him,
but because he wanted to see what he saw.

The next morning, the Armenians were summoned to Leo's
office. One of them was originally from Istanbul. "When we left
Turkey, my father made a vow never to speak Turkish again," the
soldier said. Isaac explained that these men were not Turks but
Central Asians who had been on an epic trek. The Armenian
smiled scoffingly when Isaac said the word *trek*.

"And if I refuse to translate?" the Armenian said.

"You cannot refuse," Leo said. "It's an order."

Leo and Isaac went to the room where the Uzbeks were waiting, sitting stiffly at a table. The older man was wiry and small,
his black hair streaked with gray. He had green Asiatic eyes, his
skin thick and lined from exposure to the sun and the elements.
The younger man was solid, muscular, with wide shoulders and
large, veined hands. His face was as smooth as a child's, except
for a wispy mustache and beard. His eyes were the dark green of
forests.

They asked the Turkish Armenian to come into the room and
called again for tea. The Armenian did not want to drink tea. "Let's
just get down to business," he said, but Isaac told him that he had to
drink tea, so he did. They all drank in silence, and then Isaac told
the Armenian to start speaking to them in Turkish, which he did
in a rote sort of way, without using his hands. The Uzbeks seemed
to understand something, and the older man began to speak. He
spoke for a long time. The Armenian interrupted him often, and
finally the Armenian retold their story in the most perfunctory
way, devoid of emotion or awe.

They were father and son. One day, Russian soldiers had come to their village and ordered them to transport a group of forty horses and supplies to a place far away. After a full week of travel, they arrived at a Russian army base, safe but tired. The soldiers to whom they had delivered the horses fed them and told them to spend the night. That night they were awakened from a deep sleep by the sound of gunfire, and their hosts ran in all directions; some of them were killed and others taken prisoner by the new soldiers that had attacked in the middle of the night. These were the Germans, though the Uzbeks knew nothing about Hitler's campaign to take over Europe. The father and son ran, too, and they hid in the stables with the horses, who were agitated and reared up and stomped and neighed, and try as they might, the two men could not calm them down. In the end, the Germans found them there, and they whipped the horses into silence and tied them together with one long rope, looping it around their necks so that if one fell, the others would fall with him. They tied the Uzbeks' hands behind their backs and put them with the Russian prisoners. Then they made them all walk and walk and walk. Eventually they were put on a train, and after many days they came to a camp, where they worked at various jobs, felling trees and cutting firewood, making sure the officers' fireplaces were always blazing, and cleaning the stables and tending the horses. There was not much food, and they were often hungry.

Then one day more soldiers came. These were the Americans, of course. They attacked the camp and killed the horses. The father and son were captured yet again, along with their original captors, and forced to walk for a long time, until they reached the ocean, though they did not know it was the ocean, as they had never seen the ocean before. They were put on a giant boat, the sea was violent, and they were sick for days and could not eat. Finally they landed in a big city, where they were put on another train, and after many days, they arrived at the camp in the desert in the summer of 1944.

In the fall, once it was cooler, the prisoners did logging work in the nearby mountains, and the Uzbeks had to work, too, even though it had been established by Isaac's official report that they were not the enemy. Still, they did not complain. On the contrary, they worked harder than the other prisoners; Bidor kept his pockets filled with pine needles, and when he was sad, he would take a fistful and breathe in the smell of the forest. Since they were so far from home and they were not the enemy, Leo and Isaac got permission from the commanding officer to invite them to tea once or twice a week. After tea, they often walked together in the desert. The Uzbeks walked ahead, talking softly to each other, whispering almost, and Leo and Isaac whispered, too, out of respect for the desert and for the Uzbeks who were so far from home. Once, and only once, the Uzbeks asked for something—lamb. They wanted to cook a special meal, but the commanding officer did not grant Leo and Isaac permission to buy lamb. Although Leo and Isaac knew that the Uzbeks understood that it had not been their decision, they felt they had failed them. Still, when they said there would be no lamb, the Uzbeks just smiled, as they always did.

Bidor started visiting Leo when he was on guard duty. He appeared in the deepest night, when the only sound was Leo's sick heart beating and the muffled whoosh of the ocean in his ears—which Isaac said was actually his eardrums vibrating, but he liked to think of it as the ocean, which he had seen only once in his life. On the first night, Bidor asked Leo for a cigarette; then he walked a few paces away, lit the cigarette and smoked, his back to Leo, looking up at the stars. When he finished the cigarette, Leo called to him, saying, "More?" and Bidor returned for another. "Take it with you to the barracks," Leo said, but Bidor went back to where he had been standing, lit the cigarette, and smoked, though this time he did not turn away from Leo. When he finished this cigarette, he walked back to where Leo was, said thank you, and turned toward the barracks.

The next time the moon was hidden. It would be more difficult for Bidor to find his way to the guard post, Leo thought, but then he heard footsteps, and he knew who it was, and he let him approach without shining his flashlight on him. If it had been an enemy, he would have been dead. He let the footsteps draw nearer, waiting to distinguish Bidor's figure, but all he saw was darkness. How could Bidor see where he was going? Were his eyes more trained to the night? He was humming a mournful tune. Or perhaps, Leo thought, it was a lullaby. Then Bidor's arms were around him, his breath on his neck. Afterward they stood side by side, looking out at the darkness, smoking. "How did you know?" Leo asked.

Bidor spoke for a long time, and Leo listened. It sounded beautiful, like the night, like Bidor's lips, like his green eyes that Leo could not see in the dark, but he knew they were there, and he believed at that moment that he understood what Bidor was saying, that he was telling him about the night in his village and the sound of horses approaching, the smell of fires burning and lamb cooking. He wanted to tell Bidor something soothing about his own hometown, but he could think of nothing except the fires spewing from the smokestacks of the steel mills. Sometimes, he said, if it was a really dark night like tonight, you couldn't even see the spires, and the flames looked like they were dancing in the sky all on their own. "Look," he said, and he waved his cigarette in the air. "Can you see the ball of fire dancing?"

Bidor took the cigarette from Leo and held it straight out in front of him. He began to turn, slowly at first, then faster and faster, and the fire at the end of the cigarette turned with him, drawing a circle of fire in the night.

Even after weeks had gone by and Leo awoke every morning in Ulli's bed feeling strong, he always expected that one morning he would not be able to move beyond his memory of what had happened to Bidor when Leo was supposed to be keeping him safe. Yet he kept feeling strong, and he started to believe he was cured, that the valve in his heart was not getting thinner at all but expanding, opening itself up. And they were making money, he and Ulli together, not a lot, but enough to get them started, for that is how they saw it, as a beginning, not an end in itself. It was their secret too, something Isaac was not a part of, though he wasn't stupid, far from it, and he must have suspected. But as long as they said nothing, it was still a secret. They were the perfect team, he and Ulli. Ulli was a good salesperson. She had her connections with the women she interpreted for, and through them there were more and more clients. There was, it seemed, no German in Berlin who could keep himself from American cigarettes and whiskey. Cigarettes and whiskey were what got them through the winter, through picking over the rubble and cleaning up the rubble, through dead sons and brothers and fathers and all those dead Jews. Leo procured the goods, typing out the purchase orders, taking a box here, a bottle there. It was easy. Still, they were cautious. "Never be greedy," Leo always said, for he knew all too well the consequences of greed, though later he would understand that it was not greed but desire that made him and Bidor crave carelessness, as if their lack of concern were their own secret language, as if it replaced all the words they did not share.

It was Isaac who found them in Leo's office, Bidor kneeling on the floor in front of the swivel chair. Why hadn't Isaac knocked? Why hadn't Leo locked the door? Now, as Leo sat there at the table drinking the coffee Isaac had brought him in the cup that belonged to a family that had disappeared into the rubble, Leo wondered whether that was what he had wanted, to be found out by Isaac so that the floodwaters would be released and either he would drown or Isaac would save him. But he had neither drowned nor been saved, though Isaac, he was certain, thought he had saved him. Leo did not know what Isaac had seen, nor did Leo tell him that it was Bidor who had sought him out in the night, for that would be implying that he had been unwilling or innocent, and he was neither. "It is best if you have no contact with them now," Isaac had decided, and Leo had accepted this punishment.

Isaac became the sole protector of the Uzbeks. He continued to drink tea with them and walk with them in the desert. Leo wondered whether the three of them walked together now or whether Isaac still walked behind while they talked of things that he could not understand. At first, after Leo had been banished, he watched

Bidor through his office window, watched him get on the truck that took them to the forest, watched him line up for roll call every morning, always hoping that Bidor would sense him watching, that he would turn around and see Leo's face in the window. In the beginning Leo both worried and hoped that Bidor would come to him again when he was on guard duty, and when Bidor didn't, he did not cease to hope, even though he imagined that Isaac had made it clear to Bidor as well—keep your distance. He wondered whether Bidor was hoping that Leo would come to him, despite the danger, or whether he accepted Leo's absence as he had accepted his presence, as he had accepted all the things that had happened to him, that had brought him so far from home, so far from anything he could understand.

When the war was over, all the prisoners were sent to Idaho, where they were to be processed for repatriation. The Germans were going home to their families, to their bombed-out cities and their dead. Russian soldiers who had allowed themselves to be taken prisoner had been proclaimed traitors to the Revolution by Stalin, who made it clear that upon their return, they would be put under arrest and shipped off to Siberia. It was this proclamation, this knowledge that the Uzbeks were doomed, that brought on Leo's weakness. His legs began to feel heavy, as if they were bloated with water. Walking felt like running up a mountain. His arms ached. His shoulders burned. His hands and feet went numb. If the Uzbeks were sent to work in the mines, their lungs would fill with dust. Every day the mere act of breathing would become more difficult, and at night they would lie awake, concentrating on their own wheezing, afraid that if they did not keep vigil over every breath, their lungs would give up the fight. And if they worked on laying railroad tracks, bent over, hacking at the frozen earth with picks, it would be the cold that would get them. One by one their toes and fingers would succumb to frostbite, and if they did not hack the dead digits off with the same picks they used on the frozen earth, gangrene would set in, and that would be the end.

Isaac did not want to tell the Uzbeks that they weren't going home like everyone else. "Even if we bring in the Armenian, they won't understand. Stalin means nothing to them," he said.

"We can try to tell them something, that they are going to another prison, a more difficult prison, that they will have to be strong. If not, they will think we betrayed them," Leo said.

Isaac was silent.

"We should never have been kind to them," Leo said.

"That would only make things easier for you."

"You are afraid to tell them to their faces, afraid to look them in the eyes and tell them you are sending them to their deaths. Do you think that when they are no longer here, you won't think about them, you won't hear them cursing those who were supposed to protect them?"

"There is nothing we can do, Leo," Isaac said. "Soon it will all be over."

Before the prisoners were shipped off to be repatriated, the army sent Isaac on a mission to bring the crazy Russian—the one who thought that Stalin was living in his brain—to the military hospital in San Francisco. All this time, since this man had arrived on the same train as the Uzbeks, the army had put up with his rages—the howling in the middle of the night, the throwing of dishes. Leo had written the reports accounting for the broken chairs, the smashed eyeglasses that they kept replacing because he was as blind as a bat without them. But now the army had decided that they could not send him back in this condition. Perhaps they were afraid of being censured, that the Soviets would say *Look what the evil Americans have done.*

On the second day of Isaac's absence Leo went to see the Uzbeks in the recreation hall, where they sat every evening smoking and watching the other prisoners play pool. "I wanted to say goodbye," he said, and they understood "goodbye" and held out their hands. They each shook hands with him. "Goodbye," they said.

"Tea?" he asked.

"Tea," they said. It occurred to him only then that Bidor's father probably did not know why Leo had stopped being their friend.

He led the Uzbeks to his office, where he prepared tea while they waited patiently, not talking. They sat now like men who had been sitting in chairs their whole lives, with one arm over the back, legs crossed. They had learned a few more words too—delicious, sugar, spoon, table, telephone. Once Leo was sitting with them, the tea served, they began pointing to these things, pronouncing the words carefully, smiling proudly. They continued—"please, thank you, you're welcome, work, sing, happy, sad"—listing all the words they had learned.

"Yes, very good," Leo said after each word, which he knew made the whole thing even more ridiculous, but he did not know what else to say that they would understand.

When they finished their tea, he did not offer them more, for he could not bear to look at them knowing he would not save them. After they were gone, Leo found pine needles on the floor by their chairs.

The day of the great transport came. Everyone was up early, everyone except the Russians, who refused to rise from their cots.

"Up and at 'em," the soldiers called, and they hurled curses back and turned to the wall. In the end, they had to be dragged from their beds. Leo watched it all, watched the Germans clean and crisp, eager and ready, watched the Uzbeks watching the Russians being pulled from their beds. They were not smiling. What, he wondered, was their interpretation of what they saw? Could they even imagine that there were people who did not want to go home, that home could be more dangerous than war?

Breakfast over, the prisoners lined up to get on the buses. It was Leo's job to call out the names and check them off as they boarded. "Bidor," he called. "Otabek." The Uzbeks walked straight and tall to the bus, and Leo checked off their names.

When everyone had boarded, even the Russians, who, after they had been dragged out of bed, had become strangely docile, Leo checked his list one more time—everyone was accounted for. The commanding officer gave the order to close the doors, and the buses started moving. Some of the prisoners waved and some did not. The Uzbeks waved. Leo had not wanted to look, but he knew they would not understand his coldness as shame, not until they were handcuffed on the other side, not until they knew they were not going home, so Leo waved and smiled, and then they were gone. Would it have been more difficult to drop bombs on cities, to shoot the enemy in the head or straight through the heart? If it were so difficult, Leo thought, if it were more difficult than putting the Uzbeks on the bus, then why were there so many dead?

The next day, Isaac returned from his mission, which had not gone well. The crazy Russian had gotten completely out of control and was shot dead by the military police.

"At least he didn't have to go to Siberia," Leo said.

"Not everyone who gets sent there dies, you know," Isaac said.

"It's living there that frightens me," Leo said.

"We cannot know what is unbearable unless we have lived it ourselves."

"We can imagine."

"Try to let it go, Leo. Try to think of the future. There is nothing we could have done," Isaac said, though they both knew this was just what people said when the opposite was true.

"As a matter of fact, I am thinking of the future. I've reenlisted," Leo announced.

"I thought you hated the army," Isaac said.

"I do," Leo said.

"I see," Isaac replied, accepting his answer.

When Leo thought they would be saying goodbye, wondering whether Isaac would write, whether he would ever take Isaac up on his offer to start his future in New York, wondering whether Isaac had offered only because he knew that Leo would want to run like hell from Isaac, from everything Isaac knew about him, Isaac reenlisted too.

"They're sending me to Berlin to interpret for the displaced persons," he said.

Leo was going to Berlin.

"I thought you hated the army," Leo said.

"I do, but they need interpreters," Isaac said. "They say there are millions," he added.

"What are they going to do with them all?" Leo said, thinking that these were the new numbers—the millions of dead soldiers, the millions of dead Jews, the millions of displaced persons.

Winter

In Ulli's apartment, they kept a low profile, never raising their voices no matter how much vodka they drank. "Shhh," they would say when they found themselves losing control, laughing too hard, or pounding their fists on the table. "We'll be denounced," they said. But though they made light of their precarious situation with the apartment, they understood the gravity, the tenuousness of it, as well. In the end, in the spring, after the long, cold winter, they were finally reported—by whom they could not be sure, though they blamed Frau Herscher, a dour woman who lived alone on the third floor and responded to their greetings with silent disapproval.

But they had had their winter. They had been warm and had eaten and drunk and talked. If someone had looked in on them, observed them from afar, he might have seen something different—three people talking endlessly about useless things, drinking, cooped up in a stolen apartment, curtains drawn—but they did not feel the need for the outside world. Inside it was warm, and they were friends.

Leo and Isaac had access to luxuries at the base, so they always arrived at Ulli's apartment laden with delicacies—different varieties of Scotch and whiskey, vodka, ice cream, caviar, canned tangerines and pears. They cooked elaborate meals that were always accompanied by large quantities of alcohol. Leo and Isaac told stories demonstrating the stupidity of the United States Army and its commanders. "There's the right way and then there's the army way," Leo and Isaac liked to say. The three of them talked about their childhoods, the games they played, their neighbors. They tried to imagine what they would be like when they were old.

They memorized poems and recited them dramatically. Leo acquired an anthology of British poetry from the library on base, and though he could not understand why anyone would choose poetry over song, he developed a repertoire of his own and, because of his phenomenal memory, could out-recite both Isaac and Ulli even though both of them had been reading and memorizing poems since childhood.

Their favorite was one that Leo discovered, "Dover Beach" by Matthew Arnold. They always ended their poetry nights reciting it in unison. Ulli still remembered it in its entirety, and she often found herself reciting the final stanza when she was cleaning up the rooms, sweeping old newspapers and candy wrappers into the trash, wringing out the mop with her bare hands:

> Ah, love, let us be true
> To one another! for the world, which seems
> To lie before us like a land of dreams,
> So various, so beautiful, so new,
> Hath really neither joy, nor love, nor light,

Nor certitude, nor peace, nor help for pain;
And we are here as on a darkling plain
Swept with confused alarms of struggle and flight,
Where ignorant armies clash by night.

They always cried when they recited "Dover Beach." Did they cry because they knew they could not be true to one another or because they were, in fact, true to one another?

Yet despite the warmth of winter, they longed for spring. They longed for the end of that particularly brutal winter, which lashed out angrily at all the dead dogs of Europe. It was the winter that turned so many people away from God once and for all. The bombings, the atrocities—for these, they could forgive their God—but the winter, that was a dirty trick. That could not be the work of the Divine, no matter how vengeful. Isaac, Leo, and Ulli enjoyed this sort of conversation. In fact, the small-mindedness of God was one of their favorite topics. They had a theory that if God existed, he would have to be small-minded. He would have to be the sort of God who unleashed the most brutal winter of the century on a continent of people who were already smashed into the ground.

When spring arrived, however, it was not what they thought it would be, and they realized soon enough that they missed the simplicity of winter, the limitations of their apartment. They found themselves repulsed by the new season, by the sickly yellowness of daffodils and the feel of sun on their faces and the smell of soft rain that wafted in through the open windows. Still, they were always trying to believe in it, convince themselves that they really did want to be outside in the sun with all those flowers. So they went outside. They walked and ate ice cream. They sat in beer gardens.

When spring came, Ulli could not sleep, so she began spending the longest hours of the night in the kitchen with Isaac. At first it was Isaac who talked, mostly about the people he was interviewing at the displaced persons camp. These were the released prisoners of the concentration camps as well as the refugees who had followed Hitler's retreating army out of Eastern Europe because they were more afraid of the Soviets than of Hitler. It was Isaac's job to weed out the innocent civilians from the collaborators. The former would be relocated throughout what was then called *the free world*, mostly to the United States, while the others were turned over to the Soviets. Sometimes he consulted with Ulli about his designations. Ulli was well aware of the irony in his asking her, a German, to assist him with this task, but only once did they actually broach the subject—when Isaac was examining the case of a Ukrainian man who claimed that he had hidden a family of Jews in his barn. The man had shown Isaac a ring that he said one of the women in the family had given him as a token of her appreciation.

The man told Isaac that he hadn't wanted the ring, but the woman insisted. She wanted him to give it to his future wife but, Isaac told Ulli, "I knew he was lying. I could tell by the way he handed it to me, as if it were only an object, not the ring of a woman he had saved. And then, when I was examining it, he asked me if I was Jewish, and when I told him that I was, he laughed and said, 'I knew it,' as if I were the one who was lying. Even though he knew his fate was in my hands, he couldn't hide his hatred." Isaac paused. "You know," he continued, "that was perhaps the only time in my life I have really felt Jewish. My parents rejected all that. When I was a child, I wasn't even quite sure what it meant to be a

Jew, except that I knew I was a Jew, as were my parents and their Russian socialist friends. I asked my father about Jews on various occasions, but I never got a satisfactory answer. Sometimes he would say that we were the people of the Book, the Torah, but that the Torah was nonsense, though the idea of being people of the Book was not. He often ended his explanations by emphasizing that we were an ancient and unpopular people, and then I would ask why, and he would say we were unpopular because we were chosen by God, which was completely confusing because he didn't believe in God. 'What were we chosen to do?' I asked him once, and he laughed and said we weren't chosen to do anything, no one is chosen, but we all have to choose.

"I didn't even know my parents had been raised religious until I was twelve. I didn't know one single prayer, had never set foot inside a synagogue, but that man could sense that I was Jewish, and he hated me for it. I never want to hate like that," Isaac said. "Never."

"I can't imagine you hating anyone," Ulli said.

"War can change people. Perhaps if I had not been hated, I would have learned how to hate, too, like everyone else."

"Not everyone," Ulli said.

"No, not everyone," Isaac said, "but too many, so many."

And Ulli knew he was thinking about her, about what she had chosen and done or not chosen and not done, and she could not help but feel that Isaac had enlisted her aid not only to assuage his doubts about her but to punish her as well.

Still, when Isaac could not determine from the evidence or from intuition whether a DP was lying or telling the truth, he gave the person the benefit of the doubt, acquitted him, so to speak, and Ulli wondered whether that was also partly because of her, because he wanted so much for her to be innocent, to give *her* the benefit of the doubt.

"But what if he was one of those who should not be allowed to forget?" Ulli asked on one occasion after Isaac had made such a decision.

"His guilt will follow him whether he is wasting away in prison behind the Iron Curtain or whether he is comfortable in a cozy little house in America," he said, and she knew this was true.

The Russian lessons began one night when there was a lull in the conversation. Ulli looked down and saw Isaac's book lying on the table, the unfamiliar Cyrillic letters embossed on the spine. "Read to me," she said. She thought that hearing Russian coming from Isaac's mouth might soften her memory of the night when the Russian soldiers came. Perhaps then, she thought, she would finally be able to speak about it—not to Leo, which would change everything, and that was the one thing she could not bear, but perhaps she could tell Isaac.

"But it's in Russian," Isaac said. "You won't understand a thing."

"It will be soothing," she told him. And it was. She allowed the words to flow over her, to be pure sound rather than language with meaning and memory. After three pages he stopped and asked whether he should continue.

"Please," Ulli said, so he continued, stopping every once in a while to see whether she wanted him to go on. He read for about an hour, and she concentrated on the sound of the words coming from his mouth.

"I could teach you," he said when he had finished a chapter.

"If I could understand, it wouldn't be as beautiful," she said.

"Or it would be even more beautiful," he said.

But the lessons were not about the beauty of the Russian language, nor did they turn out to be a battle against the past, for how could mastering a language ever change that? No, the lessons were simply how she survived the long, sleepless nights of spring. They were something to occupy her mind, to muffle the laughter of the Russian soldiers. Yet she believed at the time that—especially because Isaac spent his days recording the experiences of the displaced persons and thus understood that, in one way or another, no one had come out of the war unscathed—if he really wanted to know, if he really wanted to know her, he would have asked. *Tell me, Ulli, what it was like when the Red Army came.* Later, however, she understood that even if he had asked, she would not have spoken about the past. All she wanted was to make it through the nights to the morning, to that first cup of coffee and Leo with his plans and thick thighs and the silly songs and drawn-out toasts. So she chose learning a new tongue over speaking. Leo over Isaac.

II

Breakfast

In the morning, the sun filled Isaac's room at the Hotel Atlas. The avocado-colored walls were aglow with light, giving everything—the sheet that covered him, his pants folded neatly over the back of a chair, the lampshade—a greenish hue. He recognized it as morning light, though he remembered lying down in the early afternoon, before lunch, even. Could he have slept so long? So much can happen while one is sleeping, like that first night when he had let Leo go with Ulli into the bedroom, when he had sat there like an idiot, watching as he always did.

Why was the sun so strong? Who had opened the blinds?

He closed his eyes again, closed them hard. He breathed in, counting to twenty, then letting his breath out slowly. It had been months since he had made it to twenty. He did it again. He was strong, rested. It was time to get up.

That night, he had not gotten up. He had sat on the sofa watching them dance, banging into the furniture, clinging to each other while he did what he always did: observe. He had done nothing to keep them from making that terrible mistake, just as he had done nothing to prevent the Uzbeks from being sent back to the Soviet Union. *Remember Bidor*, he could have whispered in Leo's ear, and Leo would have let go of Ulli, gone with him back out into the night, away from her, into the snow. But he hadn't gotten up; he had stayed on the sofa that night and all the other nights.

But he was getting up now, going downstairs. He had not come this far to waste away the morning. "'Arise ye prisoners of starvation,'" he sang as he swung his legs over the side of the bed, placed his feet on the floor. "'Arise ye wretched of this earth,'" he continued as he put on his clothes hastily, without washing up. He took the stairs, still humming, hands in his pockets, without holding on to the rail. How long had it been since he had done that?

"There you are," Ulli said as he entered the dining room. The other guests were eating breakfast—bread and butter, jam, coffee, tea, fruit. She was wearing the yellow slippers.

"Would you like the European or the Moroccan breakfast?" she asked.

"The Moroccan," he answered.

"Coffee or tea?"

"Coffee." He had given up coffee a few years ago. His doctor's idea. He had taken his advice, though the change made him feel neither stronger nor less tired.

She brought him bread and cheese and olives. The coffee was thick and bitter. Isaac watched Ulli move from table to table, greeting her guests, laying her hand lightly on a shoulder, nodding, removing plates, conferring with Abdoul, who darted from the kitchen to the dining room and back in a matter of seconds, balancing all the guests' needs on his tray. After a while Ulli took a seat at Isaac's table.

"How long did I sleep?" Isaac asked.

"About twenty hours, I think. You got heatstroke from your outing. You were burning up with fever."

"Perhaps it's the jet lag too."

"Yes, that can be very disorienting. Maybe you'd better take it easy today," Ulli suggested. "Tomorrow, I was thinking we could go to the Roman ruins at Volubilis, and tonight we will have a special dinner. I have already been thinking about the menu."

"That's not necessary," Isaac said. "I really require very little."

"Of course it's not necessary, but this is a hotel, you remember, and it is my job to make sure you are comfortable. It will be nice. It has been a long time since I have had the chance to sit down to dinner with an old friend," Ulli said.

"I would be more than happy to help with the preparations. It would do me good, in fact, to be useful," Isaac said.

"One doesn't have to be useful every moment of one's life. That's why we invented vacations and hotels."

"I haven't come here for a vacation." Isaac looked down at his coffee cup, which was empty.

"Would you like some more coffee?" Ulli asked instead of responding to his statement.

"No, I'd better not." He looked up again. "I read about the ruins at Volubilis in the guidebook," he said, taking the guidebook out of his pocket and showing it to her.

"You see, you do imagine yourself on vacation. Otherwise you wouldn't have bought a guidebook."

"It's Juliet's. She left a box of them in the basement. She spent a lot of time here in Morocco, before you were here, of course.

She's lived in so many countries that I don't even think I could list them all, but she's settled down now. Even though California seems so far away from New Jersey, it's close compared to Paraguay and Poland. It's nice to have her in the country, though it makes me feel old that she's no longer wandering, that even Juliet is no longer young."

"Didn't you visit her when she was living abroad?"

"No. I'm afraid I haven't done much traveling, except for my research. She always came for a visit in the summer. I haven't even been to Russia since it became Russia again. When I was a boy, I read everything I could about Marco Polo and dreamed of traveling all over the world, but I am really not well suited for it. Whenever I am away from home, all I think about is returning." Isaac paused, and Ulli took a sip of coffee, lifting the cup slowly and setting it back in its saucer without making a sound. "Not now, though. Now I am happy to be here," he said.

"I'm glad," Ulli said. "I'm glad you're here, too."

"It's a beautiful hotel, Ulli. It must be nice to have something to take care of, something that provides a structure for your days. I did not realize until after the girls were grown how much I depended upon it—the bath and bedtimes, the doctor's appointments and school meetings, shopping for school clothes in the fall, homework."

"But you had your work. Even after they were grown up, you had that, didn't you?"

"Yes, but I have grown tired of my work. When I retired, I thought I would just take a break. I reread all of Balzac and Thomas Mann. I kept waiting for ideas, but nothing came. So I kept reading, but after a while I got tired of reading. I found myself nodding off in my reading chair. I found myself counting the pages left until the ends of chapters. I would sit for hours just listening to the radio."

"Then you came to see me," Ulli said.

"Yes. I'd begun to feel paralyzed, and then I lost the car. If I hadn't lost the car, I might not be here."

"What do you mean?" Ulli asked.

"I drove to New York, planning on going to the museum. There was an exhibit of Persian miniatures. It was terribly hot and humid. There was a jam on the West Side Highway, and after I'd been sitting in traffic for almost an hour, the car simply died. It didn't overheat in the usual way that cars overheat. There was no smoke coming out from under the hood, no smell of wires burning. Of course, I don't have a cell phone—though Simone has been bugging me about getting one just for emergencies like this—so I couldn't call for help. Instead, I simply got out of the car and began walking. I just left it there in the middle of all that traffic. Later I felt bad about it, about making the situation worse, but at the time it seemed like the only thing I could do. The car died at around Eighty-sixth Street, so I walked to the Seventy-ninth Street exit and down the exit ramp. My original intention had been to find a garage, but I found that I was happy to be walking, despite the heat, despite the fact that my car was sitting dead on the West Side Highway.

"In the end, the police towed it to a yard somewhere in the Bronx, and in order to get it back, I would have had to find a way to get to the Bronx, pay a huge fine for abandoning the car on the highway, and then arrange to have the car towed to a garage. I told them I didn't want it, but they informed me that I was required by law to come in and file paperwork giving up ownership of the car in addition to paying the abandonment fine. I told them I would be there within the next few days. Every day for three days I got up fully intending to make the trek to the Bronx, but every day I never got around to it. I got embroiled in a book. I decided to organize my files. I walked downtown to get my groceries. And that was it.

"For the next couple of weeks I felt triumphant, as if I had accomplished something extremely important. But soon that feeling of elation wore off, and I felt terribly selfish for contributing to the traffic, for falling prey to the absurd notion that my age gave me the right to inconvenience others, to be, in fact, a nuisance. I could not stop thinking about the people stuck there on the highway who had more important things to do than see an exhibit of Persian miniatures. Yet somehow, mixed in with this feeling of guilt was an urge to walk on the beach. I craved the smell of water and salt and sand, the smashing of waves. I had forgotten, I realized, that I had once been very fond of the ocean. I suppose I could have taken a bus to the beach. I actually considered going on one of those horrible tours to Atlantic City. I tried to convince myself that it would be amusing to go all the way to Atlantic City and not even enter a casino, but I knew I would return home in the evening feeling even more discontented. I knew I needed to do something. So here I am."

"You can stay as long as you like, Isaac. I'll even put you to work if you want."

Isaac laughed. "It will be like old times," he said.

Abdoul came to the table. "*Pardon, monsieur,*" he said, bowing to Isaac.

"*Pas de problème,*" Isaac said, nodding his head.

Abdoul spoke a few words to Ulli in Arabic. It was obvious that he was upset about something.

"Excuse us a minute," Ulli said, leading Abdoul toward the kitchen, calming him down as they walked so that the other guests did not even notice something was amiss.

After a while, Ulli reemerged from the kitchen and approached a woman who was sitting alone at a table near the window. Isaac had noticed her when he came in, her arms and hands cluttered with silver bracelets and gigantic rings with red and blue stones. As he passed her table, she had looked up from her book, and though he had nodded and greeted her softly in French, she did not smile. As the woman spoke now to Ulli, Isaac could hear the clanking of her bracelets, like chains, he thought, as she gesticulated, pointing toward the stairway and toward Abdoul, who was standing sullenly near the kitchen door, watching. Ulli put her hand on the woman's shoulder and spoke softly, but the woman's voice grew louder so that now all the guests were watching. Isaac wanted to tell them all to stop looking, that Ulli could handle it. Instead, he read up on Volubilis. According to the guidebook, the Roman ruins were exquisite and the bus ride out there charming. On the bus it was not uncommon to encounter traveling musicians on their way to the nearby shrine of Moulay Idris, named after the creator of the first Arab dynasty in Morocco. Though the guidebook described in great detail the beauty of the shrine's calligraphy and mosaics, it also warned that it was prohibited for non-Muslims to spend the night in town.

Ulli had managed to calm the woman down. Her bracelets were no longer clanking. Isaac looked up from his book as Ulli and the woman arose and headed for the stairs, the woman walking fast, as if she were proving something, but Ulli had no trouble keeping up, though she was surely twice the woman's age. Abdoul came over to Isaac's table to see whether he required anything more. "A little more coffee, perhaps," Isaac said, hoping he would not regret it later. Abdoul bowed, and Isaac made as if to stand so that he could bow too, but Abdoul put his hand on Isaac's shoulder. "Please sit, monsieur. You are our guest," he said, bowing again.

Of course he was a guest, Ulli's guest, the hotel's guest, but she had said that he could help. He tried to imagine himself chitchatting with the other guests, running here, running there, smiling as Ulli was doing, now that she had returned to the dining room. Looking at Ulli, one would never know there had been a problem. Slowly she made her way through the room. It was strange to see her so confident, so at ease. She had always approached life like someone who, surveying a stream she was about to cross, trusted neither the rocks' stability nor her own sense of balance. Yet she wasn't paralyzed by this. She stepped on the stones, crossed the river, and if she made it to the other side without falling, she was pleasantly surprised. If she didn't, that was just the way things were.

This is how it was when the landlord's agent finally came to the apartment. It was a Sunday.

Earlier Isaac and Leo had convinced Ulli to go out and enjoy the warm spring weather. They rented bicycles and rode around for hours. Each time they finished a lap, each of them secretly hoped that one of them would have the courage to suggest calling it quits, but no one did. They had paid for the entire afternoon, so they all felt obligated to keep riding. They paced themselves, like prisoners trying to make it through a day, a week, a month, a year.

The agent rang the bell just as they finished dinner. They had been drinking vodka since before the meal, so they were quite drunk.

"You are?" the agent asked when Ulli opened the door.

"Ulli Schlemmer," she answered.

"May I come in?" the man asked.

She led him to the living room. He sat down and took some papers out of his briefcase. He put on his glasses and started looking through the papers. "Just as I suspected," he said without looking up.

By this time Leo and Isaac had come into the living room too. Leo offered him some vodka.

"I do not touch anything Russian," the man replied, still without looking up.

Isaac laughed. "Perhaps you would like some beer then?" he suggested, approaching the man unsteadily. The man leaned way back into the sofa, shielding his face, as if he expected Isaac to crash right into him. "Or cognac?" Isaac said, bending over, speaking right into the man's ear, though he did not whisper. "We have quite a large selection."

"No, thank you. I will not take much of your time. Now, Fräulein Schlemmer." He looked at Ulli, and Isaac backed away, joining Leo on the green velvet sofa. "It has come to our attention that you are not the authorized tenant of this apartment."

Ulli neither agreed nor disagreed with his pronouncement.

"So you have found the authorized tenants?" Isaac asked.

"We have found one authorized tenant, a soldier. He has been in the hospital all this time," the man replied, pushing his glasses up, though they had not in the least bit slipped down his nose. "He's blind now," he added, then paused. "This paper"—he handed it to Ulli—"specifies that you are not authorized to inhabit this apartment and that you must vacate the premises by five p.m. tomorrow." He crossed his legs.

Ulli looked at the paper and then handed it to Isaac, who read it carefully and returned it to the man.

"It is for you to keep," the man said, handing Ulli the paper again.

"Thank you," Ulli said. "Will that be all?"

"Five o'clock tomorrow," he repeated, putting the rest of his papers back into the briefcase.

"More vodka?" Leo asked when the agent had gone, understanding that something serious had just occurred. He poured them each another glass.

"We always knew someday it would come to this," Ulli said.

"Come to what?" Leo said. "It's just an apartment. The important thing is that we're together and we are drinking vodka."

"Yes, to us and to vodka," they said, and they drank until the sun came up.

After she lost the apartment, Leo and Ulli moved into a hotel, and Isaac moved back to the barracks, but Ulli and Isaac continued the Russian lessons, meeting at a café once or twice a week. For a short time, before they all left Germany, Isaac had a local girlfriend, a quiet, tall nurse who sang. She was older than Isaac and had been at the front with the wounded. She wore a small gold cross around her neck, and Leo and Ulli called her "the Christian," privately as well as in front of Isaac, who didn't seem bothered by the cross. Once, the four of them went out for afternoon coffee and pastries. "Karlotte has a beautiful voice," Isaac blurted out. "Why don't you sing for us?" he said, placing his hand gently on hers.

And she did. She stood up and sang "Ave Maria," softly but quite nicely. When she finished, the other customers at the café clapped, and she smiled shyly and thanked them. She did not say a word until she and Isaac were walking to the trolley stop together. When Isaac asked why she had been so quiet, she simply said, "They are not my kind of people."

"And what exactly are your kind of people?" Isaac asked.

"People who understand that there are some things you shouldn't laugh about," she said.

"But they weren't laughing," Isaac said.

"Not out loud, but you could see it in their eyes."

"You do not understand," Isaac said, but he knew what she had felt. He knew that when the three of them got together, they didn't let anyone else in.

Isaac escorted Karlotte home after that conversation, rode with her all the way on the streetcar to the end of the line, where she lived in an apartment with her mother. He saw her a few times after that, but more out of duty than interest, and then his orders to return to the States came through, and it was easy to extricate himself. She did not cry when he told her he was leaving. "I do not think I would like to live in America. Everything is so new there," she said, as if he had asked her to come along.

Ulli returned to the table. "Sorry, there is always something," she said. "My guest was convinced that one of my employees stole a bracelet from her room, but what she doesn't understand is that they would not risk their jobs for the few dirhams they could make off a silly silver bracelet. Moroccans don't even wear silver. They think of it as primitive and backward, what Berber nomads wear. And then of course we found it. Actually, I found it, because she refused to look, just stood in the doorway with her arms crossed. It was on the floor behind the sink."

"It's a wonder she would even know she was missing a bracelet," Isaac said.

Ulli laughed. "I have found that the more possessions people have, the more obsessed they become with keeping track of them."

"That's why I've been thinking about selling the house. I think I would be content enough in an apartment in the city, especially now that I don't have a car, but I'm afraid the girls will read too much into it. Instead of understanding that I no longer want the house, they will convince themselves that I am moving because I can no longer take care of it. And then there's Iraj to think of." He

had not meant to mention Iraj so lackadaisically. The plan had been
to ease into Iraj, into all of it.

"Iraj?"

"I should have told you long ago. Juliet has a son." He paused.
"His name is Iraj."

Ulli didn't answer right away. "There is so much we have to
catch up on," she said finally.

"Yes," Isaac said.

On the plane, he had made a list of what he wanted to tell her.
But after he saw Ulli again, he imagined the two of them at a table,
he with his list, she with a cigarette, for that was how he remembered her, always with a cigarette, and he felt silly for making the
list at all, for thinking that a list was what was needed.

"You have quit smoking," Isaac said.

"Years ago. I don't even remember what it tastes like."

"I used to like lighting them for you. It was a way to come
closer," Isaac said.

"But you hated my smoking."

"I hated the smoke, not the smoking," Isaac said, leaning back
in his chair and clasping his arms behind his head.

"It's one of the things I miss about those days when everyone
smoked. It gave us all something to focus on when we didn't know
what to say. Now we just have to face it all on our own." Ulli set her
hands on the table, as if she were about to get up, but she simply
left them there.

"He's fifteen. I wanted to write to you when he was born. I
don't know why I didn't. I kept putting it off, and then, when we
realized that he wasn't quite right—"

"Not quite right?" Ulli prompted him.

"He's what they used to call *slow*. They have all sorts of other
names for it now."

"Is he in school?" she asked, leaning in toward Isaac.

"In a special program. We didn't realize something was wrong until he was about three and still hadn't begun to talk. The doctors said not to worry about it, that Woodrow Wilson didn't speak until he was four. But that was an exception. He's good at memorizing things. Every time he visits, we have what he calls our history projects. The last time we were together, he memorized all the wars of the nineteenth century and their exact dates. He loves to cook. He wants to be a chef, but he gets bogged down by details. He can spend half an hour cutting up a pepper, but he has talent, too. He knows intuitively how to blend ingredients. Once, when I was making leg of lamb, he insisted that we soak it in milk overnight to make it tender, so we did, and it was perfect."

"Do you have a photograph?"

"I should have thought about that. But we don't really take pictures. I have some, of course, but I didn't think to bring them."

Ulli looked up at the ceiling, the way students do when they are reciting something they have been required to memorize, as if she were straining to imagine Iraj.

"You would like him," Isaac added. He tried to imagine her going for a walk with Iraj. Would she have the patience to stop to pet and talk to every dog, to wait for the green light even though there were no cars coming, to count all the out-of-state license plates?

"And what about Iraj's father?" Ulli asked.

"Juliet met him when she was teaching in Turkey. He was a refugee there, a deserter from the Iranian army, but things didn't work out. Iraj thinks that his father died in a bus accident. Juliet says that when he's older, she'll tell him the truth."

"Does the father know he has a son?" Ulli asked.

"I don't think so. She didn't even know she was pregnant until she returned to the States, and as far as I know, she's had no contact with him since then."

"You're right. This would have been so much easier with a cigarette," Ulli said. "This is the point where I would remove one slowly from the pack and you would reach for the lighter." She paused. "But after it was lit and I'd taken my first deep drag, we would still have to speak." She looked around the dining room, surveying it all carefully, as if she were looking for something that needed tending to. But the breakfast diners had long since gone, and the waiters had cleared the tables. Everything was in its place—the chairs all pushed in close to the tables, the floor swept. "I never managed to convince myself that the girls were better off without me," Ulli said.

"I should not have let you slip away so easily," Isaac said, lifting his coffee cup to his lips and holding it there.

"It was my choice, mine and Leo's choice. There was nothing more you could have done," she said softly.

"Yes, but I should never have let you leave them so completely," Isaac said.

She turned toward him, using, it seemed to Isaac, all her willpower not to look away. "I am the one who ran off—"

Isaac interrupted. "I was selfish too, Ulli. I wanted them to myself—without complications."

"Well . . ." Ulli paused, still holding his gaze. For a moment it seemed as if the film had been lifted from her eyes, that they were as he remembered them, but when she spoke, it was there again. "What about Iraj? Do you think it would be best to tell him that his father is still alive?"

"I do, but I am not the one to know what is best. We always think we are doing what is best, and then it so rarely is."

"Do you regret having adopted them?" Ulli asked.

"No, of course not. I cannot imagine my life without them," Isaac said.

"You see. I could. I did imagine it without them. I chose a life without them, Isaac, and you didn't," Ulli said, putting her hands on the table, pushing down.

Now it was Isaac who looked away. He couldn't bear to watch her thinking about getting up, leaving him when they had just started talking. It embarrassed him to see her shame, her weakness, yet at the same time he couldn't let her go. "I'm afraid that in an effort to steel them for life, in order to protect them, I taught them—too well—how to be alone," Isaac continued. "They are good at that, at being alone. Even when they were young, they did not seek out other playmates, and I did not push them to do so. I thought the three of us were enough for one another, and since they never seemed unhappy about it, I believed that our little world was enough, that it was the whole story, and that somehow when they ventured out on their own, all they would need was the memory of their childhood with me."

"That is so much more than most people have," Ulli said, removing her hands from the table. "You don't think it's possible to be alone and happy? I think those who learn to be alone, who can find pleasure in their own company, are, in the end, less disappointed than most of us. I say this because it has taken me a lifetime to achieve this."

"Yes," Isaac agreed, "but not being disappointed is less than what I had hoped for them. What about love? Simone has been a live-in health-care worker for over twenty years. She's never done anything else. She has spent her life watching over the dying, bathing them, preparing meals that they hardly touch, sitting with them on park benches or in front of televisions. I don't know how she can stand the televisions. For me that is the worst of it—that constant transmission of inanities. She says she blocks it out, doesn't even hear it. I don't know how she can sit so much. It is what I hate the most about old age—the sitting."

"I wouldn't be able to do it."

Of course not, Isaac thought, but he let it go, thought instead of Simone sitting at her patient's bedside, breathing in the sour breath of the dying. "And she was such an active child—they both were—but particularly Simone. She's a runner. She's done I don't know how many marathons, not the official ones. She waits until the week after the New York Marathon is over, and then she runs it on her own. When she was seven, she was already running around the block ten, twenty, sometimes thirty times. I would watch her from the kitchen window, and every time she passed, she would wave. Juliet ran only because of Simone, because Simone said that she had to, that it would make her strong."

"How did she get into this profession?" Ulli asked.

"She started during college. Her first client was a Sephardic Jew from Salonika. He had a terrible skin disease and was in constant excruciating pain. Apparently he had had other health-care workers, but Simone was the only one who knew how to move him, how to bathe him without causing pain. During her last year of college she worked for him full-time, *lived in* as they say, and when she graduated, she stayed on until he died two years later. I would never tell her this, but I was relieved when he died. I understood her attachment to him and admired her sense of duty, but I was sure that once she was free of the responsibility, she would embark on her own life, her real life, but instead she found another live-in health-care position. And after that woman died, there was another, and another, and another. There is no shortage of old and sick people."

"You are implying that she stayed in this line of work out of some kind of weakness or fear, but perhaps the opposite is true."

"And what exactly is the opposite, Ulli?" Isaac asked.

"Maybe she is one of the few who has the strength to do this kind of work. Do you think she would have been happier or more successful if she had become a doctor so she could just swoop in, patch up a body, and send it on its way? Isn't it more difficult to listen to the same stories over and over again, to lift patients onto the toilet, to look in at three and four in the morning just to make sure they are still breathing?"

"This is what I always tell myself. This is what I know Simone wants me to believe. But I'm not sure whether it is what *she* believes," Isaac said.

"And what about life outside of work? I imagine she's not married," Ulli said.

"Simone is a lesbian," Isaac said.

"Does she have a girlfriend?" Ulli asked calmly, though she found that she was trembling. It was not that she was surprised or disapproved, but rather that she did not allow herself to think about who her daughters had become and what role she, and Leo, had in who they turned out to be.

"Not as far as I know. When I ask her about such things, she says she will let me know if there is ever somebody worth telling me about."

"Has she had someone serious in the past?"

"When she was in college, but I don't think the girl took it seriously. She ended up getting married and becoming quite a famous journalist. She won some kind of big prize for her coverage of the war in El Salvador. Simone brought her to dinner at the house once. She was a vegetarian, which wasn't common in those days, but we made a big meal—mushroom barley soup and a vegetable ragout. She knew more about history than most of my students, but it was obvious that she didn't love Simone, that she just enjoyed the attention."

"And Juliet? After Iraj's father, was there anyone?"

"Not anyone I have ever been presented with," Isaac said.

"We sound like two old women with nothing to do except worry about marrying off our daughters," Ulli said.

Isaac laughed. "As cliché as it sounds, I just want them to be happy."

"Remember how you used to say that happiness was overrated?"

"That was when I was young and believed that one had to be tortured and miserable in order to do great things," Isaac said.

"And you don't think that anymore?"

"Perhaps what I think now is that greatness is overrated."

"I don't know about greatness, but I still think happiness is overrated," Ulli said.

Isaac almost found himself saying, That's because you didn't have children.

The woman with the bracelets was back. She was leaving.

"But you are not scheduled to leave until Sunday," Ulli said.

"I have changed my mind," the woman said coldly, her bracelets still. "I will pay for all the reserved nights if that's what you want."

"I hope you don't think we want you to leave," Ulli said.

"I didn't say that. I said no such thing," the woman said, lowering her voice as if this were a secret.

"Please, why don't you sit down, have a cup of tea with us. There's no need to rush, and it's getting to that time of day when it is best to stay indoors."

"I do not want any more tea. I'm sick to death of tea," she said, the bracelets back in action. "I just want the bill."

"But only for the nights you stayed," Ulli said.

"If you insist . . ."

"I do. Can I call you a taxi?" Ulli asked.

"No. Please don't go to any trouble," the woman said.

"Abdoul will help you with your bags," Ulli said.

"I have already brought them to the lobby," she replied.

"I hope the rest of your trip is more pleasant," Ulli said, bowing ever so slightly.

"I'm sorry," the woman said.

"Come," Ulli said.

The woman followed Ulli, walking a few feet behind her, her eyes looking straight ahead, focusing, it seemed to Isaac, the anger and sadness and guilt of all her years on Ulli's back. If one bored a hole right there, one would hit Ulli's heart, Isaac thought.

"She's gone?" Isaac asked when Ulli returned to the table.

"Yes, walked off on her own into the sun with those two ridiculous suitcases. I don't know why people travel with so much luggage. I never took anything more than what could fit under the seat in a plane. Even when I was moving to a new position in a new country, I always sold off my belongings and started anew. You would be amazed at how much stuff some of the other UNESCO people would drag around with them. One of my colleagues, a mild-mannered man who devoted his life to eradicating polio, insisted on bringing his collection of cricket bats with him wherever he went. He had hundreds of them, dating back to the beginning of cricket, whenever that was."

"Why did you try so hard to get her to stay after how horrible she was?" Isaac asked.

"Because later, once she is back home, the embarrassment she feels for having left will be much stronger than the embarrassment she felt for jumping to conclusions."

"Do you even think she knows that she left out of shame? She struck me as the kind of person who does not give much time to self-reflection," Isaac said.

"Perhaps you're right," Ulli said. "Perhaps I was just projecting. The truth is, we don't know a thing about her, and now I am the one who has jumped to conclusions."

"It's only natural, isn't it, to fill in what we do not know?" Isaac said.

"Natural perhaps, but in the end, not very satisfying."

Isaac felt his air passages tightening. He reached into his pocket for his inhaler, but instead of taking it out, he held it for a moment just for reassurance. He coughed, but only once, and then he let it go. "Did you never think of replying to my letters, Ulli?"

"Of course I did. Of course I did."

"Well, that's why I came to see you. I was tired of trying to fill in the blanks on my own."

"And how did you do such a thing?" Ulli asked.

"I imagined your loneliness. I thought of you walking alone down a busy street in an important city. I saw you sitting at a table in a restaurant, surrounded by people, and everyone was laughing except you. You were looking off into space or toward the door, wondering how much longer you had to sit there before you could leave. Sometimes I pictured you lying awake in the dark next to a man who was snoring."

"Did you think of me that way because that was how you really thought my life was or because you were angry and wanted me to suffer?"

"Both." There. It was said, finally, once and for all.

Gita

IN THE BEGINNING, Isaac had not been angry with Ulli. He had
the girls to think about, and his career. During those years he did
not think of Ulli each time he looked at Simone and Juliet, though
they looked like her, and Leo too, had her blue eyes and Leo's stur-
diness. Instead he saw himself in them—in the way Juliet played
with her hair while she was reading and Simone walked with her
hands clasped behind her back. The anger resurfaced after Gita,
though he suspected it had always been there, following its own
ebb and flow.

He met Gita on his first trip to the Soviet Union, upon which
he had embarked with guarded excitement. He had no specific ex-
pectations for the journey, though he certainly had not set forth
looking for romance. In fact, the purpose of his trip was entirely
practical. He had exhausted the information available in the United
States on the group of nineteenth-century Russian intellectuals he
was researching, and since, at twelve and thirteen, the girls were

old enough to be left in the care of his old friend Katya Ladijin-skaya, he had no excuse not to seek his fortune in the archives in Leningrad. He and his parents had left when he was barely three years old, so he had no memories of the land at all, but he hoped at the very least to feel some swell of emotion upon finally returning to the country of his birth. Russian, as his parents never let him forget, was his mother tongue, despite the fact that both his tongue and his pen preferred French and English. But when he arrived, he was disappointed with the absence of snow. He had been expecting everything to be white. Instead, all he saw were gray and brown—gray buildings and gray roads, brown hats, brown coats, polluted brown skies—so that he felt the weight of those two colors on him like a heavy but not so warm blanket.

On the way from the airport he and the taxi driver did not talk except to confirm the name of his hotel. He knew that people preferred not to talk to foreigners, so Isaac did not want to make the man nervous by engaging in chitchat. Still, he was planning on looking up his relatives, though he was prepared for the fact that they might not want to see him. If they did agree to meet him, he had brought photographs of his parents and his daughters, as well as snowsuits and pantyhose, blue jeans and Palmolive soap and Bayer aspirin. He was worried that the snowsuits would be too bright, that the children would be embarrassed to wear yellow or red or blue, though he knew that children did not worry about such things.

"Do you have a hat?" the taxi driver asked him as he lifted the three large suitcases out of the trunk.

"I am not accustomed to wearing a hat," Isaac said.

"Here in Leningrad the winter is very cold," the driver said, as if he thought Isaac had never experienced winter. "You must buy a hat." The taxi driver was the first of dozens to be concerned about his lack of headgear, though the others were all old women. These women were relentless, accosting him on the street with their grave warnings about the horrors of frostbite.

"Look," he told one old woman. "There's not even any snow on the ground."

"Just wait," the woman said. "Just wait."

After that, he almost gave in and bought a woolen cap, but at the last minute he changed his mind. He would not, he decided, be bullied by old women.

What frustrated him most about the Soviet Union was the waiting. Of course he had known about the lines for buying food. Everyone knew about those. But he had no way of knowing what the waiting really meant, how it could affect you, eat you up like cancer until you became lethargy itself. Every meal involved layers of waiting. First he waited for the waiter to bring the menu. This could take up to one hour, despite his vigorous requests and gestures. Then he waited for the waiter to take his order. Even such a simple thing took some time because they had to go through the entire leather-bound menu until he happened upon the only available dish, the pork cutlet or cabbage soup that was being prepared that day. Once, he tried asking the waiter what they really had to offer, but the waiter merely nodded at the menu, and they had to go through the whole sham the way they always did, until he hit on the right answer. After the ordering was completed, he waited for the food to arrive, which could take up to two hours if the restaurant staff were so inclined. Finally, there was a good half-hour wait until the waiter brought him the check.

The first three days of his stay, he arrived at the archives promptly at nine and waited in vain for someone to let him in. He had gone to great lengths to arrange access, and he had a thick folder of signed and sealed papers to prove it, but no one actually showed up until the third day. Once he finally gained access to the archives, an old woman with a large ring of keys walked up to the door and took her time turning the key in the lock. "Wait," she told him gruffly as he tried to follow her inside. The door slammed, and it was another thirty minutes before he was allowed to enter.

He never knew when the archives would open, though the sign on the door clearly said that the archive hours were from nine o'clock to five thirty, Monday through Saturday. Sometimes they opened at ten, sometimes at nine thirty, sometimes at eleven. He never knew when they would close, but usually, at about three—three thirty if he was lucky—the woman told him it was time for him to pack up his things. Once—perhaps she had fallen asleep—it was almost seven before she told him she was closing.

Because of the erratic schedule at the archives, in order to make full use of the hours that they were open, he did not have time to waste on breakfast and lunch, so he was ravenous by the time he ate his dinner, which he always had in the hotel restaurant. He thought sometimes of trying out another hotel restaurant to see whether it was more efficient, but by the end of a long day he was always too debilitated for such experiments.

In the morning, instead of eating breakfast, he ran. He thought he would call a great deal of attention to himself with his running, for exercise of this type was certainly not popular among the Soviets, but he soon found that no one seemed to pay him any attention at all. In the mornings, he noticed, people were quiet and slow, as if they were still dreaming in their warm beds. It was at night that the old women stopped him about getting a hat.

As far as he knew, there were only three other guests at the hotel during his entire two-month stay. There were two portly Romanians who, whenever he passed them on the stairway or in the lobby, switched from Romanian to loud, heavily accented French. *"Bonjour, monsieur,"* they said to him.

Isaac would bow slightly and reply, *"Bonjour, Messieurs."* He did not know what their business in Leningrad was.

The other guest was a handsome African who always wore traditional African clothing and, each time they met, inquired in English after Isaac's health and the health of his family. Once, they drank tea together in the restaurant and talked about how they missed their children, though Isaac did not say that he worried about how they were getting along with Katya Ladijinskaya, who was not always easy to get along with. Still, he found a rhythm to his days and was content to immerse himself in the stories of people who had died before he was born. There was safety in knowing that their lives would never touch his, that he could learn the intimate details of their business anxieties or troubles with the authorities, yet they would never demand anything of him in return. On Sundays the archives were closed, so Isaac walked. He walked from one end of Leningrad to the other. Then he would write the girls a long letter about what he had seen. He put off calling his relatives.

Isaac realized that he was waiting for a snowstorm, that he thought somehow a snowstorm would make him realize that he really was in the Soviet Union, not just in a dusty library reading through the personal papers of minor intellectuals. He was sure that once it snowed, he would call his relatives and they would invite him to their humble apartments where they would drink plenty of vodka and eat good black bread and something special that they had waited in line for hours to acquire. They would talk about his parents and his grandparents. He would learn things about them he had never known, and in the end, the children of his cousins and second cousins would don their new snowsuits and they would all walk him back to his hotel in the snow.

It did snow, but instead of calling his relatives, he met Gita. It was snowing when he emerged from the archives, so instead of heading to the hotel for his usual bad and prolonged dinner, he walked in the opposite direction. He walked without paying any attention to where he was going—turning abruptly onto small lanes when he felt moved to do so, walking in the middle of the large boulevards, which had become impassable to vehicles. Noisy groups of men invited him to join them for a drink. He wished them a joyous evening and continued on his way. Sometimes they ran after him, trying to convince him.

Every once in a while he passed another lone walker, and they smiled at each other. When he had walked for almost two hours, he realized that he was cold, so he looked around for a place to have tea or a piece of bread and cheese. But he was in a residential district, and there was nothing. Still, he did not turn around. He was not ready to return to the hotel. And then he saw the lights—not hundreds of lights like at the opera, although to him it seemed like hundreds of lights—illuminating the first story of a large, square building. He climbed the stairs to the building and pulled on the massive iron doors. He had not expected them to open, but since they did, he walked in. Inside, there was music. He followed the music and came upon a large hall filled with tables at which were sitting men and women in brown suits. Everyone was enshrouded in cigarette smoke. At the end of the hall on a small stage was a string quartet playing a waltz. Above the stage was a banner that read ACADEMY OF AR-CHITECTS ANNUAL BANQUET. There was a dance floor, where half a dozen couples were dancing. The men whipped the women around much too forcefully, and still the women laughed.

No one seemed to notice him, so he stood in a corner. He grew braver and took an empty seat at a table whose occupants seemed particularly drunk. Someone offered him vodka, and he accepted. He grabbed a piece of bread from the breadbasket, and no one seemed to mind. Someone filled his glass again. One of the men at his table showed him a plaque he had received for twenty years of service to architecture. "Congratulations," Isaac said, and everyone at the table clapped, and more vodka was drunk. He ate what was left of the bread and announced that he was going to look for a dance partner. Someone slapped him on the back, and off he went. He was actually planning to leave, but the music stopped. A fat, important-looking man stepped onto the stage and started giving a speech about how architecture was the most glorious of socialist endeavors because it represented both the greatness of the socialist ideal and the strength and sweat of the Soviet worker. The man droned on. Isaac stopped listening, but he felt that it would be rude to leave during the speech. The members of the string quartet were sitting very straight and quietly in their chairs, but then the only woman in the group dropped her bow. Everyone ignored it except for him. He smiled at her, and she smiled back, and that was Gita.

He sat through the fat man's speech and another speech and through the final toasts to architecture and the Soviet Union, to Lenin and Marx and a lot of people whose names were unfamiliar to him but who must have been members of the Academy of Architects; when their names were called, they stood up and bowed, and everyone clapped. Then it was over, the members of the string quartet packed up their instruments, and Isaac followed Gita out the door into the snowy night.

"Excuse me," he called after her. At first she did not turn around, although he knew she had heard him. "Miss," he tried again, and this time she turned.

"Yes?" she said, and then he didn't know what to say. She was about to turn back around when he noticed that she was not wearing a hat.

"You really should wear a hat in this weather," he said, and she laughed and told him he should take his own advice, and that was how it started.

They walked for several hours, and when they were too tired to go on, she sneaked into his hotel with him.

"It's so warm in here," Gita said as soon as she stepped into the room.

"Too warm almost," Isaac said. "Either the heat is on too high or it's hardly on at all."

"Let's open the windows," Gita said. They opened all the windows, and they made love on the floor beneath the windows, and the snow fell on their naked bodies. "It's always warmer when it snows," Isaac said.

"Yes," Gita said, pulling him closer.

On that first night, the phone rang late, long after they had fallen asleep. "Are you sure you are in the right place at the right time?" a voice said in heavily accented English.

"Excuse me?" Isaac answered in Russian, but the man had already hung up.

He told Gita it was a wrong number—the caller had wanted room 602 and his was 601. She stayed with him at the hotel almost every night until he left, and every night the phone rang. The calls were always in English and always in the form of a colloquial question or a cliché. Once a man asked, "Is everything good to go?" and another time, "Is it always darkest before the dawn?" Each time, he told Gita it was a wrong number, and she told him he should complain at the front desk, but he said it wouldn't do any good.

He had expected to be watched, but he hadn't planned on doing anything worth watching. He asked her once whether she was afraid that something would happen to her after he was gone, and she told him that the chairman of the Academy of Architects was a close friend of her late husband, who had drowned himself in the Neva River three years earlier. That was how she got the position as the head and only librarian of the Academy of Architecture. Still, he knew how precarious such connections could be, and he wondered whether the Academy of Architects itself was responsible for the phone calls. Perhaps because of these concerns, he felt that their happiest times together were when they were not in the room, though he knew how much she enjoyed the privacy she had at the hotel, for she lived in one room with her two children and her mother in a communal apartment shared by four other families. On many evenings he sat at his desk in the meager light, reviewing his notes while she soaked in the bathtub.

They talked mostly about their children. Her son, Shura, she told him, was quiet and thin and already proving to be a talented oboist. Her daughter, Vera, had little interest in music and books but was devoted to swimming. She practiced every day after school for hours, after which she came home and devoured huge amounts of food. Gita was surprised that his girls did not take music lessons, and he explained that they liked music but preferred the written word to all other forms of artistic expression. He told her that sometimes he worried that they liked to read too much, that neither of them talked about their classmates or their teachers, and that on Simone's last birthday he had suggested that she invite some of her classmates for a party, but she just wanted to have a quiet dinner *en famille* instead.

He did not tell Gita that his daughters were motherless and he wifeless. He knew that she assumed, because of his silence, that there was someone besides his daughters waiting for him to come home, but he could not tell her the truth—that being with her reminded him that Ulli did not love him, never did, and never would. Instead he gave Gita all the gifts he had brought for his relatives, the snowsuits and pantyhose, the soap and aspirin. On their last evening together Gita presented him with a photograph of Shura and Vera standing stiffly in the park, dressed up in their new snowsuits, and Isaac gave her the photo of Simone and Juliet, which he had brought to show his relatives.

It was only now, sitting across from Ulli all these years later, that Isaac understood, finally, that it was wrong not to have written back to Gita. He should have told her about Ulli, and that he was sorry, terribly sorry, for he had truly believed, at the beginning of things, that the memory of Ulli would recede and he would be left only with Gita. But when he was home again, listening to the Mozart Oboe Concerto with his daughters as dusk turned to night, it was Gita who receded. As the sky went dark and the last movement began, he closed his eyes and gave in to thoughts of Ulli, until the record was over and Simone or Juliet turned on the light.

Perhaps if Gita had not said that she loved him, if she had asked for money, if she had asked for anything at all, he would not have thrown the letters away. Perhaps then he would have written back, kept in touch in a paternalistic sort of way. When his colleagues went to the Soviet Union, they could have brought her money. The dollars would have made her life easier. But there were no demands, just reports about the flowers in the Summer Garden and her children's latest accomplishments and the last line, which simply and always read *I love you*.

After Gita's letters finally ceased, about a year after Isaac returned from the Soviet Union, he wrote to Ulli about his sojourn behind the Iron Curtain. *The girls are asking about you more and more*, he wrote, though this was not true. He suggested that Ulli come for a short visit. She would not have to stay with them. She could stay in New York and they could meet in the city. He missed her. He told her that. *It has been too long*, he wrote. He carried the letter around in his pocket for weeks, until he could almost feel it pressing on him, weighing him down, but he could neither mail it nor throw it away. At night he put it in his night table, and he almost heard it beating from inside the closed drawer, like Poe's telltale heart.

One evening in early spring, when the air was especially pungent, he and the girls went for a long walk through the quiet streets of their town. They looked into picture windows at the purple glow of televisions. "What a pity to spend a beautiful evening like this in front of a television," Isaac said, and the girls agreed.

"Let's walk until the sun comes up," Juliet suggested, and so they walked, up and down hills, around suburban loops, through silent downtowns. When the sun came up, they were far from home, and by the time they made it back to the house, the birds had already settled down and worshippers were arriving at the Lutheran church up the street. After he had settled the girls in their beds and kissed them good night, breathing in the smell of spring in their hair, he understood that Ulli was not capable of appreciating the smell of spring in her daughters' hair, so he tore his letter into pieces so small that not one of them contained an intelligible word.

"I don't know why I didn't leave you and Leo that first night," Isaac said to Ulli at the breakfast table after a long silence during which he wondered why she didn't jump up to attend to something rather than sit there with him, thinking about his anger. "I could have walked back to the barracks by myself, but instead I lay awake listening to you and Leo—and then silence, which was even worse. I should have told you then about Leo before you . . ." Isaac paused. "Before you fell in love with him."

"I don't know whether I would have listened. I would have said that none of it mattered. I would have believed that my love was enough. That's what people always believe, that love is enough. But it isn't."

"I think that on some level I wanted to see everything fall apart. I wanted you to come running to me when it happened, though I suspect that if you had run from Leo, you would have run from me too. And you would never have come to the United States and we wouldn't have had the girls."

"Maybe that would have been better."

"Not for them, not for me. It wasn't always easy, of course," Isaac continued. "Especially when they were teenagers."

"I missed all that," Ulli said.

"Yes. You did," Isaac said. He remembered that he had forgotten to pull the shades down in his room as Ulli had told him to do. "The room will turn into a furnace if you let the sun in," she had said, and he had been reminded of an article he read in *The New York Times* about indentured servants in Brazil who produce charcoal. The workers had to go inside the ovens, into the furnace, and shovel out the charcoal. Sometimes they fell onto the burning embers, so they wore thick clothing, which made the heat even more unbearable.

"I forgot to close the shades in my room," Isaac said.

"I'll send Abdoul to do it," Ulli said, but he was already getting up.

"No, I'll go," Isaac said.

"You'll come down again for lunch?" Ulli asked, looking at her watch. "I usually eat at one."

"One, yes. That will give me some time to rest. I am feeling tired, Ulli," he said, though he wasn't feeling physically tired at all.

"It's from the trip and the lingering effects of the sunstroke. You'll be fine after a rest," she said, jumping to her feet, relieved to be excused from the conversation. "If you need anything, just call the front desk," she added as he headed for the stairs. He would use the banister this time, take it slowly, one step at a time, but he wouldn't stop until he reached the landing, and he wouldn't turn around to see whether she was still sitting at the table, watching him to make sure that he was all right, which of course he was. He didn't feel the least bit out of breath, just a little tired. Where, he wondered, did she get all her energy?

A dry breeze brushed his face when he opened the door to his room. She was right about the blinds. The room was already hot, but he went to the window to pull down the blinds anyway. He lay down on the bed and closed his eyes, then remembered that he had left his inhaler in the pocket of his jacket, which he had hung on the chair. It should be by the bed just in case. But he was too tired to move, so he closed his eyes again and slept.

Footsteps

Around dinnertime, Ulli checked in on Isaac. He was breathing steadily, one of his long arms hanging over the side of the bed. Peaceful, as if all he had wanted was to say what he had come to say, to be here with her, and now that he was, he could rest.

Ulli did not sleep that night. She went to bed at her usual hour after checking on Isaac one more time, after doing the books and going over the chef's order for the next day's supplies. She read for a while, but that only made her more awake. And it was so hot, even at midnight, as if the earth had ceased to spin and night was just a sham, nothing more than a curtain lowered between her and a sun that still raged in full force behind it. She went to the window and stood watching, feeling a strange excitement, as if she were waiting for someone, but then she remembered that Isaac was already there, sleeping in room number fourteen. He should have written first, given her some warning, some time to prepare. But he was here, and she could not sleep. She leaned out the window, breathed in the air, but it wasn't enough. How frightening it must be for Isaac to be always at the edge of suffocation. How could he even sleep at all?

In the lobby, the night guard, a boy really, one of Abdoul's nephews, was sleeping, but she didn't wake him. He was not supposed to sleep when he was on duty, of course, but he always did, and really it didn't matter. Before him, there had been no guard. She hired him only as a favor to Abdoul. The boy had had a hard time. His father had died in a mining accident and his mother was ill.

She walked through the medieval stone gate that surrounded the old city and onto the road that led down the hill to the Ville Nouvelle. She thought it would be cooler once she was out of the narrow streets of the old city, but the air was still, and she could smell sheep dung and diesel, though there were no cars now, no vehicles at all. In the distance a dog barked once and then was quiet.

In the Ville Nouvelle she stopped to look at shopwindows, though there was nothing in any of them that she wanted. She liked that—looking at things other people wanted and then not wanting them. It made her feel young and old at the same time, as if she were both full of idealism and too old to care. She came to a fountain and sat on the edge, running her hand through the water, which was warm, like bath water. It had been years since she had taken a bath or gone for a swim, and in all those years she had never missed it, the feeling of floating, of letting one's limbs succumb to water. She heard footsteps approaching. She pulled her hand from the fountain, but did not get up or turn around. She sat with her wet hand in her lap and looked up at the stars. She was not afraid, she told herself. They are only footsteps. But she was afraid, and then the man was standing in front of her, and she could smell the alcohol on his breath, and he sat down next to her.

She stood up and started walking back toward the road that led to the walls of the old city. At first she thought he was not following her, and she could feel her heart slowing down, her limbs unstiffening. She wanted to look back, of course, but she kept walking, and after a while she was no longer afraid, and a car drove by, carrying with it a warm breeze but a breeze nonetheless, and by the time she reached her street, she was feeling sure that now she would be able to sleep.

And then there he was, grabbing her arm, pulling it up behind her back. "Quiet," he said, and she could feel the blade on her neck. "Walk." They came to the hotel, and he told her to open the door. Had he been waiting for her all these years, waiting for her to walk out into the night so that he could attack her? How did he know? But everyone in Meknes knew her, the old lady of the Hotel Atlas. That's what they all called her. What a ridiculous name, she thought, as if anyone could hold up the weight of the world. I should have awakened the boy, she thought as she turned the key in the door. "Shhh," the man said into her ear. "Shhh," he said again, pressing the knife to her neck. She tiptoed past the boy, who was still sleeping, his head resting on his arms on the reception desk. The man pushed her gently now, through the lobby and the dining room to the kitchen. "Shhh," he said. This is how it will end, she thought, and she closed her eyes and was calm. From far away she heard the Russian soldiers approaching, whistling and laughing. He stopped in the middle of the kitchen, as if surprised that they had come so far, as if he did not know what to do next, and his grip on her arm relaxed for just a moment, and then he gripped her tightly again. But that moment of hesitation had occurred and could not be undone. She lunged for a pot sitting on the counter, knocked it to the tile floor, where it landed with a deafening clatter, and Ulli, unable to regain her balance, fell too, pulling her attacker, who did not let go of her arm, down with her.

Abdoul and the boy at the reception desk were there in a moment, switching on the lights as they came, running. Abdoul grabbed Ulli's attacker, pulled him up from the floor, punched him so that he fell to the floor again.

"Enough," Ulli said, and Abdoul left him on the ground, weeping.

Ulli knew that if she called the police, the whole town would know about the attack by morning unless she paid a bribe. But she had learned over the years that paying bribes for intangible favors like silence was a waste of money, that eventually they would sell the information to one of her competitors in the Ville Nouvelle who would spread the word about the dangers of the old city. They would, of course, neglect to mention that he had followed her from the Ville Nouvelle, that if she had stayed in the old city, she would have been safe.

Abdoul pulled the man from the floor, dragged him out of the kitchen to the lobby. Ulli came as far as the lobby, where she gave him the keys to the Mercedes. "Take him far away from here, but do not hurt him."

"I will do what must be done," Abdoul said.

"You will not hurt him," Ulli said sternly. "I don't want to be responsible for his fear," she said, loudly enough for the man, who was still crying, to hear.

"As you wish, madame," Abdoul said.

"Here," Ulli said, thrusting two hundred dirhams into his hand. She did not know exactly what the money was for, except that she had grown accustomed to solving problems with a few dirhams here and a few dirhams there. She hoped, perhaps, that it would keep the man away. All she wanted was for him to be gone. As soon as they were out the door, however, Ulli realized that Abdoul must have thought that the money was for him, to ensure that he would follow her orders, and she thought that was probably for the best. She imagined her attacker lying on the side of the road, his head aching, his pockets empty and his throat dry, and for a moment she allowed herself to take pleasure in his misery. But she did not allow herself to linger there, in his fear.

When Abdoul returned an hour later, he sent the boy home. "I never want to see you again," he said, turning away from him dramatically, waving him off, and the boy—who in Abdoul's absence had prepared tea for Ulli and waited silently in attendance—left without a word. In a few weeks, Ulli was sure, Abdoul would ask to have him reinstated. He would apologize for acting rashly, remind her of the boy's poor mother, and Ulli would take him in again, for he was a sweet boy and would never again, she was sure, fall asleep while on duty.

After the boy was sent away, Abdoul wanted to take Ulli to the hospital. He was sure that she was injured. Her arm ached. That was all. There would be a bruise, of course, but not until morning. Now all she could think of was sleep. Abdoul wanted to keep watch outside her door, but she knew she would not be able to sleep with him there. In the end he agreed because it was his job to do what she required.

"In the morning, you will not be able to tell that anything happened in the kitchen," he said.

"Thank you," Ulli said. "Thank you."

It was after three in the morning. She passed Isaac's room on her way to her own quarters, but she did not stop to check on him, though she wondered whether he had been awakened by the noise, whether he was restlessly counting the minutes until morning.

When she got to her room, she called Abdoul to make sure he would not speak to anyone about what had happened. Now that the tourists were finally coming back, she did not want to risk losing them again. Only after hanging up did she let herself give in to sleep. She would rest now, and she would awaken when the sun was shining and take care of what needed to be taken care of, and that was the end of it. After all, nothing had happened. She was tired, she reminded herself, and tomorrow would be a busy day. The hotel would be full, and there was the wedding in the evening that she had to attend, the daughter of her most important meat and wine supplier. What on earth had she been thinking to go out alone in the middle of the night?

She couldn't sleep, of course. The moment she closed her eyes, she could hear the soldiers laughing and whistling, smell them as they got closer, their clothes thick with war. She saw Simone and Juliet crouching in a corner, shaking, clutching each other. She tried to run to them, but she stumbled, fell again on the hard kitchen floor, and the soldiers came closer and her daughters were whimpering. Ulli sat up, turned on the light, forced herself to think of her attacker lying on the kitchen floor, weak and vanquished by an old woman. "We are safe now," she said out loud. "We are safe now," she repeated, as if the words would change everything.

Isaac was just finishing his breakfast, eating the last scoop of his soft-boiled egg, when Ulli came into the dining room. "Good morning," he said to her cheerfully.

"Isaac," Ulli said, as if she were surprised to see him, had forgotten he was staying there.

"What's wrong, Ulli?" Isaac asked.

"Nothing," she said. "Sometimes I have a hard time sleeping."

"Have a seat," he said, standing up and pulling the chair out for her.

"I'm sorry, Isaac, but I am already behind," she said. She left him there, standing with his hand on the back of the chair.

"Ulli," he called after her, and some of the guests turned to look.

She couldn't face him now. She stopped, smiled at her guests, and continued on to the kitchen, where everything was back in place, as Abdoul had said it would be. She stood for a moment, staring at the spot where they had fallen to the floor. She could still feel his weight on her.

"*Madame?*"

"Ah, Dris," she said, pulling herself together, throwing her shoulders back, breathing in. "It smells wonderful," she said. "Wonderful."

"Please, have a seat. You are not well," the cook said. He took her arm in order to lead her to a stool in the corner.

"No!" Ulli said, breaking loose.

"*Madame—*"

She heard the cook calling after her, but she did not respond.

Isaac was still at the table when she came back through the dining room. He did not get up this time, did not pull out a chair, but Ulli sat down across from him.

"I'm sorry, Isaac. There is so much to do. We will be completely full by evening."

"Of course," Isaac said.

"I want you to go home," Ulli said.

Isaac did not respond.

"It's not you, Isaac. It was never you. It's just too much. I don't have the strength," she said. "I'm sorry."

"The strength for what?" he said.

"Forgive me. Forgive me for everything," she said, and walked away.

Don't be sorry, just don't do it, Isaac thought. It was what he used to tell the girls when they apologized about something they had done, though he knew they would make the same mistakes again and be sorry again. "Ulli," he called, but she was already gone.

III

America

THE HOTEL ROOM where Leo and Ulli lived after the eviction had a peculiar smell. It wasn't specific or strong, like mildew or urine, old sweat or cheap perfume, but it was there, and it seeped into Leo's clothes and skin, reminded him too much of the anxiety that he could hear in his parents' voices when they talked about the swelling river: "It's up an inch already, and if we have any more rain . . ." It wasn't even an unpleasant smell. There was something sweet about it, like cake, but Leo couldn't figure out where the hell it came from, and that was what bothered him, the mystery of it, not the smell itself.

Ulli couldn't smell anything. "It's a clean place," she said, which it was. Every day a woman came to sweep and mop, and in the mornings they opened the windows to let in fresh air. The smell drove Leo out into the world. He no longer wanted to linger, to luxuriate in sleep and Ulli's warmth beside him. All around, hammers were banging, cement was mixing; out of the rubble, a new city was growing. People no longer bent to winter. They opened their arms wide to embrace the sun and stood tall now that they were free of the heavy weight of overcoats. There was meat in the grocery stores, and oranges. It seemed as if, overnight, streetlights had sprung from the pavement, filling the darkness with new light. It would not be long before there was no rubble left, no street unlit. Stores would be overflowing with vegetables and eggs, soap and beer, and cigarettes would become as plentiful as air. Already, forgetting was winning over remembering. Soon the displaced people would all have found their places, and the Germans were filling their shopping carts with delicacies.

In order to avoid the brightest lights and the people walking arm in arm in the evening, Leo walked from the hotel to the base along the darker side streets. Sometimes, as he walked alone, there were men who looked at him as if they knew him. Sometimes the men followed him, keeping their distance, but he would continue walking at the same even pace until his pursuer gave up and he was alone.

On one night, however, a man did not veer off into the night. He kept following at a steady pace, so Leo veered, but still he followed. Leo stopped abruptly and turned around, and the man stopped right under a streetlamp, so Leo could see not just his shadow but his smile, half like a child and half like a tired old man who had done this so many times before. The man thrust his hands deep into his pockets and stared right at Leo, waiting.

"What do you want?" Leo called to him in English.

"*Komm*," the man said.

Leo started walking toward the man, who smiled smugly, as if he were sure of what Leo wanted. Leo stopped just a few feet before him. Who is this man? Who does he think I am? Leo thought, his desire turning to anger.

Again the man whispered, *"Komm."* Leo came closer. Now they stood face-to-face. The man said it again, *"Komm,"* and Leo punched him hard, felt the bone in the man's nose give. The man clutched his nose, and Leo punched him again in the stomach. The man staggered back, and Leo struck him in the jaw. The man fell to the ground. Off to the side, near the streetlamp, was a vacant lot. Along with stacks of lumber was a pile of brand-new bricks. Leo grabbed a brick off the top of the pile and returned to where the man was lying on the ground, clutching his stomach. Leo raised the brick. *"Bitte,"* the man said. Leo turned toward the streetlamp and threw the brick at the lamp with all his might.

The next day, he asked Ulli to marry him. It was time to go home, and he wanted her to come with him, not to Johnstown with its fire-spitting spires and menacing river, but someplace new.

"Where?" Ulli asked.

"I've been thinking about California," Leo said.

"I would like to go to California," Ulli said. It was, she thought, the most American place in America, the newest, the least burdened by history, the exact opposite of Berlin. "Do you think we could live by the ocean?"

"We can live wherever we goddamn want," Leo said, for at that moment he was sure that anything was possible.

"In California you have to drive everywhere," Isaac said when they told him.

"I like driving," Leo said.

"You'll miss the winter," Isaac said.

"I hate the winter," Leo said.

"What will you do there?" Isaac asked, and Leo said he would figure it out.

"You could go to college," Isaac suggested, but Leo didn't want to go to school. He was tired of sitting on the sidelines. He was go-

ing to be part of the action now. He was going to make something
of himself.

An army chaplain conducted the ceremony. They made it clear
that they didn't want any mention of God, but the chaplain could
not help himself and spoke of God more than once. Isaac was more
annoyed about it than Ulli or Leo.

"What the hell," Leo said, patting the chaplain on the back
when Isaac insisted on bringing it up after the ceremony was over.
"It's just words, right? We're leaving tomorrow, going home," Leo
said.

"I wish I were going home," the chaplain said sadly.

"God is everywhere," Isaac said, but nobody laughed.

In 1950, the year Ulli arrived in the United States, one still de-
boarded a plane right onto the tarmac, and so she walked down the
metal stairs and right into a New York City summer. The temperature was ninety-seven, the humidity ninety-five percent. She was
wearing high heels, gloves, and one of those silly pillbox hats with
a mesh veil. Leo wore a seersucker suit. Their plan was to move
to Los Angeles, but first they were going to visit Leo's family in
Johnstown. He said that they might as well spend a couple of days
in New York. Ulli did not remember much about those two days
except the heat and the bartender at the hotel bar, a surly Hungar-
ian who was scared to death of nuclear war. They spent most of
their time there with him because they both agreed that it was just
too hot to venture outside, though they did go to the top of the
Empire State Building since it was just a few blocks from the hotel.
They stood smoking at the window at the top of the tallest building

in the world, looking out over the city. The next day, they took the train to Pennsylvania.

Leo was the kind of man who loved to surprise people, so he had not written to his parents about his marriage or about his return to the United States and civilian life. On the short walk from the bus station to his parents' house, they stopped three times so Leo could introduce Ulli to the owner of the grocery store, the owner of the diner, and a high school friend who worked at the post office. "This is my wife," he said proudly each time, and she shook hands with all of them and told them she was glad to meet them.

"You're a lucky man," the grocer said, and Leo agreed.

Leo's father, it turned out, was home from work with a bad back and could not get up from bed, so Ulli was presented to him in the bedroom. "Sit," he said, so they sat down beside him.

"You remember Joe Ricardi?" he said to Leo. "He brought home a German wife too. She already had a baby. As a matter of fact, I think they got married for that very reason. You're not pregnant, are you?" he asked Ulli.

"Oh no," she said.

"Then you must be in love," he said.

"Yes," Leo said, and he meant it.

They went into the kitchen, where his mother served them tuna fish sandwiches and pickles. She did not eat with them.

In the evening, they visited his older brother, Ivan, and his wife and children. Leo's brother had been in combat in Europe, but Leo and Ivan didn't talk about the war. Ulli wondered whether it was because Ivan did not want to think about what he had seen and done, or because he didn't want to make Leo feel inadequate for having spent the war behind a desk. She could feel the distance between them, and the objects in the room—the worn sofa, the drapes, the coffee table upon which sat a single bowl of mints—all stood like sentries, keeping the delicate peace. While the brothers drank beer and talked about baseball, Ivan's wife showed Ulli her garden. She broke a flower from a bush and handed it to Ulli. "Honeysuckle," she said.

"Thank you," Ulli said.

"You can eat it," the wife said. "Like this." She broke off another flower and sucked on it. "Try it," she said.

Ulli tried it.

"What do you think?" the wife asked.

"It's sweet," she said.

"Yes, like honey," the wife said, and they went back into the house.

Later, Ulli cried when she told Leo about the honeysuckle. "She was so kind," she said.

"Why are you crying, then?" Leo asked.

"Because there is so little kindness in the world."

"Well, things are different now," Leo said. "I know they are."

That night, Leo's parents insisted on letting them use the only fan in the house. "But what about your back?" Ulli protested to Leo's father.

"My back hurts whether it's hot or not," Leo's father said.

After a couple of days, even though his back still hurt, Leo's father had to return to work at the steel mill. He had worked there since he finished high school. All the men in his family had worked in the steel mill ever since they settled in the area in the mid-nineteenth century. Ivan worked there.

"There's no rest for us steelworkers," Leo's father said, half complaining and half proud. "It's the steelworkers who won the war, you know. We made the U.S. Army what it is. Do you think you can fight a war without steel? Not that I don't appreciate the soldiers, the ones who shed their blood. Don't get me wrong about that. It's just that people have got to understand that there's more to a war than the fighting."

"I think they do understand," Ulli replied, as if he had been looking for confirmation.

Ulli wanted to say more, that she was sorry for what her country had done, but she knew it was too soon for that, especially since Leo's sister, whom Ulli did not meet because she was living in Pittsburgh, had been engaged to a man who had died on the Western Front.

Leo's mother showed Ulli photos of the members of their family—both on her side and on Leo's father's side—who had "perished," as she put it, in the flood. They had a special leather album just for them. On the cover, embossed in gold, it read *Our Beloved Victims of the Johnstown Flood, May 1889*.

"The river will flood again, you know," she said after they finished looking at the album. "It flooded in 1936, and it will flood again. There's no stopping nature."

"Do you ever think of moving?" Ulli asked.

She looked at Ulli as if Ulli had asked her whether she hated her mother. "Where would we go?" she said.

"You could come to California with us," Ulli offered.

"What on earth would we do in California?" she said. "California," she repeated, as if it were the most absurd place in the world.

During the day, Leo and Ulli helped his mother with various projects, cleaning out the kitchen cabinets and lining them with new shelving paper or going through all the boxes in the garage and carting off what was to be discarded to the dump. Ulli found these tasks terribly tiring: the measuring and cutting to make sure that everything was exactly right, his mother's insistence on looking through every last yellowed newspaper because there might be a recipe or an article she could not live without. Leo, on the other hand, was energized by this midsummer spring cleaning. It was something concrete he could do with direct and obvious results.

It would do no harm to linger here for a while. Who knew when they would have a chance to visit again? California was so far away. And Leo could think things through while he worked, take the time to get it all straight in his head, though he was sure everything would work out. He had a plan now, too, a plan beyond California—insurance. They had met a guy in New York, Jimmy was his name, who was in insurance, and he was rolling in money and insisted on buying drinks. Jimmy had been in the Pacific. He had a foot-long scar on his thigh—shrapnel. After a few rounds Jimmy pulled up his pant leg and showed them the scar, made them touch it.

"Does it hurt?" Ulli asked.

"When it rains," Jimmy said.

The war, Jimmy said, had made people more interested in holding on to what they had. He had given Leo his card. "If you want to get into insurance, just give me a call," he said, and that was Leo's plan, to call Jimmy. Maybe he knew some people in California.

Before they left Johnstown, Leo took Ulli to the cemetery to see the graves of his ancestors who had died in the flood. He knew where they all were buried, and he and Ulli walked slowly from gravesite to gravesite. At each stop, he looked up at the sky and recited from memory every word on the tombstone. Each time, he asked her whether he had gotten it exactly right, and of course, he had.

"When I was a kid, we used to come here every Sunday af- ter church, but then, the Sunday after my twelfth birthday, my mother was sick, so we didn't go, and then we never went again. I wonder whether they talked about it, decided that we didn't need to make the pilgrimage anymore, that enough time had passed, or whether they just got lazy about it. This is the first time I've been here since that last Sunday. I wasn't sure I was going to remember everything," he said.

"I know the names of all the other victims too," he added. He recited all of them. There were two thousand two hundred and nine names, and as Leo spoke the names of the dead, Ulli tried to imagine what it was like to be swept away by a wall of water that was at the same time as hard as rock and as ungraspable as air. By the time Leo got to the end of the list, they were both crying, and they held on to each other like a drowning man holds on to a lone tree. "I won't ever let you go," Leo said, and that made Ulli cry even harder.

They did not make it to California. The plan was to spend a week or so with Isaac in New York, just for old times' sake, Leo kept saying, and then head out to Los Angeles on the Greyhound bus, but Leo met another guy in a bar, another insurance salesman, and he also said to give him a call, which Leo did, and the next day he met the boss, who said that Leo was going to be a natural, he could tell. Leo told Ulli that he would just get some experience in the business, learn the tricks of the trade, and then they would go to California.

They stayed with Isaac for three weeks, during which time

Isaac kept reminding them that they were welcome to stay as long as they liked. Isaac was hardly ever home anyway. He was in the thick of graduate school at Columbia and would often spend the entire night at the library, coming home at dawn only to shower and change. But they couldn't stay with Isaac forever. Leo and Ulli had to make their own way, especially since Isaac disapproved of insurance, which was obvious from the way he nodded without commenting every time Leo brought it up. What bothered Leo, however, was not that Isaac disapproved, but that he thought what Leo was doing was so insignificant that he didn't even want to argue with him about it. So they left Isaac to his books and got their own place in Yorkville, near the German restaurants and delis that Ulli never entered, not even once, for she was done with Germany, done with wurst and black bread, but the apartment was cheap, and through the bedroom window they could see a sliver of the East River.

Leo, it turned out, was more than a natural at selling life insurance—he was a genius. In fact, he sold more insurance than anyone else on his team, and the company soon made him the regional manager. For the first time in his life he saw the advantages of having grown up in the shadow of the flood. Johnstown gave him insight that the other salesmen, most of whom were from Queens or the Bronx or Brooklyn, lacked. They had been raised in what they all assured him was the greatest city in the world, had not known that kind of lurking danger.

"The first rule," he told the new hires, "is never, ever talk about danger. That's what the big bosses will tell you to do. They'll tell you to start listing all the possible things that could happen—car accidents, train accidents, a brick could fall from a building onto someone's head, cancer, heart attack, murder, drowning. You might think that's the way to go, but if you get them thinking about the dangers all around them, they're just going to start feeling out of control, and when people feel out of control, they give up. They just let things happen. They don't prepare. The trick is to sell them the benefits without ever mentioning death. So what do you do? You get them talking about their dreams and their families and what they're saving up for—a house, a car, maybe a trip. You've got to commend them on how hard they're working to make a good life for their families. You get them imagining where they're going to be ten, fifteen years from now, and you get them talking about their kids, what they want to be when they grow up, how smart they are. You never mention danger. You make them feel like there's nothing in the world that could stop them from being happy, and then you just take out the form and set it in front of them. 'This will keep you safe,' you say. And then you hand them the pen."

People liked Leo, and he and Ulli were often invited to the homes of his colleagues, where the men drank whiskey while the women busied themselves in the kitchen. Ulli did not mind domestic tasks and would have been happy enough to do them on her own, without the company of the other wives, whose talk about their children, or their plans for having children, or where they had bought a certain dress or a hat or underwear, bored her. They talked in low voices, as if they were telling grave secrets.

Leo and Ulli did their share—too much, according to Ulli— of entertaining as well. Ulli and Leo cooked the meals together, though they did not tell their guests that. "Your wife is quite the cook," his colleagues said, and Leo would laugh and say, "Damn right she is," and everyone would laugh. When they had guests, Ulli drank steadily and practiced speaking with an American accent. As soon as the guests were gone, she went straight to bed, leaving Leo to clean up, which he did graciously—his *penance*, he called it, for having such boring friends.

It was after one of their dinner parties that they had their first real fight. That night Ulli had been drinking more than usual, and she started imitating one of the wives' strong New York accents. When no one seemed to notice except Leo, Ulli started parroting the woman, repeating every single thing she said, and she was a talker.

"My wife is quite the linguist," Leo said. "She speaks Russian, you know."

The wives nodded, and the men smiled.

Ulli did not smile or nod.

"Why don't you say something in Russian for us," Leo suggested.

"I'd rather not," Ulli said.

"Aw, c'mon. Don't be like that," one of the husbands said.

"Why don't you recite 'Dover Beach,'" Ulli said, glaring at Leo. "He knows hundreds of poems by heart. Have you told them that?"

"I'll do it if you say something in Russian," Leo said, so she recited the numbers to one hundred, slowly.

"Bravo," Leo said, and started clapping. The others clapped too, until Leo stopped.

"Now it's your turn," Ulli said.

He stood, cleared his throat, and began to recite. When he got to the final line about ignorant armies clashing by night, one of the wives started laughing, and then the men started laughing, and one of them slapped Leo on the back and Leo started laughing too. After that, Ulli was silent. When the guests were gone, she started throwing the glasses against the wall, and Leo grabbed her arms and pulled them behind her back until she said, "Enough, Leo," and she broke away and started picking up the broken glass.

"You'll hurt yourself," Leo said.

"I don't care," she said.

"I do," Leo said.

"That was our poem," Ulli said.

"But you wanted me to recite it."

"You laughed," Ulli said.

"I was trying to make them comfortable after that nonsense you pulled with that poor woman."

"She's not a poor woman."

"There was no reason to be cruel," Leo said.

"Of course there's no reason to be cruel. I was drunk," Ulli said.

"Why don't you get some rest?" he said.

While he cleaned up the broken glass, he could hear Ulli crying in the bedroom, but he did not go to her, not because he was angry, but because she was angry. He knew that she was tired of waiting for him to come home at night and having to be pleasant and polite and say things like "More potatoes?" or "Here, let me fill your glass." He didn't go to her, because he did not want to change his life. He was building something, and eventually, she would see.

From that night on, Leo went out with his colleagues by himself. "You missed a great party," he would say when he came home, and he really meant it. He enjoyed himself with the insurance salesmen and their wives. It was fun being successful. Later she wondered why she did not put up more of a fight, why she did not either demand her equal share of happiness or make an effort to enjoy her husband's success like the other wives, who seemed to want so little. Was it because that was just the way things were after the war, during peacetime—the women safe and sound at home, the men swinging their briefcases toward prosperity? Or was it that she did not know how to be happy?

Ulli began going out on her own. She learned that the city was full of people who were on the lookout for human contact. She found those people in the dingy bars on Tenth Avenue and in isolated corners of Central Park, in coffee shops tucked in under the elevated, on trains. She never had any trouble, was never even afraid, not even for a moment. No one ever demanded anything she could not give. The most she did was listen or relate the superficial details of her life. None of these people ever became her friend. They spent a morning, an afternoon, together, and then they each disappeared back into the city. She had no particular stomping grounds, preferring far-flung neighborhoods toward the ends of subway lines, and she avoided returning to a place more than once.

Once, she met a man at a Chock full o'Nuts. He was an ugly man, with folds of fat on the back of his neck and razor nicks all over his face. He was a salesman too. What was it about her that attracted salesmen? Did she look like an easy sell or a difficult one? He sold fire extinguishers and believed vehemently that every household should have one. "And if there are children in the house," he said, "it is a crime not to have one. Imagine their tiny, helpless bodies burning up."

"I don't have children," Ulli said, thinking that Leo would have disapproved of his pitch. What did he think he was doing, talking about children burning up?

"Don't worry, I'm not trying to sell you anything," he said. "How about we could go to the beach?"

Ulli agreed to go with him if he gave her a driving lesson.

"Look at this baby," he said as they approached his car. "Dodges are the best. I wouldn't buy anything but a Dodge. Don't ever buy anything but a Dodge."

"I won't," she said.

They drove out to Long Island and stopped at a Howard Johnson's for lunch. They had milkshakes and hamburgers. "So where are you from anyway?" he asked.

"Germany. Berlin," she said.

"You don't sound German," he said, which was what everyone said.

"My mother was English."

"Well, that explains it."

They drove to the beach, took off their shoes, and walked along the shore. His feet were terribly white. He hadn't cut his toenails in a long time, so they curved like talons. "It's been years since I've walked on the beach," he said, swinging his arms.

After a while, he wanted to sit down and have a smoke, so he laid out his jacket for her and they sat on the sand and smoked a few cigarettes and looked out at the water.

"So you married a soldier?" he asked after they had been sitting there for a while.

"Yes," she said.

"Do you love him?" he asked.

"Yes," she said.

"Hope he's not a drinker."

"Not really," she said.

"Good. I used to drink, but I stopped when my wife died. I should have stopped before, but that's the way it is."

"I'm sorry about your wife," she said.

"Cancer," he said, shaking his head.

They walked back to the parking lot. "How about some driving now?" he asked.

She hadn't forgotten but had decided not to bring it up. It seemed like a foolish request after he told her about his wife.

"I'd love to," she said, feeling that he would be disappointed if she changed her mind.

Although the day had not been particularly hot, the sun was strong, so the steering wheel was hot to touch. "That's why I always have my driving gloves," he said, reaching into the glove compartment. "They'll be a little big, since I've got such big hands."

He explained how everything worked in the greatest detail—the clutch, the brakes, the emergency brake, the gears, the mirrors. The mirrors, he said, were extremely important. Then he went on to the dials and levers—the heat, the lights, the windshield wipers—and only after he was sure that she understood the purpose of them all, were they ready to begin driving. Slowly he led her through the steps and, following his directions, she managed to slip smoothly from first to second gear. "You're a natural," he said. She drove around the parking lot, once, twice, three times, following his instructions. "Always keep your eyes on the road," he said, even though she was.

Ulli was afraid to tell him she had had enough. He seemed to be having such a wonderful time, so she kept driving round and round the parking lot. Finally he said they should probably be getting back to the city, and she agreed because she wanted to be sure to be home—in time for Leo.

She insisted that he drop her off at the Chock full o'Nuts because she did not want him to know where she lived. "I guess we've come full circle," he said.

"I guess we have," she said. "Thank you for letting me drive."

"My pleasure," he said. "Here's my card. Call me when you feel like driving."

"I will," she said, but she never did. She thought about calling him, but she knew better, knew that the day could not be replicated, though for weeks after their outing, she awoke every morning thinking of him shaving in a tiny bathroom in a dark studio with windows facing the air shaft, telling himself he must pick up some razors on the way home. In her version of his life, he never got around to buying new razors, so every morning the bleeding got worse, blood dripped onto his clean white shirt, and he tried to wash it out with soap and a washcloth, but it always left a yellowish stain.

During this period, when Leo was rising to the top of the insurance world and Ulli was wandering around the city, they saw Isaac only once a week—every Sunday afternoon at three. Isaac provided the pastries, always éclairs and Napoleons. They did not have the heart to tell him they were tired of éclairs and Napoleons, that they were ready for something new. There was something about Isaac's apartment, about the pastries and the coffee in the middle of the afternoon, about the dominance of books, that left Ulli feeling like a child again, enduring her parents' interminable Sundays. Ulli spoke little during these gatherings, letting Leo and Isaac do most of the talking. They reminisced about Berlin a lot, remembering the meals they prepared, the cold. They liked talking about who might be living in the apartment now. They hoped it was someone nice, a young couple with a baby. Ulli didn't want to think about the apartment, but she didn't tell them that. Sometimes Leo asked Isaac to tell them about his work, but Isaac always said he didn't like to talk about it. "You wouldn't be interested," he said, and Leo didn't push it. By six o'clock Ulli would be asleep on the sofa, and

Leo would have to wake her, prod her to the door, hold her up as they waited for the elevator. It was only when they were back in the street again, when the air hit her face and the noise of passing cars entered her consciousness, that she could stand on her own, and then she wanted to walk and walk and walk until she was exhausted. Leo obliged her. They often walked all the way down to Battery Park and back up to their apartment, where they would fall into bed with relief, clutching each other, making love like soldiers about to be sent forth from the trenches into battle.

On Monday mornings she lingered in bed while Leo jumped up, excited about the week's prospects. Was he going over his appointments in his head, adding up the figures—the premiums, the percentages? Was there a moment while he was drying off after his shower or tying his shoelaces that he wondered what it was she did all day, or did he just push that out of his head? Still, she yearned for him, waited for him to come home, counted the hours, and no matter how far she wandered, she was always home at six, despite the fact that each day it became clearer that what had seemed so attractive, so simple when they were in Germany, was not at all what she wanted. She tried not to be waiting for him, to stop on the way home for just one more drink or one more cup of coffee, to walk rather than take the bus, but then she would end up rushing, all in a tizzy about getting home in time. She wanted to be home before him, not out of any sense of duty, not because she was trying to be a good wife, but because she missed him, because she loved him even if he was an insurance salesmen selling people a security they both knew could never exist.

She didn't understand it, this love for him, but it was there, and if seven o'clock passed, then eight, then nine, the only way she could calm herself was to remember the bomb shelter, the waiting, the silence, the planes overhead, the buildings crashing down around her. I am safe, she repeated to herself over and over again. He will return, and he always did, smiling, full of stories, tired from a hard day's work, hungry.

At one point Leo bought Ulli a phonograph, and every night for three weeks he came home with a new record. After dinner they listened to the record, and sometimes they danced. The figure in their bank account grew.

On weekends they went to the Metropolitan Museum, to the theater, to movies. They went out to steak houses and ate more beef in one night than Ulli had eaten during the entire war. They went to see Frank Sinatra. They went up to Harlem to see Billie Holiday at the Apollo Theater. "That is the saddest woman I have ever seen," Leo said, and Ulli wanted to tell him that she was sad too, that she wished she could take her sadness and turn it into song, into something that people were not afraid to look at, into something they could touch and hold in their arms, not out of pity but out of love. But she did not know how to talk to him here, and she found herself longing for the quiet of snow-covered rubble and the pleasure of that one cigarette after having gone for so long without them.

The Pink Parakeet

LEO WAS GOOD at not thinking about what Ulli did all day. He knew that she spent a lot of time listening to records. That's why he bought her so many of them. When he came home, the apartment was thick with smoke, but he never complained, never asked her why she didn't open the windows even on warm days. They would be going to California soon, he told himself, and they would have children. Then there would be so much to do. He liked thinking of children all bathed and clean and in their pajamas, running to the door to greet him after a long day at work. He liked thinking about buying them gifts. And then one evening after work he discovered the Pink Parakeet.

The doctor had suggested that regular and mild exercise would be good for his heart, so when the weather was nice, after going out for a couple of drinks with his team, he often walked the twenty blocks home. The walk also helped him ease his way from the world of insurance policies and pitches to their apartment, to

Ulli's world, to Ulli. He did not allow himself to think of how different he had felt when he and Ulli were walking home to the apartment in Berlin.

One damp, cold evening in February, as he was waiting to cross the street, a man who was standing next to him coughed. Leo turned, and the man looked right at him and nodded, as if he were giving him permission for something. The light changed, and Leo and the man walked abreast without turning to look at each other, until they got to the opposite side of the street, where Leo dropped behind. The man kept on at the same pace, and Leo followed. At the next corner the man crossed Lexington Avenue and headed down Forty-sixth Street. At Third Avenue the man turned uptown, and so did Leo, but he kept his distance, hanging back when they came to a red light so that he would not have to stand next to the man again, but when the light turned green, he quickened his pace so as not to lose sight of him. Just before reaching the corner of Fifty-third Street, the man entered a bar. Leo followed him inside.

He knew right away what kind of bar it was, even though he had not known of their existence until that moment, and he felt both a sense of relief and a terrifying dread, the same kind of dread he felt when he lay awake at night thinking about his damaged heart, the time bomb ready to go off. I should leave, he thought, just turn around and walk out, but the man he had followed was just taking a seat at the bar, nodding to him again, and Leo nodded back, but he did not move. The man ordered a drink, and the bartender brought it, a cocktail with an umbrella in it. The man took the umbrella out of his drink and set it on the bar, took a sip, set his drink down, lit a cigarette, but he didn't turn around.

What did one say when one went up to a man at a bar? Leo

thought. Did one not speak at all, just sit down next to him? Did one just order a drink with an umbrella, take the umbrella out, take a sip, light a cigarette, and look straight ahead at the giant pink parakeet painted on the wall behind the bar?

"I've never heard of a pink parakeet before," Leo said, sitting down a few stools away from the man.

"I don't know anything about parakeets," the man said.

Leo didn't know anything about parakeets either. "I don't like birds," Leo said, which he realized was true. There was something unpredictable about them, nervous, stupid, though he had never really thought about it before.

"I don't like birds either," the man said, turning toward him. "But here we are in the bird circuit nonetheless."

Leo laughed so that the man would not suspect that he didn't have a clue what the bird circuit was or why it was funny.

The man called the bartender over. "What are you drinking?" he asked Leo.

"Jack Daniel's," he said. "On the rocks."

The man paid for Leo's drink, and Leo did not protest.

"I hope it won't rain," Leo said, not knowing how to thank him.

The man, whose name Leo would never know, was older than Leo, but not old—in his mid-thirties, Leo guessed. He wondered, as he always did whenever he met someone new, whether he had been in the war, but he didn't ask. He never did, and the man didn't ask him. Instead the man asked him whether he was from Pennsylvania.

"How did you know?" Leo asked.

The man said that it was the way he pronounced the word *hope*.

"So how do you say it?" Leo asked, and the man said "hope," and Leo said "hope" again, but he couldn't hear the difference.

"Say *coke*," the man said, and Leo said "coke," and the man said, "See?"

Later, when Leo was back home with Ulli, after he had changed into dry clothes because it had rained after all, Leo asked Ulli whether he pronounced words funny.

"All words or just some words?"

"Some words, like *coke* and *hope*. Words with *o*'s."

"Say them again," she said. He repeated the words, and she repeated them each two or three times.

"Say *suppose*," she said, and Leo said, "Suppose."

"The *o* is longer, drawn out, like you're yawning when you say it."

After that, Leo watched his *o*'s, though rather than shortening the sound, he ended up just saying those words more softly, so that his speech took on a new cadence that sounded like a shortwave radio coming in and out of range.

He stayed away from the Pink Parakeet for three days, going home after work—by train. But on the fourth night, he could not help himself. The man he had followed the first time was not there, but another man was sitting at the bar, so he sat next to him. After a while, the man next to him got up and headed toward a back room. Leo followed. When the man reached the door, Leo stopped and waited until he had entered and the door closed behind him. Then Leo opened the door and went inside.

It was not long before he understood what the man had meant by the bird circuit. There were other bars on Third Avenue with bird names—the Blue Parrot, the Happy Cockatoo, the Egret. He tried them all. Each bird bar had its bird painting. Each bird bar had a back room.

The next time he stopped by the Pink Parakeet, he drank too much with an older man called Howard. Unlike the other men at the Pink Parakeet, Howard introduced himself and looked Leo right in the eye when he offered to buy him a drink. This was due, Leo learned, to the fact that Howard was an optometrist and spent his days up close to people, looking into their eyes. "A lot of people are afraid of eyes, but if you look at them enough, you realize there's nothing to be afraid of," Howard said.

"I don't think people are afraid of looking into eyes. They're afraid of people looking into *their* eyes. They're afraid they'll see something, some weakness," Leo said.

"Look into my eyes, Leo. What do you see?"

Leo wondered whether this was a line Howard used all the time, whether he was always hoping that some young man would see something in his eyes that no one had seen before, something mysterious and alluring or, perhaps, the remnants of his youth. Leo pulled the bar stool up closer, leaned forward.

"See anything?" Howard asked.

"They're brown," Leo said.

"Anything else?"

"I see the blood vessels. There are more in your left eye than in your right eye."

"Anything else?"

"No."

"No deep, dark secrets, no tortured soul, no evil or kindness?"

"No."

"You see. All that windows-of-the-soul stuff is just nonsense."

"But they're beautiful, eyes are, or can be."

"Beauty is not what it's cracked up to be," Howard said, sighing deeply. "I'm tired of caring about beauty. At my age it just makes me a lecherous old man. Whatever you do, don't end up a lecherous old man. That is the most difficult part about being a homosexual," he said.

The word *homosexual* hit Leo hard, as if it were a demented bird that had flown into his quiet room and was thrashing about, squawking. He lit a cigarette and hoped Howard wouldn't see that his hands were trembling, though he knew he would. He could tell that Howard was used to looking carefully. "I have a bad heart. I probably won't make it to old age," Leo said.

"Then you must live your life now, which is what we all should do, but we don't. We spend our lives grinding lenses so other people can see, but they don't really want to see. What do you do, Leo? What are you wasting your life on?"

"I'm in life insurance," Leo said.

"I see. I imagine you're quite good at it," Howard said.

"Yes. I've been the number one salesman in the region two years in a row."

"Well, I suppose that could be something to be proud of, if one cared about such things."

"I am proud," Leo said.

"That's good, son," he said. "I'm sorry."

"That's okay," Leo said, though he did not know what Howard was apologizing about.

"So tell me about your heart, and then I will tell you about mine," Howard continued.

"It's a murmur, a harsh murmur. That's what it's called. My aortic valve is inflamed, and it will keep getting more and more inflamed so that eventually the blood won't be able to get through."

"Is there nothing that can be done about it?"

"No, but the doctor in the army told me they were working on it, that someday they might be able to do something."

"That's something to hope for, isn't it?" Howard said, putting his hand on Leo's hand, not holding it, but just letting it rest there lightly.

"Yes," Leo said.

"Sometimes," Howard continued, lifting his hand to pick up his glass, taking a sip, setting the glass down, not returning his hand to where it had been, "sometimes I think about all those people before they invented lenses, walking around half blind, the world a blur, never even hoping that one day they would be able to see."

"They probably still hoped," Leo said. "People always hope."

"Not always, not when it's hopeless," Howard said.

"Nothing is hopeless," Leo said.

"Now you sound like an insurance salesman."

"You said you were going to tell me about your heart."

"I did indeed, but not tonight," Howard said. "It's late, and you have to get home to your wife. If you want to hear about my heart, you will have to see me again."

"How did you know? About my wife, I mean?"

"I'm an old hand at this, Leo. Here," he said, giving Leo his card. "If you want to hear the story, stop by the shop just before six. We're closed on Sundays, but any other day you'll find me there, if you want a friend. I am done with being a lecherous old man."

Leo waited two weeks before going to Howard's store. The night of their meeting at the Pink Parakeet, Howard had been wearing a deep blue Italian suit and a colorful Indian scarf, and Leo had imagined the store would look like Howard—velvet drapes, the walls lined with gold cases in which the glasses were displayed like items in a museum. But it looked more like Leo's mother's living room than a museum, and Howard—who had gotten up from the table in the back where he had been attending a customer and was walking to the front to greet him—was now sporting a plain gray suit, white shirt, and a thin black tie. And he was wearing glasses.

"Leo, I'm glad you could come," Howard said, as if there had been an appointment. "Have a seat. I'm just finishing up with Mrs. Bauman. She's chosen the most horrid glasses. I couldn't talk her out of them," he said under his breath.

And they were horrid—pale pink cat-eye glasses that, despite their flamboyant upward swoop, were dwarfed by Mrs. Bauman's large, fleshy head. "Leo, come have a closer look at Mrs. Bauman's new glasses. Aren't they lovely?" Howard tipped her chin up with his fingertips, then moved her giant head gently to the left and then the right. "How do they feel?"

"Perfect," Mrs. Bauman said. "Thank you."

After Mrs. Bauman left, Leo waited while Howard went through the closing routine. Leo offered to sweep, but Howard had refused indignantly. "I didn't ask you here to be my *Putzfrau*," he said. So Leo left him to the sweeping, which he did very thoroughly, starting at the back of the store and making his way to the front. When he was finished, Howard counted the money in the till, pulled the blinds, and turned the sign to closed.

"Good night, my optical illusion," Howard said as he shut the security gate.

That night Howard took Leo to the Village—"*the real thing*," he called it. The birdy bars on Third Avenue were for cowards. In each bar they had one drink, no more than one. Otherwise, Howard said, they wouldn't have the stamina. In each bar Howard knew someone who came up and threw his arms around him and said, "Howard, it's been ages." In each bar, Howard made Leo ask someone to dance, and then they went on to the next bar, where Leo also danced and Howard watched. At the last bar there was a show. A man dressed up like Marlene Dietrich sang "Johnny." After her performance she threw a rose into the crowd and Leo caught it. "Careful of the thorns, sweetheart," Marlene Dietrich said, blowing him a kiss, and Leo blew her a kiss back.

Leo didn't keep the rose. He left it in the taxi he took back uptown to his apartment. He wondered how long the rose would ride back and forth, up and down Manhattan, before someone took it. Perhaps the taxi driver would find it at the end of his shift. He liked thinking of the taxi driver alone at dawn, finding the rose in the back of his cab.

Leo knew the moment he opened the door that Ulli was awake, sitting on the sofa in the dark. "I missed you," she called when he was still in the entryway hanging up his coat and hat.

"You're still up?"

"I'm still up," she said.

Leo did not turn on the light but felt his way slowly through the hallway to the living room couch. "Come here," he said, drawing her close, kissing her the way he wanted to kiss Marlene Dietrich.

"Don't go," Ulli said. "Don't go."

"I'm here," Leo said, closing his eyes, putting himself back in their apartment in Berlin, where they had been protected from both the past and the future. He thought about what Howard had said when Leo asked why he had chosen him to be his friend: "You seemed like a man who wanted to be happy."

"Doesn't everyone want to be happy?" Leo asked.

"I have come to the conclusion that unhappiness is so much easier, and most people, frankly, are lazy and scared."

"Scared of what?"

"Of being happy."

"And what's scary about it?"

"It requires you to be who you really are even if people despise you."

"It's not easy to be happy if people despise you," Leo said.

"Exactly. That's why unhappiness is easier."

"And what about you, are you happy?" Leo asked.

"I'm afraid I have lost the energy and the courage to pursue it."

"Were you happy in the past?"

"At times," Howard had said.

As they lay on the couch afterward, Ulli sleeping on his chest, Leo believed that what he wanted more than anything else, more than he wanted to kiss Marlene Dietrich, was to protect Ulli from unhappiness.

After the night in the Village, Leo did not return to Howard's store or to the bars on Third Avenue. He walked home on Lexington, avoiding Third Avenue altogether. Sometimes when he was walking, he thought he heard someone calling his name, but when he turned around to look, there was never anyone there. He was home by six, the latest seven if he went out for a quick drink with his colleagues after work. Sometimes when he came home, there was an elaborate meal waiting for him, with candles ready to be lit. On other nights he found Ulli sitting on the couch listening to Billie Holiday and no food waiting at all, and he accepted this lack of food as graciously as he accepted the three-course dinners and the candlelight. He tried not to think about Howard methodically sweeping his shop at the end of the day, hoping that maybe tomorrow Leo would stop by again. He tried not to wonder whether Howard needed glasses or not, and what it was that had happened to his heart.

Words

I N WAITING FOR her husband, Ulli found that even the simplest tasks, such as making the bed and buying groceries, were as difficult as burying the dead. Still, every night when Leo walked in the door, everything changed. There he was, hanging up his coat and his hat, and there were his lips on hers, his tongue in her mouth, and the day became a blur, a nightmare, the unspeakable past. All there was was Leo.

How long, she wondered later, after she found herself once again out in the world, would she have gone on like that, trying to pretend that all she needed was Leo? Instead, Isaac had called. "I found the perfect thing for you," he said. He did not say, *I found the answer to your unhappiness*. He did not say *I know you are unhappy*. He did not say *Leo is not enough*, but she knew that was what he meant.

"A car?" she guessed, though she knew that something as banal

and concrete as a car would never occur to Isaac as being the solution for anything.

"A car? What would you do with a car in the city?" he asked.

"I don't know," Ulli said. "Plenty of people have cars, you
know."

"I didn't call you to discuss cars," Isaac said, and he proceeded
to tell her about an announcement he had seen at Columbia for
a yearlong training program for simultaneous interpreters. "Meet
me tomorrow at eight on the steps of Butler Library," he said. "I'll
give you all the information then." He did not ask her whether she
wanted the information or whether she was free to meet him at
eight. Of course he knew she was free. Of course he knew that she
had nothing in the world but time.

There were twenty of them when they started out, and by the end of
the day, only six, all men except for Ulli. As soon as the tests began,
a confidence came over her, similar to the calm she had felt while
sitting in the bomb shelter, listening to the planes flying overhead,
watching the shaking hands of her neighbors and their rocking
back and forth, wishing she could tell them that she was sure, abso-
lutely-without-a-doubt sure, that they would not die that night. The
test had gotten harder throughout the day, starting out with basic
translations of vocabulary and phrases, eliminating those who did
not know the words for *peacock* or *quagmire*, and culminating in an
almost impossible task: for thirty minutes she had to sit in a booth
wearing earphones and repeat into a tape recorder, word for word,
the stream of sentences in English, Russian, German, and French
flowing into her ears, all while writing the numbers from one to one
hundred backward. She accepted the requirements, lost herself in

the challenge, felt that she could go on forever, for hours, days even, simply speaking and writing out numbers. She felt unfettered—she would almost dare to say free—for the first time since she was a child, when freedom was so much easier to come by.

The key was to keep up a rhythm, to take the words in and spit them out again without allowing the mind to get bogged down in meaning. They tried to trick them, she learned later, spewing out pages and pages of Nazi propaganda and nihilistic religious tracts, trying to trap them in their own beliefs, in anger, in meaning, but she did not grasp the meaning of what she heard and what she repeated. To her they were only sounds. She came home from the tests, which lasted more than eight hours, physically invigorated, as if she had spent the day hiking in the mountains.

Ulli had not told Leo about the program, and she made Isaac promise not to mention it, not because she thought Leo would be opposed, but because she did not want his sympathy if she were not accepted. When she got the official results a few weeks later, Ulli called Isaac, and he insisted they celebrate. "We will tell Leo at dinner," he said.

"Isaac has invited us for dinner this Friday at his favorite Czech place on Second Avenue," she told Leo a few nights beforehand.

"What's the occasion?" he asked.

"Apparently it's a secret," she said.

When they arrived, Isaac was already ensconced at a table in the corner next to the fireplace. "*Prost*," he said, raising his glass to them. "I've ordered goose, for old times' sake."

They had cooked a goose for New Year's in Berlin. Ulli had traded three bottles of commissary American whiskey for it. The butcher was ecstatic and claimed to have ridden his bicycle sixty kilometers to his uncle's farm in order to acquire the goose. They spent the whole day cooking, making a special prune and orange sauce, but ultimately they were disappointed by the bird, which turned out to be fatty and tasted vaguely of grass. At midnight they had gone up to the roof to toast the New Year, the first postwar year, and they left the rest of the goose up there for the crows. Leo insisted that the crows would eat the goose with pleasure, but Isaac and Ulli were not convinced, because it seemed a form of cannibalism. In the following days, she thought of going up to the roof to check on the goose, but she never did.

At the restaurant, they did not remind Isaac of their disappointment, and when the goose came, surrounded by baked apples on a yellow platter, they marveled at it and consumed the bird gleefully, although it too was fatty, but at least this one did not taste like grass. The plum dumplings, however, were perfect and the slivovitz went down smoothly. During dessert, it began to snow, and they watched it through the window from their warm table beside the fireplace. Isaac would not let Ulli announce her achievement until the very end, after they had eaten strudel and finished off the slivovitz. Then he stood and proclaimed, so that the entire restaurant could hear, "It is with great honor that I announce that Ulli Schlemmer has been accepted into the simultaneous interpreter training program at the United Nations."

The other diners broke into thunderous applause, and Ulli stood and thanked everyone, and Leo picked her up, lifted her high into the air, insisting that everyone in the restaurant drink a toast to her and to the United Nations.

"To Isaac," Ulli said, raising her glass. He had moved to the other side of the room, and she thought she noticed his lips trembling, as if he were trying to keep back tears, but Leo swept her up again and kissed her hard, and when she looked back at Isaac, he was clinking glasses with a portly diner and laughing.

For the first few months of training, there were only words, like water surrounding her, holding her up yet capable also of doing her in. Even when she left school for the day, she translated every word she saw or heard or thought. She translated the hundreds of conversations she heard every day: on the bus, in the subway, in shops, on corners, on telephones. At night she stuffed cotton into her ears and walked from their apartment to Columbus Circle and back, repeating the word *blank* over and over again so that she could rest. "Blank, blank, blank, blank," she said while she brushed her teeth, while Leo caressed her breasts. In the middle of the night Leo would have to shake her. "You're talking again," he would say, and Ulli would force herself to stay awake so that he could sleep.

Gradually, however, as she became a swifter and more accurate interpreter, meaning returned to her, and by the time she graduated and got her first job, she no longer dreaded waking up in the morning or spending the day longing for sleep. In fact, she slept very little. It seemed to her that the less she slept, the faster she was able to interpret and the truer she was to the words.

In those first years as an interpreter, her colleagues were all men. One would expect that the men would not have been pleased by her presence and would have made it their business to belittle her, but she experienced nothing of the sort, perhaps because she was the best among them. She never stumbled, never hesitated, never resorted to paraphrasing. After work they often went out drinking together, and they treated her more as an honorary man than as a woman. When Leo came along for drinks, they were friendly toward him, and he always made an effort to enjoy their company.

He had started his own business by then, specializing in insurance plans for the booming construction industry. They had moved out of the apartment in Yorkville to a larger, sunnier place on Central Park West. From the living room and bedroom they had an unobstructed view of Central Park. Ulli's work often took her to Vienna, and when she returned to New York from a conference, she always brought Leo a gift. His favorite was an Ottoman snuff-box, on the cover of which was a bearded sultan. He used it for his cuff links and kept it on the night table next to the bed. She liked to think of him lying in their bed with the box on the table next to him. Sometimes she wondered whether he was always alone in that bed when she was away, but mostly she was too busy to think about that.

Howard's War

LEO WAS PROUD of Ulli's accomplishments and admired her
ability to concentrate so intensely. She never missed a beat, never
let a word slip through her fingers, Leo liked to tell his clients,
who out of politeness asked about his wife, never expecting a whole
lesson in the workings of the United Nations and the importance
of the interpreters. We're a team, he would tell them, both of us
protecting the world in our own way, Ulli keeping war at bay, Leo
guarding financial security.

"I wouldn't want my wife traipsing around the world. I like
to know that she's safe at home," Leo's partner was always saying.

"My wife can take care of herself, that's for sure," Leo said,
proud of being proud of Ulli.

Now it was Ulli who did not come home until after midnight.
It was Ulli who returned tired from a long journey, full of stories,
full of words. Missing Ulli brought Leo a strange kind of comfort.
When she was gone, he stood at the window looking out at the

darkness of Central Park and the ring of lights around it, imagining her in her hotel room in Vienna. In his imaginings there was always a balcony, and he pictured her on it, looking out at the city, smoking the last cigarette of the evening. By the time she finished her cigarette, her hands and face would be numb, for she would not have put on her coat just to stand out on the balcony, but inside it was warm, and the sheets were soft, and soon she would fall asleep thinking of him. Leo imagined that she was thinking also about their bed in Berlin. If he concentrated on Ulli in their room in Berlin, on the cold outside and the sound of wooden beams loosening and crashing to the ground, he could not imagine his life without her.

With Ulli strong again and Leo's business growing, all was stable, peaceful, secure. There would be no harm in going down to the Village every once in a while when she was gone or when important talks were going on and she practically lived at the UN. It was like having a special meal out, a treat. It was, he told himself, another form of insurance, a way to keep the longing contained so that he and Ulli could continue what they were building. And it worked. His forays downtown helped him stay strong for Ulli, for when she returned. Until one night, in a dark bar in the Village near the docks, Howard found him. "I knew we would meet again," Howard said.

"So did I," Leo said, for deep down, or maybe not so deep down, he had known that he could not run from Howard forever.

They did not stay at the bar by the docks, but walked through the quiet streets of the West Village to an Italian café far from all that commotion, as Howard put it. "Of all the places, why did you choose that dive?" Howard asked.

"Why did you?" Leo asked, and they both laughed.

The Italian café became their regular meeting spot. Sometimes they went to a bar afterward, where they would part ways, going solo into what Howard called "the bowels of earth." "We're like miners," he liked to say, "going down all clean and full of vigor and coming up to the surface again with blackened faces and burned-out lungs." Other times Howard took Leo to the theater or the opera, for which he always insisted on paying, no matter how much Leo protested. Leo enjoyed going to the theater, but he didn't get what Howard, or anyone, saw in opera. Once, after an excruciatingly long performance, Leo started to tell Howard how he really felt, but he knew that if he were truthful, Howard would no longer take him to the opera and that would mean Howard would go alone. The thought of him alone at the opera was more than Leo could bear.

At first Leo thought that Howard told him things because he was lonely and had no one else to talk to aside from his customers, with whom he could not possibly talk about what he talked about with Leo, but gradually Leo understood that he, too, needed to tell his story, and he realized that he had never really exchanged secrets with anyone, not even Ulli. What secrets, he wondered, was Ulli keeping from him?

It was easier to talk to Howard about Bidor than about Ulli. What he had felt for Bidor was something Howard understood. It was what Howard called situational love. "If you had met him under different circumstances, if he had not been condemned to the cold cruelty of Siberia, you would hardly remember him," Howard said.

"Perhaps I would remember him better. Maybe if I didn't have that image of him bent to the ground, hacking at the frozen earth, I would remember the green of his eyes and the power in his arms."

"Perhaps," Howard said, but he was not convinced. "You are confusing guilt with love."

"I didn't say that I loved him, but I cared about him. That's something, isn't it?"

"Of course it's something," Howard said. "There was nothing you could have done, you know."

"That's what Isaac always said."

"In war there are no solutions, but we keep on thinking that war leads to solutions."

Howard had not sat out his war—the Great War, the war in which more people died than any other war in the entire history of mankind. Howard had killed. Howard had medals, which, one muggy summer evening, he and Leo tossed from the Palisades into the Hudson River. "Thank you," Howard said when it was over. "I could not stand the weight of them any longer."

"To valor," Howard said, raising his glass, for he had brought champagne to mark the occasion, to send his medals to their death.

Howard said that the worst thing was that he had never cried for the young boys he killed. He hardly remembered the feel of flesh giving in to the thrust of his bayonet. But he had cried for the boy who died in his arms, who did not feel the kiss Howard planted on his lips when they were already blue.

All people, Howard said, had one moment in their lives, one moment that distinguishes them from all the other poor fools who walk this earth. That was his moment. After that, there were just the days of his life, the steady stream of eyes, the opening and closing of gates, the dinners and lunches, the back rooms.

"Who was he?" Leo asked.

"A boy who was too young to die," Howard said.

"So you didn't know him?"

"No, but after that, there could be no other."

"But how can you live without love?" Leo asked.

"One can live with the memory of love," Howard said. "One can get up every morning, boil an egg, put it in a wooden cup, crack it, scoop out the nourishment. One can wash the wooden cup and set it back in the cupboard, put on one's hat and coat, open a store, sell glasses, grind lenses, sweep, balance the books. One can keep on living because dying is not an option."

But Leo didn't want to live with the memory of love. He wanted to breathe it in, wrap his arms around it, feel it in his bones.

IV

The Shrine of Moulay Idris

Isaac walked up the stairs to his room, where he began to pack his bag carefully, making sure not to waste any space. It was a small bag, and everything had to be folded just right; otherwise he would not be able to close it. When all that was left was the leather toiletry case, the one Simone and Juliet had given him when he went on his first trip to the Soviet Union, he stopped. Simone had warned him that things might not go well, that Ulli might not want to see him. "If it's something you have to do, then you must do it, but you have to be prepared. People don't change, not really. They just become more and more like themselves."

"Ulli is not one of your clients," Isaac said.

"I just don't know why now, after all these years, you want to see her."

"Don't you have any interest in knowing what happened to her, how she's doing?"

"Not really," Simone had said. "I don't see how it would make a difference. And the asthma." She paused. "You have to be careful."

"Maybe the dry air will be good for it," Isaac said. "Maybe I will be cured again as I was in Arizona."

Simone put her hand on his shoulder. "I just don't want you to get hurt," she said.

But Isaac was tired of being careful, tired of sleeping in the afternoons, tired of counting his breaths, tired of memories.

"I am prepared," Isaac said, holding up his inhaler like a torch.

And he had been prepared, and then Ulli had seemed so pleased to see him, and she had given him the best room, with a balcony, and he had bought her those silly *babouches*. She just needed some time to get used to his presence. He had not come all the way to Morocco to be left again with nothing. Still, she needed time. He understood that, and he could entertain himself. He had always been good at that. He would go to Volubilis by himself. It wasn't the pyramids, but it would be spectacular nonetheless. "'Arise ye prisoners of starvation, arise ye wretched of this earth,'" he sang, as he used to do when Simone and Juliet were reluctant to get out of bed.

"Enough, enough!" they would scream, burying their heads under the blankets, but he would continue singing until they had no choice but to rise, rub their eyes, and get ready for the day.

He did not think it would be so easy to slip out of the hotel un-noticed. He thought the employees would be all over him, warning him about the sun and about not staying out for long. He had planned to make up something about going to the souk again to buy gifts for his daughters now that he was leaving. *Don't worry about me*, he thought he would have to say, but he made it to the lobby, through the lobby, and out the door without encountering anyone.

Abdoul caught up with him before he got to the first corner. "Monsieur," Abdoul said.

"Abdoul," Isaac said.

"Where are you going, monsieur?"

"To Volubilis," Isaac answered proudly, forgetting his plan to lie about his outing.

"I will call a taxi," Abdoul said.

"No. I will take the bus. In the guidebook it says that there are buses to Volubilis at the market." He took the book out of his pocket, as though offering proof.

"It is a very old bus," Abdoul said.

"I like old buses," Isaac insisted.

"It is not a good idea," Abdoul said.

"I will be fine. I assure you," Isaac said, adding, "I take full responsibility."

Abdoul shook his head and explained how to reach the market. When he finished, he made Isaac repeat the directions, which he was able to do without error. "There are many small streets," Abdoul warned. "You will not be able to read the names, so you must pay close attention, and when you get to the market, you must ask for the bus to Volubilis." Abdoul went over the directions a second time and made Isaac repeat them again.

"I will be fine," Isaac assured him. "Please tell madame that I will not be having lunch at the hotel," he added, bowing.

He found the gas station and the store that sold used televisions, just as Abdoul had said, and the grand taxi station, the school. He followed the directions carefully, stopping at every intersection to assess his progress, and he arrived at the market without any glitches. "Volubilis?" he asked a toothless man who was probably quite a bit younger than he was, and the man pulled him by the sleeve toward a bus. After speaking to the bus driver, he pushed Isaac onto the bus. "*Troi dirhams,*" the driver said, and Isaac paid him. He was the only passenger on the bus, so he had his pick of seats. He chose one next to the window about a quarter of the way back. "*Ici,*" the bus driver called to him, pointing to the seat right behind him.

"Thank you," Isaac called back. "I am comfortable here."

"*Ici. C'est mieux,*" the driver insisted, and though Isaac didn't see what was better about it, he moved up to the seat behind the driver.

The driver was smoking, and the smoke wafted slowly toward him, riding on the thick, hot air. Isaac opened the window and leaned out, but the smoke reached him anyway, mixing with the smells of diesel and hot fruit. He concentrated on not coughing, counting his breaths—in and out, in and out—for he did not want the bus driver to think he was a nuisance, an old man, a foreigner who wanted to deprive him of one of his few pleasures. After a while, passengers started to board the bus, and the smell of smoke mingled with the smell of sweat. A young man with a duffel bag sat down next to him and lit a cigarette. This was the true test of endurance. The young man tapped Isaac on the shoulder, and when Isaac turned to him, he offered him a cigarette.

"*Non, merci,*" Isaac said. "*Je ne fume pas.*"

"Pff," the young man snorted.

"I have asthma," Isaac explained, and the young man smiled skeptically.

The bus was full now. The latecomers were standing in the aisles. Isaac was thirsty. He had forgotten to bring water, but as the bus finally set forth, the breeze diluted the smoke, and Isaac could feel his air passages relax. They stopped often, picking up more passengers, until there was no more standing room. As the bus finally picked up speed, the young man reached over him and closed the window.

"But why?" Isaac asked.

"The draft carries disease," the young man explained.

Isaac did not argue. If he were the praying sort, he would have prayed for the young man not to smoke again. Instead, he prepared himself for the next cigarette—which didn't come. Perhaps it was too hot to smoke. The driver put on a tape, and the bus seemed to move in rhythm with the music. The scenery was pleasant—olive groves, dry earth, hills. They came to the town of Moulay Idris, and Isaac disembarked. "Not Volubilis," the bus driver told him.

"I know," Isaac said. The bus driver said something in Arabic, and some people laughed.

Isaac found himself in the middle of a small square. The green-tiled pyramids of the shrine loomed ahead. Why had he gotten off here? He had little interest in religious shrines, especially those he was not even allowed to visit, and he had been looking forward to seeing Volubilis after learning from the guidebook that the Romans "had dreamt of penetrating the Atlas but they had never managed to subdue the Berbers." At Volubilis their imperial road had ended.

Strangely enough, Isaac was not approached by anyone when he got off the bus, and even as he headed toward the shrine, no one paid him any attention. He felt invisible and consequently emboldened—courageous, in fact, though danger was not on his mind—

and though he still could not give a reason for stopping here rather than continuing on to Volubilis, he was pleased with his decision. The shrine was there, right in front of him, and he found himself walking toward the entrance. NON-MUSLIMS PROHIBITED BEYOND THIS POINT, a sign said, but Isaac felt compelled to go inside, to see what it was that he was not allowed to see, to disobey the rules for once, after all these years of doing what he was supposed to do.

Inside, there were men praying. He walked along the perimeter of the hall. What if I have an asthma attack here? he thought. He reached into his pocket. The inhaler was there, ready like a gun. He completed a full circle and began to walk around it again. Someone was following him, but he did not turn around. He could hear the man's breathing—hard, as if he were running. Or were those only his own labored breaths? He realized then that the man was not following him, but was merely walking as he was, round and round. Is that what is done, like at the Kaaba in Mecca?

He felt the phlegm rising, lodging itself in the back of his throat. He tried to clear his throat without coughing. He would sit awhile, in a corner behind a column, where he could use the inhaler, pull himself together.

He could feel the coolness of the floor through his pants. He leaned forward and pressed one cheek against the column, then the other. In the distance, he heard water. The fountain, he thought. He breathed in deeply: there was a smell of cathedrals without the incense. It must be the stone. One would not think that stone had a smell, but Isaac knew it did, knew the way it lingered in the air.

He thought of his mother. She would be waiting on the sidelines. When the treatment was over, she would take him to the chaise longue and wrap him in a wool blanket that smelled of animals. He liked lying in the sun. He liked the murmur of voices around him. He found it comforting. It was like listening to music.

The place where his mother brought him to take the waters was in the mountains. There would come a day, she told him, after five, six, ten summers, when the waters would finally wash away the asthma. He had to be patient, though, very patient. He liked the mountains, but he would have preferred being near the ocean. He had the feeling that swimming in the sea would truly make him strong.

The treatment took place in a room made of all marble—marble ceilings and floors and walls. He stood facing the wall and held on to a copper handle with both hands. Next to him, spread out along the wall, were the other "special cases." One summer there was an old bald man whom Isaac imagined was being treated to make his hair grow back. He and the bald man were generally joined by a fat gentleman who wore a huge ring with a green stone. The three of them stood, clutching their copper handles, barebacked, with towels wrapped around their waists. Behind them were three men in white who aimed the fire hoses at them and counted in unison— "One, two, three." Then the water was upon him, pressing him up against the wall.

In the afternoons he spent long periods by himself. After lunch, his mother disappeared. She preferred to take her nap in her room rather than outside in the fresh air that she insisted was so good for him. He had his books to look at and paper and colored pencils. Often, while sitting peacefully on the chaise longue, he would have an asthma attack. Sometimes he had three or four attacks in an afternoon, but he never told his mother. He did not want to disappoint her, for she seemed to enjoy the hotel. There were some other Russian ladies who were different from the Russians they knew in Paris. They did not talk about politics. His mother drank coffee with them, but she did not speak much in their presence, though she smiled when she was with them and seemed to enjoy their company.

If someone had asked him whether he liked taking the waters, he would have said that he did not, but the truth was, he could not imagine spending his summers any other way. He could not see himself riding bicycles or playing soccer. He could not imagine sleeping outside and singing songs way into the night and going for days without bathing, which is what the children of his parents' friends did all summer long at a camp for young socialists. His father had wanted to send him to camp, along with all his medicines and strict instructions about not overexerting himself, but his mother would not have it. Secretly, Isaac was glad he did not have to spend the summer with the children of his parents' friends. Although he considered them friends, he had enough of them during the year and was perfectly happy to spend two months without them, and without the noise and excitement that children brought with them wherever they went.

Still, he did not think his summers were easy—the weight of an angry river crushing his back, pushing him up against the marble wall. He began to think of the men who controlled the water hoses as his enemies—they were the Bolsheviks, and he was the brave Menshevik, holding on for the true revolution. He muttered to himself, "Bolshevik pigs," and chuckled as the first blast of water hit his spine. Though he did not really have a clear understanding of the difference between the Bolsheviks and the Mensheviks, he knew the Mensheviks were good, because his father was one, and he knew the Bolsheviks were bad, because they stole the revolution and killed many of his father's friends and forced Isaac and his parents to flee Russia when he was three.

It was toward the end of his last summer of taking the waters—he was seventeen—that one of his fellow patients, a Dutchman, died during the treatment. Isaac was in his usual place, and the patient stood to his left. The man was his parents' age, neither young nor old. They had never spoken, though they endured the hoses together every morning. Not even five minutes into the treatment, the Dutchman fell to the floor, and the man in white lowered the hose so the water would still hit him right in the middle of the back, just as he always did when someone fell. He would not have stopped until the end of the session if it had not been for Isaac, who knew immediately that the Dutchman was dead. He could see the man's eyes staring blankly at the wall. Isaac turned around and faced the water head-on. The water hit him right in the chest, and though he had nothing to hold on to, he did not lose his footing. "He's dead!" Isaac screamed over the noise of gushing water. "He's dead!" he screamed again, pointing to the man slumped on the marble floor.

Now, as Isaac opened his eyes and saw the arches of the shrine above him and the crowd of men around him, as their faces went in and out of focus in time with the throbbing of his head, he realized that he could have simply walked away, refused to be subjected to the water. Holding on had not been the only option. Sometimes escape was an act of strength.

"*Monsieur, monsieur*—" The voice of a young boy reached him from what seemed like very far away, but the boy was standing over him, pulling on his sleeve. Who was this boy with sleep in his eyes, shimmering almost in a shaft of light?

"You collapsed, monsieur," the boy explained, and then Isaac remembered getting off the bus, the shrine.

The others were talking, arguing, pointing at him. They were not pleased. The boy said something to them, and they lowered their voices, shaking their heads, still not content.

"Please," Isaac said to the boy. "Help me up."

"But you are too weak," the boy answered, so Isaac got up by himself. The boy tried to help him then, but Isaac pushed him away.

"I am not a child," he said, realizing that this must sound strange to the boy, who was, in fact, a child. The men surrounded him, moving in. "What do they want?" Isaac asked the boy.

"It is nothing," the boy said. "Come." He took Isaac's hand, and they walked toward the door. When they reached the door, Isaac had to fight off the urge to turn around, to wave at the surly crowd they had left behind. "Go now," the boy ordered him, and Isaac walked out the door.

On the bus back to Meknes, there were musicians. They did not stop between songs, or perhaps what they were playing was one continuous song folding back on itself, repeating rhythms and melodies and then diving into the unknown without warning. One of the musicians squeezed through the standing passengers, collecting money. Isaac was generous, as he was pleased with their performance and imagined that it was not easy to play so vigorously while standing in a moving bus, especially when the temperature was surely over one hundred degrees. They were on their way to a wedding, they told him, an important wedding of the daughter of an important man. "You must come. You cannot leave Morocco without having gone to a wedding," they said, and the drummer wrote the address on the inside cover of a matchbook and handed it to Isaac.

"Thank you," Isaac said, putting the matchbook into his pocket.

They began playing again, and he kept his eyes closed, concentrating on the music. There was something about it—the combination of all the seemingly contradictory sounds—that was strangely peaceful, almost like Berlin after the war. He could see Ulli at the kitchen table, leaning in like a woman in a Vermeer, but it was nighttime and there was no light coming in through a window, no scene outside a window. There was no window at all. There was just Ulli sitting at a table, conjugating verbs. He always imagined it like this: he would be lying on the sofa in the living room, listening to her studying, and he would get up quietly, go to the kitchen, watch her from the doorway. Leo would be in the other room, sleeping, unaware of what was about to happen. Isaac would not say a word as he approached, but she would know he was coming. She would be waiting, and he would pull her up from her chair, turn her around. There was always the wall. He was ashamed of the wall, the harshness of it, but he could never think of it any other way. He always pulled her hands above her head. Yet there was a tenderness to it always, a slowness, slow the way dreams are slow, and then they stayed standing, clutching each other until they felt cold, for, though it was warm in the apartment, it was still winter and there were drafts. They wrapped themselves in Isaac's blanket and lay on the rug, holding each other until they were warm again. After a while they fell asleep, and in the morning Leo found them there and did not wake them. He showered and got dressed and slipped out the door, and they did not hear any of it because they were sleeping.

When the bus finally reached the marketplace, Isaac was drenched in sweat, but he stood up without having to hold on to the luggage rack above his head. He even lingered awhile and bought a thin wooden *kif* pipe from an old man whose fingers were stained yellow from tobacco. "If you want something for your pipe, I will send you to the right person," the man said as he was wrapping it up in newspaper.

"No, thank you," Isaac said. "I do not smoke."

"*Comme vous voulez*," the man said, going back to the pipe he was carving, bending his head, it seemed to Isaac, more deeply over his work than necessary.

"I bought it because it's beautiful," Isaac said, but the man did not look up.

"Have you been to the shrine of Moulay Idris?" Isaac asked.

"Yes, everyone has been to the shrine of Moulay Idris," the man said, still not looking up from his work.

"I have just come from there," Isaac said.

"You are a Muslim?" the man asked, looking up now from his carving.

"No," Isaac said.

"Then you are not allowed to enter," the man said.

"No one stopped me. I simply walked through the door," Isaac explained.

"God will not be happy with you," the man said, waving him off with a kingly impatience, and Isaac turned away. What would be the point of trying to explain that he had not been testing God or his laws, but testing himself?

He set forth in the direction of the hotel. He wanted to see Ulli. Perhaps she had changed her mind. Perhaps she had been worried all this time, wondering where he was, and she would be standing at the door, wringing her hands.

He heard music, and he thought at first that he was merely remembering the sound of it from the bus. He turned around, and then there they were, walking abreast down the street toward him and the medieval gate through which he was about to pass. It was as if they were coming to get him. "*Monsieur*," the drummer called to him, waving.

"Where are you going?" asked the fat fellow who played the violinlike instrument.

"My hotel is just down there," Isaac said, pointing down the street.

"The Hotel Atlas?" the fat fellow asked.

"Yes, how did you know?"

"We play there once a year for the owner's birthday. It's a lavish event, and all the important people of Meknes are invited," one of the others said.

"In the winter," Isaac said.

"Yes, in the winter," the same fellow responded.

"But you must come with us to the wedding," said the oud player, who had been standing off to the side, seemingly disinterested.

"Thank you, but I must return to my friend," Isaac said.

"But your friend is invited too. Everyone is invited," they said in unison, as if they had rehearsed it.

"My friend cannot leave the hotel. She has her guests to look after," Isaac said.

"Your friend is the owner?" the drummer asked.

"Yes, Ulli, Madame Schlemmer." He did not know how to refer to her. "So you see, it is not possible," Isaac said, bowing slightly.

"Surely she will be there too. Everyone who is important will be there," the portly musician said. "It would be a great insult if she did not attend."

"Very well, *comme vous voulez*," he said, laughing at his own joke, and as soon as he said it, he felt invigorated. "To the wedding, where the important people are."

And hooking arms with Isaac, the portly musician and the oud player led him down the street toward the wedding.

Family

ABDOUL HAD RUN back to the hotel to tell Ulli that Isaac was on his way to Volubilis, all alone. And he was going by bus. Abdoul wanted to go after him in the Mercedes. If he left right away, he would be able to catch him before he boarded. Part of Ulli wanted to let Abdoul run after Isaac, but if he wanted to go to Volubilis alone on the market bus, who was she to stop him? "He is old, Abdoul, but not an imbecile," she said instead.

"I did not say he was an imbecile, madame, but not only imbeciles make unwise decisions," Abdoul replied. "Remember the sunstroke?"

"I am sure he will be fine. If something happens, people will look after him."

"*Insha'Allah*," Abdoul said. "But I still do not think it is a good idea."

She did not, of course, tell Abdoul that she was the one who had sent him away. Had she really expected him to take the next train back to Rabat simply because she asked him to leave? He would be fine. There was nothing dangerous about Volubilis.

Ulli went about her usual morning tasks, and at three she inspected the rooms that had been vacated that day, making sure they were ready for the next wave of inhabitants. Soon the new guests would begin to arrive. As she walked down the hall toward the staircase, she stopped at Isaac's room and put her ear to the door. It was quiet. Of course it was quiet. He was in Volubilis. What had she expected to hear—weeping, the girls chattering away about the silly things they chattered about? She opened the door, looked in. On the stand in the corner near the window, Isaac's suitcase was open, freshly packed, his clothes folded neatly. On the sink in the bathroom lay a wooden baby's hairbrush with half the bristles missing. She picked it up and held it for a moment, imagining Isaac looking in the mirror, running the brush through his thin hair. How long had he been using this brush? Did he find it one day among the girls' baby things, tucked away in a box in a closet or in the basement? Had he laughed at the thought that his hair was now thin enough for a baby brush? Ulli did not even remember the feel of her daughters' hair, the contour of their scalps. She was sure, however, that Isaac did.

After examining his bathroom, she sat for a while at the desk, upon which were some coins and the hotel stationery she continued to provide for guests despite the fact that no one wrote letters anymore. From the desk she moved to the bed, first sitting on the edge, both feet on the ground, as if she had just woken up and were taking a moment to contemplate the tasks of the day. She slipped off her shoes and lay down without disturbing Isaac's pajamas. Ulli always pictured Isaac sleeping on his back, ready to jump up in case the girls called to him in the night, trembling from a nightmare or a strange noise, though when they still lived with her, they both slept through the night, waking only at dawn like birds.

She closed her eyes. She had hardly slept after all, and perhaps here in his room she could. She imagined the girls sleeping in their beds, safe and warm while Isaac sat in his study reading, but this image didn't comfort her, for she was the one who was supposed to have been awake, watching over them while they slept—and then there was the smell of him, the sound of his footsteps behind her, though she knew it was only the tap dripping. She rose, tightened the faucet, but it kept dripping. She would have to get Abdoul to fix it; there was nothing more annoying than a leaky faucet. Perhaps, she thought, if I tire myself out enough, when I go to bed tonight, I won't hear the footsteps or smell the cigarettes on his breath. Perhaps I will sleep like a child, the way my children once slept in Isaac's house.

Ulli and Leo neither decided to have children nor took precautions to prevent their conception. Perhaps this attitude was a carryover from the war. If there were carrots in the market, they ate carrots. If a bombed-out building collapsed on a small child playing in the rubble, the child would be buried. This did not mean that mothers did not warn their children not to play in the rubble, but it also did not mean that children heeded their mothers' admonitions. She and Leo took a similar approach to having children: if a child was conceived, it would be born, and if a child was not conceived, there would be no child. For a long time, almost ten years, there was no child, and though children were vaguely part of Leo's plan for the future, Ulli was sure that he gave their childlessness little thought. As for Ulli, she did not long to be a mother the way some women do, but she was not opposed to it either, so when she finally became pregnant, neither of them was alarmed. It would be another stage of their lives, another part of the future.

Ulli did not remember much about the birth. In those days they pumped women full of anesthesia, so she had no recollection of being in pain, not after the initial contractions. A nurse came by every once in a while, but until it was actually time, she was alone. She did remember the nurse counting and telling her to breathe, but she had not been prepared for any of it. Leo sat out in the waiting area with the other men. There was something she liked about that, about men waiting outside. She didn't think she would like the way it was done today, with a roomful of cheerleaders and video cameras and breathing coaches.

The day Simone was born, there was a blizzard. When they took her home a few days later, Leo spent hours with her at the window, holding her up to see the snow and the park and the sky. Whenever she cried, which was not often, Leo took her to the window, and she would immediately calm down. Even when she was obviously hungry, looking out the window held her attention, took her mind off whatever she needed.

Since both Leo and Ulli worked long hours and traveled a lot, they hired Mrs. McDonnell to take care of Simone. During her interview she made a point of telling Ulli that her ancestors were among the first settlers, not at Plymouth but at another colony whose name Ulli no longer remembered. Mrs. McDonnell had been forced to leave her native Massachusetts because her husband was a New Yorker. She had met him at a dance during the war. His family owned a small grocery store in Brooklyn, and his father was ill and could not run it on his own. Her husband, Mr. McDonnell, was a very good man, she assured Ulli several times during the interview.

Leo and Ulli were grateful to Mrs. McDonnell for taking such excellent care of Simone. "Such a sweet, sweet child," Mrs. McDonnell always said when they returned and asked how the day had gone.

With Simone in such good hands, Ulli was able to keep working and traveling. When Ulli came home from abroad, Simone was always peeking out the door as she emerged from the elevator. No matter what time Ulli's flight came in, Leo allowed the child to be up and waiting for her mother, and Simone would jump into her arms as soon as Ulli put down her bags. She helped Ulli unpack her suitcase, putting the toiletries away in the medicine chest carefully, item by item, climbing on the toilet seat in order to reach. Simone was always a careful child. Ulli did not remember her ever breaking or spilling anything, and she learned to wash her hands and brush her teeth by herself right after she learned to walk. It was as if she were trying especially hard to make things easy for Ulli, to make sure her mother would have nothing to worry about when she was at work.

When Ulli was getting ready for a trip, Simone sat with her while she packed her suitcase, handing her items as she asked for them. Ulli's work was taking her farther and farther into the world—Jakarta, Singapore, Delhi—and the more of the world she saw, the more she wanted to be out there where things were happening, where decisions were being made. The longer she stayed away, the easier it was for her to be away from her daughter. When she was back in New York, she told Simone about the places she went, and Simone, being a curious child, asked questions. Ulli answered her questions patiently, providing her with as many details as possible. She hoped that with these details Simone would be able to picture her when she was gone, see her in her hotel room with the windows wide open and the fan spinning, hear the horns honking and rain falling on the roof, just as Ulli could picture Simone sitting on the living room rug paging through her favorite book, whispering the story to herself as she went along.

Simone was especially fascinated by the fans. Ulli had likened them to helicopters. "Helicopters in the room?" Simone had asked.

"Just the blades," Ulli explained. "The things that spin and move the air around."

"Can I see the helicopters?"

"Someday," Ulli said.

Of course, Ulli knew that she could not take Simone with her. Still, she liked thinking of them together, walking hand in hand through a busy market, eating a breakfast of tropical fruits on a sunny patio, and Ulli hoped her absences would inspire in Simone a sense of adventure, a desire to go out and see the world, though it turned out that it was Juliet who ended up being the restless one.

Juliet was born in September of 1961, just eighteen months after Simone. The pregnancy was a surprise, though Ulli knew it shouldn't have been.

"I hope it's another girl," Leo said when she told him.

"Why?" Ulli asked.

"Girls are better," he said.

"Why are girls better?" Ulli asked.

"They don't have to go to war," Leo said, and Ulli thought about what the Russian soldiers had done. Leo was right. Girls don't have to go to war; the war comes to them.

They named her Juliet after Leo's grandmother, who died in the flood, not after Romeo's Juliet, though that is what people always assumed. Perhaps if Simone and Juliet had been clinging children who woke up in the middle of the night shaking with fear of monsters, or if one of them had been sickly, born with a bad heart like Leo or suffering from asthma like Isaac, Ulli would have given up her work. Perhaps not. But her daughters did not cry out in the night. Even when they got sick, when their bodies were burning up with fever, they were calm.

Sometimes when Ulli was far away, a sudden shot of fear would run through her, hit her right in the stomach, and she was sure that something had happened to Simone or Juliet, that one of them had fallen and hit her head on the corner of the glass coffee table or that Mrs. McDonnell had forgotten to raise the bars of the crib and the baby had tumbled onto the floor. The only way Ulli could calm down was to imagine running through the streets to their apartment, running up the stairs, for the elevator was always so slow, bursting into the living room, only to find Juliet sleeping soundly in her crib and Simone playing with her stuffed animals on the living room floor with Mrs. McDonnell nearby, sitting in the armchair, listening to one of her radio shows.

As much as Ulli missed her daughters, when she was home in New York for long stretches at a time and immersed in the day-to-day drudgery of her family's existence, she was often overcome by an overwhelming desire to flee. It was not uncommon that sometimes, when she was in the middle of bathing them or when Simone wanted Ulli to read her the same book over and over because it was raining outside and they could not go to the park, Ulli had to summon all her willpower not to scream or run out of the room. Sometimes, after work, the dread of going home was so great that she would stop first at a hotel bar to have a drink, to ease the transition from words that carried with them the weight of nations to words like *silly Billy* and *pajamas* and *nighty-night*.

Ulli wondered whether her mother had felt this too, the day-in-and-day-out drudgery of motherhood, but she did not write to ask her, nor did she tell Leo how she felt. He was working more now too and often did not come home until late. What he did when Ulli was gone she did not know, did not ask, but that was something she did not let herself think about. She worried, instead, about his heart, imagining him collapsed in the street or at his desk at the office, and her own heart would start to beat faster.

When Leo was home, however, he cheerfully helped out more than she supposed other fathers did, much more than her colleagues, whose wives were all home safe while they were on the other side of the world, much more than her father, who had always come home late and, as far as she could remember, had never even tied her shoelaces.

Once, when she was out with her colleagues and they were talking about their children, bragging about the usual things—their athletic accomplishments, their grades and musical talents—Ulli asked whether they thought their wives were happy just taking care of the children. "Don't you think they get bored?" she said.

The men all looked at her as if she were asking whether they thought their wives were having affairs, and then they laughed, as if they suddenly realized that she was joking.

"I'm serious," Ulli said. "I get completely bored if I have to spend an entire day with them alone. Don't you?" Of course they had never spent a day alone with their children. All they had to do was take their kids out for ice cream or bring them an exotic gift from India, and—when they were all having drinks halfway around the world—talk with their colleagues about how wonderful their kids were.

"I guess I never thought about it that way," one of them said. Ulli lit a cigarette and called over the waiter. "This round's on me," she said, and her colleagues did not protest.

She wondered now what Isaac would have said if she had talked to him about what she was feeling. Perhaps he would have had some good advice, but perhaps not. Perhaps he would not have understood at all. Neither Leo nor Ulli, nor Isaac himself, could have known that he would be so comfortable with children—a natural uncle, Leo called him. When Simone was a baby, Isaac lay on the rug like Gulliver, his long legs and arms stretched out, and let Simone crawl all over him, grab his glasses, pull his hair. Then he scooped her up and galloped around the house.

One day shortly after Simone turned three, Isaac asked if he could take her for the weekend. There was a special exhibition at the Brooklyn aquarium on sharks from around the world, which he thought Simone was old enough to enjoy. Mrs. McDonnell disapproved. It was not right, she said, to leave the child in the hands of a bachelor, but Simone enjoyed spending the weekend with Isaac so much that weekends with Isaac became a monthly tradition.

When they were together, Isaac and Simone spent a lot of time in the library. He would find a remote corner of the stacks and set her up on a blanket while he worked. She liked the books, the smell of them, Isaac said. She would make her way up and down the rows, sniffing every volume, carefully taking them out the way Isaac had shown her. In the evenings they listened to music, and after dinner he took her out for a long walk. She liked the night, he told them. When Ulli asked him how he could get any research done with a child around, he told her that Simone never disturbed him. "She's always so quiet. She can sit on the rug in my study without making a sound. I asked her once how she could be so quiet, and do you know what she said?"

"What?"

"She said that she was thinking. 'There's so much to think about,' she said. 'Like what?' I asked her. 'Like why it gets dark at night,' she said."

Why, Ulli thought, did Simone not say things like that to her? Or maybe she did, but Ulli just didn't recognize the wonder in her words the way Isaac did. Maybe she was too busy thinking about work or trying so hard not to think about how long it had been since Leo had pulled her toward him in the middle of the night or woken up singing one of his silly songs.

Open-Heart Surgery

NOT LONG AFTER Simone started spending weekends with Isaac, Leo got a new heart, or rather a new valve for his old one. He preferred, however, to tell people that he had gotten a new heart since a new valve didn't sound particularly impressive or dangerous, and the operation had been both—so cutting-edge that they filmed the whole procedure, during which Leo's blood had to be rerouted to an external pump so they could cut out the damaged valve and replace it with a new one that would last, the doctors assured him, for a hundred years.

"You will live longer than all of us," Isaac said when Leo told him about the valve's durability.

"The valve will live longer than any of us," Leo said. "That is all we know."

They were all there when he woke up—Ulli, Isaac, and Howard. Ulli sat on the bed next to him, holding his hand. Isaac and Howard were standing, one on each side of the bed. Now we are four, Leo thought, and then he closed his eyes again, not knowing how to be among them all.

What had Howard told them? Why had he come? Of course Leo hadn't told him not to, hadn't thought to take that precaution. All he was thinking about before was, what if I don't wake up, what if they botch it? But they hadn't botched it, and there he was, alive, but he wasn't ready to be awake yet, to embrace the life he had before him. He would rest. He needed rest. Later, when he wasn't so tired, he would live, so he let their voices, the three of them, lull him to sleep.

"He's still tired," Isaac said.

"Yes," Ulli said, squeezing Leo's hand. He squeezed back, and he could tell by the trembling in her hand that she was crying. He wanted to comfort her, say that everything was fine, that he wasn't tired at all, just confused.

When he awoke the next time, he was alone. "What time is it?" he called out, but no one answered. Since speaking those few words had used all his strength, he closed his eyes again and slept, and when he woke up, daylight filled the room, and they were four again.

Later, Ulli would look back on that first awakening and wonder about Howard, about his presence there, about how he trembled when he put his hand on Leo's shoulder. Leo had opened his eyes and said, "Are you there, Howard?" and Howard had said, "Of course I'm here. Where else would I be?" Why had she accepted Howard's explanation—a fellow salesman, Leo's competitor in the life insurance business. Before Leo arrived on the scene, he told her, he had been the salesman of the year, ten years running, but now Leo had his own business and was far ahead of him. "So far ahead," Howard had said. "But I'm back in first place again for life insurance, so I shouldn't complain."

At the time, she hadn't thought about Howard, about who he was or why he was there. She simply appreciated his kindness, the way he put his hand on her shoulder and told her that everything was going to be all right, that Leo was safe. That was all that mattered.

During Leo's convalescence Ulli liked thinking about him at home with the girls while she was at work. She imagined them sitting on the floor together, building castles with blocks, even though Mrs. Donny, as Simone called her, was there since Leo was not supposed to exert himself. Ulli liked coming home to the girls freshly bathed, ready for bed, the table set for dinner by Leo, who had taken up cooking and made elaborate dinners, which they ate after the girls had been put to bed.

At one point, when Leo was strong enough for company, Ulli asked whether they should invite Howard for coffee some Sunday afternoon. Since the long-ago work parties, they had never invited anyone over except for Isaac. Howard had been so kind when Leo was in the hospital. It was, she said, the right thing to do.

"I'm not up for it quite yet," Leo said, and Ulli didn't insist.

"Of course. When you feel up to it," she said, and she did not notice that Leo had turned toward the window, where there was a cardinal perched on the ledge, watching them.

Sometimes Ulli woke up in the middle of the night and lay awake for a while just listening to Leo's quiet, even breathing, the breathing of a man with a new heart, and she allowed herself to think, then, that she was happy, but she did not let herself dwell on it, on this happiness. Now, as she lay on Isaac's bed in her hotel, she shook off the memory of a happiness that had once been, for there is nothing more painful than the memory of happiness. But Isaac was here now, and though he had stirred it all up again, she was not displeased that he had come. It had been too long since someone had demanded more of her than hospitality.

Leo had grown stronger. He spent most of his afternoons sitting on the same bench in Central Park. The sun, he felt, did him good, warmed his bones, which had been cold with fear, he realized, ever since the doctor suggested the valve replacement. When he first came home from the hospital, he worried about the business and checked in with his partner several times a day. Once he was able to go outside, however, he grew lax, and days would go by before he called in for an update, which was always the same—everything was great.

When he felt even stronger, he started taking the girls to the park with him—though not all the time, for he liked being alone—and the three of them rode the carousel on the same horse, as neither Simone nor Juliet was old enough to ride by herself. "Soon," he told Simone, "you will be able to have your own pony."

"I don't want my own pony," Simone said.

"Why not?"

"I might fall," she said.

"Not if you hold on tight," he said.

"What if I can't?" she asked.

"You will," he said.

"I will try," Simone said. "I won't be scared. I promise."

"You can be scared and still do it," Leo said. "I was scared when I went into the hospital, but I did it."

"That's because you're brave," Simone said.

"But you don't have to ride your own pony just yet," Leo said. "There's still time."

"Good," Simone said, lifting her head to the breeze. When

they were back in the apartment under the watchful guidance of Mrs. Donny, Leo wondered whether he had told Simone the right thing.

On one of the days that he did not take the girls with him— when he was feeling particularly strong, could feel not only the even beat of his new heart but the blood circulating through his veins like a kind river—he decided to explore the park, and he branched off from the main road to one of the minor dirt paths that ran through the trees. He found, as the trees grew thicker, that he was whistling, noting that he didn't really whistle much anymore, so he started singing. He was singing "Henrietta's Wedding" when he saw the man leaning against a tree, one hand deep in his pocket, and then he saw that there were more men—together—in the cover of the trees. Leo stopped walking and singing, but they had already scurried deeper into the woods like cockroaches when you turn on the light. It was so quiet, he could hear them breathing. He wanted to tell them that he would not hurt them, that he of all people would not hurt them, but he ran instead, though it was still too soon for running. He ran back to his bench and wiped the surface with his handkerchief before sitting down, something he never did, just to make it seem that he had not been running at all, though everyone had seen him, holding on to his hat, his jacket flapping. He sat on his bench, trying to collect his thoughts, taking his pulse as the doctor had told him to do, but he could not concentrate because someone sat down next to him, though there were plenty of free benches all around.

"Are you okay?" the man asked.

"Yes," Leo said without looking toward him.

"I thought maybe you'd been robbed."

"No," he said.

The man did not answer, but he did not get up.

Leo's heart would not slow down. In fact it seemed to be beating faster now than when he first sat down, though he couldn't be certain, for he knew that if he timed his pulse, the man would say something like, *So you're not okay, because if you were, you wouldn't be taking your pulse.*

"Did something frighten you?"

"No," Leo said emphatically, too emphatically, but it was said and he could not take it back.

"Good," the man said.

What if he had done damage to the valve, ripped it out of place? But he would feel that, the blood overflowing the banks. *Be brave*, he said to himself, *be brave.* He turned to look at the man, but he was gone.

He did not remember walking home, did not remember stopping for a traffic light or riding in the elevator. Once he was inside and had gone straight to the bedroom, pulled the drapes, burrowed into the safety of his bed, refused Mrs. Donny's offer of tea and melba toast, her remedy for all ailments, he was not sure that any of it had been real—the men like trees in a forest, the man on the bench. What he really wanted was a drink, but he knew Mrs. Donny wouldn't allow it. She had her orders. He had his orders, so the only escape was sleep, but he couldn't sleep, even with the curtains drawn, even with the door closed and the girls being extra quiet as Mrs. Donny admonished them to be because their daddy was not feeling well. "Is it his heart?" he had heard Simone ask.

Leo didn't hear Mrs. Donny's answer.

Eventually he did fall asleep, and he awoke hours later to the smell of smoke. The room was dark now, and Ulli was there, lying on the bed next to him in her work clothes. "What time is it?" he asked.

"Late."

"How late?"

"Past midnight."

"How long have you been lying there?"

"For a while."

"I got scared," Leo said.

"I know," she said. "But everything's fine. Feel it," she said, pressing his fingers to his wrist. "Can you feel it?"

And he could feel it, his heart, beating as it was supposed to beat, steadily, in time with the clock at his bedside ticking off the seconds, the seconds that made minutes that made hours and days and weeks, months and years, all the years that he had left to live with his guaranteed-for-one-hundred-years valve. "Yes," he said. "I can feel it."

That night, they made love for the first time since his surgery. "Are you okay?" Ulli asked as soon as they were finished.

"Yes," he said.

They lay in the dark in each other's arms without speaking. It had begun to rain, and the smell of water wafted in through the open window. "I went to the park today," Leo said. He wanted to say more.

The next day, despite the doctor's orders, Leo went back to work. His heart could not bear all this resting any longer. It was time to be productive.

Oliver

DURING LEO'S CONVALESCENCE Howard had telephoned regularly, offering his services, his friendship. "Mrs. Donny takes good care of me," Leo told Howard, assuring him that as soon as he felt strong enough, he would love to meet for lunch. Howard never questioned Leo's excuses, and Leo was grateful to Howard for not making a scene, for not showing up at the apartment unannounced.

Leo had not wanted to hurt Howard, but after the convalescence he was busy getting back into the swing of things, and the business was expanding, always expanding, taking over more and more territory, like a peaceful army bringing protection instead of death and destruction.

Eventually Howard wrote Leo a letter—eleven pages of minuscule, often illegible letters that seemed to belong to a different, long-forgotten alphabet. But Leo got the gist of it. Howard loved him, had loved him since he first set eyes on him. Leo had broken his heart. It was signed thus: *Come to me, my Leo.*

Leo sent the following reply, not on a card but at the very top of a white, unlined piece of paper: *I am sorry.*

Howard did not reply, and Leo worried that Howard would do something desperate, so every few weeks Leo went to the Upper West Side to make sure Howard was still there, was still pulling the gate shut at the end of the day, glancing back over his shoulder one last time to make sure everything was in order before walking away. Leo was sure that one day he would have the courage to walk into the store to apologize, but he never did, and most of the time he believed that he was being kind, that it was best for Howard not to see him, not to start believing that maybe there was hope for his own heart, that maybe with Leo he would have another chance at love. And then, not even a month after he had gone back to work, Leo met Oliver.

It was because of Isaac that Leo met Oliver, though it wasn't Isaac's idea in the same way that meeting Ulli had been. It was Isaac who had gotten the tickets to see Billie Holiday at Carnegie Hall without checking in with Ulli about her travel schedule, which meant that he and Leo had to go to the concert without her. Leo had wanted to sell the extra ticket when they got to the concert, but instead Isaac gave it to one of his colleagues, who also ended up not being able to attend and who, in turn, gave it to his friend, a clarinetist.

Oliver was already there when Leo and Isaac arrived at their seats. "You must be Isaac," he said, getting up and clasping Leo's hand in his.

"I'm Leo," Leo said. "That's Isaac," he said, turning toward Isaac.

"Isaac." Oliver leaned over Leo and, embarrassed by his mistake, shook his hand in a more formal way. Then he offered to pay for the ticket.

"Don't be absurd," Isaac said.

"Well, thank you, then," Oliver said. "It's very generous of you."

Leo ended up in the middle, with Isaac on his right and Oliver on his left. They talked briefly about how Oliver knew the professor to whom Isaac had originally given the ticket. Later that night, after Isaac had left Leo and Oliver at the bar where they had gone, upon Oliver's insistence, for a drink after the concert, after Leo had told Oliver about his heart and Ulli and the girls, when they were lying in bed in Oliver's apartment on West End Avenue listening to Artie Shaw—the world's greatest clarinetist, according to Oliver, even though he had given up on the instrument and escaped to Spain, leaving only silence—Oliver told Leo that until the moment Isaac stood up and announced that he was going home, he had assumed that Isaac and Leo were lovers.

"Don't be absurd," Leo said, and Oliver laughed.

"And during intermission, as you were navigating the row, squeezing by the knees of the people who were seated, Isaac lost his balance for a moment and steadied himself by putting his hand on your shoulder. If you could have seen yourselves, you would have thought the same thing."

"I guess it's because we've known each other for a long time. We were in the war together," Leo said, but he did not want to talk about war that night, that first night with Oliver. There would be time for all that. He knew there would be, and he knew, after Oliver played "All of Me," standing naked in the bedroom, his eyes half closed, as if the sound of the music were visible, as if it were too bright, too raw and beautiful to look at head-on, there would be plenty of time to tell Oliver everything. On that first night with Oliver he wanted only to lie there with him and not think about everything he would eventually tell him and about the fact that soon he would have to get up, put on his clothes, and go out into the night to his apartment, where Mrs. Donny was keeping watch over his children.

He kept Oliver a secret until one muggy summer evening when Ulli was out of town and Isaac stopped by without calling first. After they had finished the quart of pistachio ice cream that Isaac had brought and the girls were in bed, Isaac and Leo sat in the living room with the windows wide open, hoping for a breeze, drinking Jack Daniel's on the rocks.

"Things cannot go on this way," Isaac said, jiggling the ice in his drink as he always did.

"What things?" Leo asked.

"Whatever it is that's making Ulli miserable," Isaac said.

"Did she tell you she's unhappy?"

"She doesn't have to tell me, Leo," Isaac said.

Of course he knew, Isaac, his goddamn conscience.

"Even the girls know something is wrong," Isaac added.

"How do you know that?"

"Simone told me that when she gets up in the middle of the night, she finds you asleep on the couch. She says she watches you sleep."

"She gets up in the middle of the night?"

"She's very quiet, walks on her tippy toes."

"How long has this been going on?" Leo asked.

"A while."

"Why didn't you tell me?"

"It was a secret. Simone made me promise not to tell."

But Leo suspected that it was Isaac who had wanted to keep it a secret, hoping, perhaps, that if no one intervened, things would get so bad between him and Ulli that they would separate and Ulli would come running to Isaac, who would, Isaac believed, love her forever and never leave her, never betray her as he had done.

"So why are you telling me now?" Leo asked.

"I'm telling you because I want to help," Isaac said. He did not say that he could not bear to think of Simone waking up in the middle of the night with that feeling in her gut that something was wrong, that what she had held as true—her parents' love for each other—might not be a truth at all. "Why don't I take them this weekend, so you and Ulli can talk."

"I don't think so," Leo said.

"You have to tell her," Isaac said. "That's a beginning."

"I don't know how to begin," Leo said.

"Is it Oliver?" Isaac asked.

"Yes," Leo said.

"I knew it," Isaac said sadly, as if he had sensed that someone he cared about had died and now it had been confirmed.

"It's different this time, with Oliver."

"Different from what?"

"From the others."

"There have been others?"

"They didn't mean anything."

"Not Bidor? He didn't mean anything?"

"No, I mean, yes, he meant something. He was the first."

"If only you had left Ulli alone," Isaac said.

"But I loved her. I did, I do."

"That is not love," Isaac said.

"What do you know about love?" Leo asked.

Isaac set his glass down on the coaster and walked to the door, where he paused, turned toward Leo, and said, "You must tell her."

"I'm sorry," Leo said, but Isaac had already pulled the door shut, gently, the way he did when he closed the door to the girls' room after looking in on them.

Ulli came home a few days later, and on Saturday she and Leo dropped the girls off at Isaac's. Once they were back home, once they had poured drinks and were sitting across from each other at the dining room table, where Leo had insisted they sit because the sofa was too soft, like water, he began with Bidor. He told Ulli about the night, the desert, the moon, and Ulli listened, smoking, saying nothing, so he kept talking.

She was on her sixth cigarette when he finished with the Uzbeks, and still she said nothing, so he told her about the bird bars and the back rooms and Howard, and how he didn't know whether Howard really needed glasses or whether they were just part of his disguise, but Ulli was not interested in Howard. She wanted to know about the back rooms.

"Are you sure?" Leo asked, and Ulli said she was sure, so he told her, because now that he had started, there was no point in trying to protect her. Perhaps, he thought, if she could imagine the sex itself, she would understand that he could not change who he was no matter how much he loved her, and he did love her. He kept telling her that, but she did not want to hear about love.

He described it all, hoping that when it came time to tell her about Oliver, the real reason he had to leave, he would not have to talk about Oliver in that way. He did not want to talk about what it felt like to be inside Oliver. He did not want her to think about how difficult it was after a long afternoon and evening in bed with Oliver for him to come home to Ulli and the girls. He did not tell Ulli about how, after they made love, Oliver played the clarinet, but he did tell Ulli that Oliver was a clarinetist.

"A sad instrument," she said.

"A sad and beautiful instrument," Leo said. But there was nothing sad about Oliver playing sad music on the clarinet.

Leo did not tell Ulli that he and Oliver walked in the park at dusk or that, even though Oliver was with the New York Philharmonic, he played those silly songs for Leo—"Yes! We Have No Bananas"—the songs they had sung in Berlin, drunk on vodka and the cold and being alive. That, he thought, would have been worse for her than imagining their lovemaking.

Switzerland

WHAT ULLI THOUGHT about when she thought about Leo and Oliver was passion, the taut muscles, the sweat, the hardness of it all, and she could not help but think that all the time they had been together, Leo had been longing for her opposite. It made her sick because it negated her. Yet she could not stop herself from imagining them together. She clung to Leo, forced him to touch her, to be inside her. "Just one last time, so I can remember," she said, and he obliged her again and again, the desperate act ending always in tears and regret. "When we were making love before, in Berlin, was it ever only us, was it ever just me?" she asked time and time again.

"Of course," Leo said, which was not a lie, though they both knew that it was also not the truth.

Ulli went one evening after work to the Pink Parakeet. She sat in the corner watching the men come in and out of the back room. At one point an elderly gentleman who was sitting at the bar bought her a drink.

"I hope you like Manhattans. I couldn't decide whether you were a Manhattan or a martini gal."

"I like both," Ulli said.

"Are you waiting for someone?"

"Not really," Ulli said.

"That is the story of my life—not really waiting for someone," the elderly gentleman said, laughing, though there was, Ulli thought, nothing funny at all about what he had said. On the contrary, it struck her as one of the saddest things anyone had ever said to her, and for just a moment she allowed herself to be relieved that this would not be Leo, that Leo would not be an elderly man in a bar not really waiting for anyone, but that meant that she would be the old woman alone in a bar or a café or a bedroom, waiting for no one. "Thank you for the drink," Ulli said, getting up abruptly. "I must be going. My husband will be waiting."

But he wasn't waiting. Isaac was, and Leo was gone. *I don't want to cause you any more suffering*, said the note from Leo.

Ulli wanted Isaac to leave her alone. "I'll be fine," she said, but Isaac stayed anyway, though he did not disturb her, retiring to the girls' bedroom, where he slept on the floor on a pallet made of blankets. Ulli could not bring herself to lie down on their bed, so she poured a drink and sat in the dark in a chair by the window. She was hungry, but the thought of food repulsed her, so she sipped vodka, looking out the window, focusing on the light of a streetlamp that was in her direct line of vision, trying not to imagine Leo's body against hers, trying not to remember his smell, but the more she tried to put him out of her mind, the more he was there.

She went to the bathroom, put down the toilet seat, and sat to wait for morning, when she could go to work and lose herself in other people's words. She closed her eyes, but it made her dizzy, so she opened them again, and there was Leo's razor on the sink, as if it had been waiting for her. Her hand was steady despite the vodka. She made six tiny slits on the inside of her thigh, and for the first time since Leo's revelation, she felt calm, the kind of calm, she imagined, that comes at the threshold of death, when all one can feel is pain. It was as if she were standing at the edge of an abyss and knew she was going to jump, and then Simone opened the bathroom door. "I saw the light on," she said without entering the bathroom. Ulli knew she should say something comforting, but she couldn't bring herself to do it, to assure her daughter that everything was fine when it wasn't. She should have gotten up, carried her back to her room, and read her a story about a mermaid or an orphan who discovers that his parents are alive and have been looking for him for years and now they have found him and taken him home to the palace where they live.

Finally it was Simone who spoke. "Go to bed now, Mommy," she said calmly.

"I will in a minute," Ulli said. Simone lingered, waiting for Ulli to leave the bathroom with her. Ulli looked down at the floor, counting the tiles, until Simone whispered, "Good night" and she could hear the soft rustle of slipper pajamas on the wooden floor. For a long time Ulli stayed in the bathroom, holding the razor blade in her hand, not moving. Finally she put the blade back in Leo's razor and went into the bedroom.

In the morning, she was glad Isaac was there to take care of getting the girls ready for Mrs. Donny's arrival while she drank coffee and ate a piece of black bread with butter and honey that Isaac had brought from the Ukrainian bakery. "It will make you strong," he said, and she ate it obediently because she had not eaten a thing since the day before.

As Isaac and the girls went about the morning routine, she could hear Simone calling out gleefully, "Long may she reign, long

may she reign," and each time Isaac responded with an even more
gleeful "long may she reign."

"What was that all about?" she asked Isaac after the girls were
dressed and Mrs. Donny had taken over.

"Oh it's just something we say," Isaac said, "something silly
we read in a book about a queen who baked a cake that reached
the clouds and was big enough for everyone in the kingdom to
enjoy."

"That's why she's been asking us lately if we could bake a cake
as tall as our building."

"What did you tell her?"

"I told her it would be very difficult, almost impossible. I suppose that wasn't very encouraging."

"As long as there's hope," Isaac said. "Children must be able to
hope that they could someday bake a cake that reaches the clouds
and believe that if they did, they would share it with everyone."

"But they never do. Share, I mean."

"No," Isaac said, "but that's what I love about being with the
girls. It reminds me of my own childhood, when I believed that
kings and queens could be good and that soldiers were brave."

"I don't remember believing that as a child. I remember believing in heaven and that if I was good, I would get to go there one day
and fly around with angels."

"My parents made sure that I didn't believe in heaven," Isaac said.

"But they let you believe in the goodness of kings and the bravery of soldiers?"

"Because they believed it themselves. Maybe the only way they
could continue believing that some causes were worth dying for
was by passing that belief on to me, though they didn't do a very
good job, I'm afraid."

"You don't think there are some causes worth dying for?"

"No," Isaac said.

"I don't want them to be afraid to stand up for what is right." She did not say that she wished she had been strong enough to do so, but Isaac understood.

"These are different times. Their lives will be different from ours, more hopeful," he said.

Maybe there was hope for others, but not for her, Ulli thought. She had survived a war, found Leo, moved to a new continent, had children, and now Leo was gone, like the family who had lived in the apartment in Berlin. How easily they had faded. How quietly their photographs had remained tucked away in the backs of drawers while the apartment took on the rhythms of her life. Yet Leo's presence was even stronger now than before he left. His smell was in the towels and sheets; his laughter clung to the walls, reminding her that what she had thought was real had been only a dream, and she felt that if Leo no longer thought about her, she would cease to exist.

"Why don't I take the girls for a couple of weeks until you and Leo figure out what to do," Isaac suggested.

"Are you sure it won't be too much for you?" she asked, though she knew it wasn't. Isaac was so good with them, so calm. He could carry them both at the same time—Simone on his back, her arms wrapped around his chest, Juliet in his arms.

"Of course not," Isaac said. "I think it's for the best."

"We could tell them that Leo and I have to go away for business, but that we'll return in two weeks, in time for Simone's fourth birthday. I don't want to tell them anything until we know what's going to happen."

"Of course not," Isaac said.

The birthday celebration was the first time Ulli and Leo had been together since Leo left the note, left all his clothes, even his toothbrush to remind her of him. On the day of Simone's fourth birthday, Ulli, Leo, and Isaac took Simone and Juliet to Radio City Music Hall and then out for ice cream at Schrafft's. Ulli and Leo bought Simone a set of handmade puppets as well as a colorfully illustrated book of myths from around the world. Isaac's gift was the simplest. Another child would not even have thought of it as a present, but he knew Simone, knew her better than Ulli did. His gift was a telegram. Isaac sent it with the following message: HAPPY BIRTHDAY, MY DEAREST SIMONE. LOVE, ISAAC. Leo read it to her, and Isaac said, "When you are all grown up, you will have this telegram to prove that you once were four." She slept with the telegram under her pillow every night for months afterward.

The day after Simone's birthday party Isaac helped Ulli pack up Leo's things. She wanted to send them to Oliver's place so that they both would have to participate in the gravity of his departure, but Isaac called the Salvation Army and they came and carted everything away. "Fine-quality goods," the driver said as he tore the receipt from the pad with a flourish.

"Can you take it all?" Ulli asked.

"Everything, like the furniture?"

"Yes."

"Not today. We'd have to get a bigger truck," he said.

"Then when?"

"Are you sure?" Isaac asked.

"I can't stand to have any of it," Ulli said, so they came back and took the lamps and sofa, the crib, the bookshelves, the books she had brought with her from Germany, the *Gourmet* magazines, the ashtrays (there were so many of them), the record player and the Billie Holiday records, the pillows and sheets and dishes and pans, everything except the girls' toys, which Isaac brought to his apartment, though he had already accumulated a menagerie of stuffed animals and an entire arsenal of games and books for Simone and Juliet to play with when they stayed with him. When everything was gone, Ulli sent the girls away with Isaac. "Just for a few days," she told him, and he said that he would keep them for as long as she needed. That night she slept on the floor in the empty apartment without blankets or cushions.

Ulli found another apartment near the UN. It was on the thirty-seventh floor, the windows almost all floor-to-ceiling glass, and one could see the East River from every room. At first she avoided getting too close to the windows, and when she did, she never looked down, let alone stepped out onto the balcony, but little by little she grew more comfortable with the drop. Rather than something to dread, it became a comfort. She moved her bed as close to the window as possible and ate her dinners alone at a table, also glass, looking out and down at the city. Ulli outfitted the new place with modern furniture made of chrome and leather and glass. She put in thick white carpeting. All the walls, even in the girls' bedroom, were white and bare except for one large abstract monochrome painting that hung in the living room above the sofa.

Isaac hated the apartment. "The girls will be afraid to go near the windows," he said when she showed it to him just after she got the keys.

"They will get used to them," Ulli said.

But the girls weren't afraid of the windows. On the contrary, they were drawn to them, spending hours sitting on the floor, their noses pressed to the pane, counting taxis, watching the clouds.

"They'll spill their juice on the white carpet," Isaac said, but they never did. Perhaps, if they had not been so adaptable, if they had shaken with fear when she held them up to the window, Ulli would not have allowed herself to focus so fervently on missing Leo, on loving him still, even though nothing had been at all the way she thought it was.

Her only respite was when she was in her cubicle and the words took over, rinsing her mind of thought, submerging her very self. Then she could breathe. But as soon as the words stopped, Leo filled her mind, and she did not know how she would survive the rest of her life. She did not know how she could keep riding up the elevator, unlocking the door, preparing coffee, bathing, putting on shoes, taking them off, making sure the girls brushed their teeth, cutting their fingernails. Sometimes late at night when Simone and Juliet were fast asleep, she called Leo just to hear his voice. "Ulli?" he would say. "Are you all right?" and then she would hang up.

Often she woke up in the middle of the night thinking that someone was in the apartment. Even though one could not hear footsteps on the plush carpeting, she heard footsteps. She heard wood creaking. Accompanying the footsteps was the smell of Russian tobacco and whistling. The footsteps drew nearer, but she could not bring herself to rise from the bed. Instead she sat stiff and trembling, soaking the sheets with her sweat, counting the steps as they drew nearer. Every time the soldiers came, she lay paralyzed in her bed instead of running to the girls. She could not imagine how she would ever be able to protect them from real danger when she could not even protect herself from her own memories. She lay awake waiting for dawn, when she could escape into the unfixable problems of the world—the threat of nuclear destruction, drought in Africa, starvation.

With Isaac acting as diplomat, the divorce went through in just a couple of months. Isaac was pleased with the results of his negotiations, and he pointed out on more than one occasion that if all ambassadors had such an easy time of it, there would be no need for armies. It was decided that the girls would live with Ulli. When Ulli was out of town for work, the girls stayed with Isaac, and Leo would take them every other weekend when he was in town, which he rarely was, owing to getaways with Oliver and business trips to California, where the need for insurance seemed to be growing at an exponential rate, or so he told Isaac. "It would be a crime not to take advantage of the building boom," he said, to which Isaac replied that he did not think that not making large amounts of money was a crime, and Leo laughed and slapped Isaac on the back, something he had started doing since he met Oliver, though Oliver was not at all the backslapping sort. Instead Oliver greeted everyone, men and women alike, with fluttery kisses on both cheeks, sometimes even returning to the first cheek for a final peck.

Four months after the divorce, Ulli was offered a supervisory position as lead interpreter for UNESCO—in Geneva. As her boss, Mr. Sengupta, was telling her about the position, she suddenly felt hungry, voraciously hungry. "Of course we would be sorry to see you go, but it's an excellent opportunity, even though Geneva is not New York—nothing is, but Switzerland is . . . ultimately, so much more civilized than America, don't you think? Take your time. You don't have to decide today," he added, putting his hand on her shoulder.

"Can I have until tomorrow?" Ulli asked, though she knew she would accept the offer.

Within a month Ulli was on her way to Geneva. Simone and Juliet, now five and four, were to stay with Isaac for another few weeks until she got settled in her job. Isaac and the girls came to the airport to send her off. The four of them sat at the gate waiting for the boarding announcement. When it was time for her to go, Simone and Juliet presented Ulli with a small box. "Open it on the airplane," Simone said.

"Are you sure this is the right decision?" Isaac asked. There were tears in his eyes.

"Isaac," Ulli said. "We will visit; you will visit."

"Of course, but I've grown quite fond of them," Isaac said, pulling out his handkerchief to dry his tears. She had never seen him cry.

They were still there, the three of them, looking out the window, waving as she walked up the stairs and into the airplane. The plane took off, and Ulli opened the box, which was lined with tissue paper and contained honey-roasted peanuts and a note from Isaac: *They made them themselves with just a little help from me. Isaac.* All around the note were the imperfect circles that Juliet was fond of drawing, and Simone had written her name in thick blue crayon letters. Ulli had no idea that Simone could already write her name. She imagined Isaac teaching her, cupping her hand, guiding the pencil across the page. They are better off with him, she thought as she ate the honey-roasted peanuts and watched the city disappear beneath the clouds.

The Hurricane

ULLI SENT POSTCARDS to her daughters from the various places she visited for her work. She spent a great deal of time picking out these postcards, feeling that the perfect image would have more meaning than the few words she wrote on the back: *Greetings from Yogyakarta. This is the sultan's palace. Wouldn't it be fun to live here?*

Isaac wrote faithfully, reporting on the girls' progress, always including their scribblings—rows and rows of Juliet's crooked circles and sometimes two entire pages of the latest letter that Simone was practicing. At the bottom Simone always added a line of *q*'s because that was her favorite letter.

Ulli returned to New York often. She kept her apartment there, and the girls stayed with her when she was in town. She told herself that since she was coming to New York frequently, it might be best to wait for the summer to bring them back with her to Geneva. She could take them to Berlin then to meet her parents. Isaac did not pressure Ulli about making a decision. When she

talked about bringing the girls to Geneva for a visit, Isaac agreed
that it would be good for them to see where they would be living
before making the final move. "The scouting expedition is just as
important as the battle itself," he said. But Ulli did not make concrete plans for them to visit, and Isaac did not bring it up. Later she
realized that this must have been a difficult time for him, that it
was unfair of her to take advantage of the fact that he would never
push her to make a decision because he was afraid that if he put
pressure on her, he would never have a chance, though, of course,
he never did have a chance.

Eventually Ulli moved from the furnished apartment provided by UNESCO to her own place. She bought Scandinavian
furniture and decorated the walls with textiles she bought on her
travels. She liked the geometry of textiles, the lack of complications. On the weekends she was in Geneva, she went hiking in the
mountains. She got her driver's license, though she did not make
the leap and buy a car. Yet she was restless. The work, which had
once required so much concentration that she would emerge dazed
from the interpreter's booth, now required barely more effort than
walking. She needed a new challenge, something that would keep
her from thinking about the decision she had made, something
that would keep her from wishing she could go back, for she knew
she wouldn't, that she was not strong enough, not brave enough
to repair the damage she had done by leaving. So when a position as chief reporter for UNESCO's education projects opened
up, she applied and, to her surprise, since she had no experience
in either education or reporting, got the job. The first time she
had to give a presentation to her colleagues and superiors on her
findings, she was trembling so much that she thought she would
not be able to go through with it. Everyone was sitting around the

conference table, waiting attentively, pens poised to take notes, and she wanted more than anything to run to the safety of her booth, but she didn't. She gave her report, beginning slowly, softly, then picking up speed and strength as she went along, as her colleagues nodded in approval and their notepads filled with her words.

During her time as an interpreter she had traveled to many third world countries, but she had seen only the presentable parts—official buildings and conference centers, hotel rooms and the posh bars and restaurants frequented by the elite. It had never even occurred to her to explore further. Her interest was only in sitting in that booth, poised to spit out the ideas of the officials and negotiators whose words she believed were so very important. Now she asked to be posted to the most isolated areas, and instead of falling asleep to the hum of an air conditioner in hotel rooms with windows that could not be opened, she slept on a mat on the floor and fell asleep to the sound of lizards clacking and insects calling to each other in the night. Maybe, when she was stationed somewhere for a longer period of time, Simone and Juliet could join her and attend one of the UNESCO schools. They could learn to speak Wolof or Malay. It was in this way, by imagining the future with the girls, that she abandoned them in the present and, ultimately, forever.

There came a time when she traveled to New York on UNESCO business but did not call Isaac, though she believed this was an anomaly, that on her next trip to New York she surely would. Perhaps she was waiting for Isaac to tell her that she must come to see them, that they had asked about her, missed her even, but he left it entirely in her hands. Was he trying to protect his daughters—for at some point that is how she had begun to think of them—from the complications of her unsatisfying visits, or did he continue to believe that Ulli would come through, that she would wake up one day and realize she wanted to be with them, with him? Or perhaps—and this was probably the most accurate interpretation of his behavior—he was afraid of losing them. She understood now that he had been holding his breath, waiting for the appropriate moment to suggest that it would be much easier for all of them if he officially adopted the girls.

After several years as a projects reporter, Ulli became a field project manager, setting up educational projects first in Latin America, then in Africa and Asia. Since her work rarely took her back to Geneva, Ulli gave up her apartment. She sold the Scandinavian furniture and gave her textiles away to friends. They had served her well, but she did not need them anymore. She thought, at first, that she would miss her things, miss having a place to return to, but she did not. On the contrary, it comforted her to know that as soon as she was feeling settled in a place, it was time again to leave.

Most of the projects she developed were in rural areas, which she preferred because she liked living simply, as the villagers did, though she was obligated by custom and UNESCO to hire someone to keep house for her, wash her clothes in the river, cook meals, clean. When the project was in a city, she was not permitted to live in the slums, where the education centers were located, but she insisted on modest quarters, though they were always quite spacious, more than enough for one person. There would certainly have been room for the girls.

Five years after she left, Ulli was in a small village in Guatemala when it started to rain. They were celebrating the first graduating class of a school Ulli had been in charge of setting up. When the rains and winds grew ominous, the villagers, including the UNESCO teachers and Ulli, took cover in the church, which was by far the strongest structure in the village. The church was damp and cool, like the bomb shelters, and the rain and wind sounded like planes approaching. Except for the steady rumble of the women praying, no one spoke. Even the children were quiet. When a baby cried, the mother pushed its face into her bosom, muffling the sound. They waited, listening to trees crashing, listening to the wind and rain, waiting for the hurricane to lose its strength. For thirty-six hours they remained in the church, and then slowly, the wind died down, the rain withdrew, and they filed out of the church and into the square.

Everything was covered with mud, thick and alive, like blood. The houses on the hills had been swept away. The air was so filled with mosquitoes that they had to keep their mouths closed lest they fly in. All around them were dead chickens and pigs, mangled bicycles, dishes, pots and pans, and felled trees.

There was no escape for her, for any of them—the roads would be impassable for weeks—but she did not remember feeling trapped. Perhaps there was no time for that, for the cholera came on the heels of the rain. Slowly at first, the villagers began to get sick. They vomited blood and their insides churned and cramped and they lay in their own excrement. The church became a makeshift hospital since it was the only place free of mud. Ulli and the others who were not sick boiled water and spooned it into the mouths of those who were sick. Some of them became delirious and thrashed and flailed, so they had to tie them down and hold open their mouths, trickle the water in slowly so that they would not choke.

After a few days, only a handful of people were still strong enough to tend to the sick and bury the dead. At night it was pitch-black in the church, so they waited, listening to their patients crying out in the night, waiting for the daylight. They survived on mangoes and avocados, and they slept in shifts, but one by one, everyone except Ulli fell ill, so she was left to care for them on her own. By day six, eight had died—three babies, three young children, and an old couple who, Ulli learned later, were both ninety-seven and had been married since they were fourteen. She carried them outside—the old man and woman were as light as children—and buried them all in the mud, thinking that later, once the villagers were well, they would find a better, more permanent place. On the seventh day, Ulli's stomach revolted, and the fever started, but she refused to succumb, even as she heard the Russian soldiers approaching, their boots, always the boots, and the smell of cheap tobacco and their laughter filling the church. She had never been so cold, not even during the winter of 1945. It was a cold that nothing could have warmed, not vodka, not Leo's arms around her, not music playing on the radio or coffee in the morning. It was a cold that came from inside.

On the eighth day, the Red Cross finally reached them. The Red Cross nurses found Ulli pacing up and down the aisle of the church, muttering, "I cannot rest, I cannot rest." When they tried to calm her, she fought back. "You can't take them. I won't allow it," she said, and she kicked a nurse hard in the belly, knocking her down so that she broke her arm on the cold stone floor of the church. They had to give Ulli a sedative. But she did not remember this, nor did she remember the Red Cross nurses caring for her while she hovered at the edge of death for almost a week. In the end there were twenty dead. If it had not been for Ulli, the Red Cross workers said, there would have been many more.

"You are a very strong woman," they told her.

When Ulli was well enough to travel, she flew to Geneva, where, at a special UNESCO ceremony, she was presented with a plaque commemorating her service and bravery. As they handed her the plaque, she thought not of those she had saved but of the ones who had died, and she wondered whether it was this terrible impotence that soldiers feel as medals are being pinned to their breasts, whether they think not of the ones they have saved, but instead of the ones they have killed. Ulli thought of Simone and Juliet, saw them smiling and waving to her as she boarded the plane for Switzerland, and she wanted to cry out, *I'll be back soon*, but she knew they couldn't hear her, not then and not now. So as the UNESCO official droned on about her dedication and sense of duty, she focused on the work that still needed to be done, on all the schools that needed to be built, all the people who would learn to read, and she knew that she would never go back to the responsibilities she had abandoned. This was her life now, her purpose, and it was time to write to Isaac. Of course she knew that the idea of her, the mother who was no longer with them, would become part of who they were, part of their longing, their anger, but it would have been worse to take them from Isaac, who would never waver, never even dream of fleeing. Leo, she knew, would agree.

California

AFTER ULLI LEFT, Leo still took Simone and Juliet every other weekend in accordance with the divorce agreement. Instead of the usual bedtime stories they got at Isaac's house, Oliver played for them once they were bathed and tucked into their beds, even though the clarinet, rather than lulling them to sleep, kept them wide awake and giggling in their room. But always, by the second night of their stay with Leo and Oliver, they started to become homesick. "Are we going home today?" they would ask, though they never cried when Leo said, "Not just yet."

When Leo dropped the girls back at Isaac's apartment, they jumped into Isaac's arms as soon as he opened the door. "Isaac, Isaac, we're home!" they said, and they ran off to their rooms, to their books and toys, their world, without saying goodbye to Leo, who stood at the door thanking Isaac again for his help and kindness until Isaac called to the girls, "Come say goodbye to your father," and they came dutifully to kiss Leo good night and thank him for taking them wherever he had taken them.

Despite his new life with Oliver, New York bore down on Leo. His own happiness oppressed him, though he knew, of course, that it was not the city itself but the constant reminder of his betrayals. He felt the weight of suits and ties and hats, of the cold, and the drone of the subway underneath, of umbrellas, all of it pressing on his chest so that he was sure something had gone wrong with his heart; but his heart was tip-top, his doctor assured him, showing him the even lines of his electrocardiogram. "You need a vacation," the doctor told him. "Get out of the city." Which he and Oliver did, but outside the city there were too many trees blocking his view, closing in on him like water. Even his business bored him, though it continued to grow steadily. Leo and his partner had twenty salesmen in their full-time employ and four secretaries who typed the ever-increasing volume of policies and contracts in triplicate at breakneck speed. Leo imagined that Ulli had felt a similar suffocation, though in her case it was unhappiness that oppressed her, and he was not angry with her for fleeing, just sad for Simone and Juliet, for all of them.

A year after Ulli left, in 1966, Leo sold his half of the business to his partner, and he and Oliver moved to California, where Oliver played the clarinet for the Hollywood studios and Leo started a new business. Within three years he had a team of fifty full-time salesmen and offices in both Santa Monica and Beverly Hills. They bought a house on the beach. They bought a car and then another car. At night they fell asleep to the sound of waves crashing on the shore. The waves did not sound like Dover Beach's "melancholy, long, withdrawing roar" or the thunderous rush of the Johnstown flood, but they produced a steady song that played whether Leo and Oliver were there to listen to it or not. It was a comfort to Leo to know that the waves would keep on coming, keep on pounding the shore long after he could no longer hear them.

Every morning, Leo took a long walk on the beach, picking up shells and sea-polished stones that, for the first year of his life in California, he sent to his daughters once a month. He grew used to missing them, and it was almost as if this act of missing them were more powerful, more real, than having them with him.

Not even a year after Leo moved to California, Isaac and the girls moved to New Jersey. There, Isaac hoped, they would begin anew, away from reminders of what they had lost, surrounded by quieter sounds of birds chirping and crickets. He got his license, bought a car. In the winter they shoveled snow; in the fall they raked leaves and the girls jumped into the piles, and when he kissed them good night, their hair smelled of autumn.

From Ulli there was only silence. On the girls' birthdays, Leo sent presents. They recorded, according to Isaac's instructions, each gift on a card, noting the date and the title of the gift. For the sake of history, it was important, he told them. The cards were then placed in chronological order in a shoebox labeled IMPORTANT ITEMS IN THE LIVES OF SIMONE AND JULIET BUCHOVSKY. The girls kept the gifts safely tucked away on a shelf in their closet—not, Isaac imagined, because they did not like or appreciate them, but because they did not think of them as real, but rather as artifacts from a parallel life they would never live. When Leo visited, Simone insisted that they remove the gifts from their place in the closet. "We don't want him to feel bad, to think we don't like his presents," she said. Isaac agreed it was the right thing to do.

They set up the stuffed animals and dolls on their beds as if that is where they had been all along, and they propped the hula hoop up in the corner of their room behind the door. They consolidated their *National Geographic* maps and the charts of the Greek gods and dinosaurs, making room on the walls for the signed photographs of famous actors, friends and clients of their father, most of whom they did not recognize. The only gifts that were always on display were the Inuit statues Leo had bought on a trip to Alaska, which he presented to them on what none of them knew would be his last visit. They liked the smooth solidness of these artifacts. They appreciated their weight. "They feel like the cold of Alaska," they said, holding them up to their cheeks.

When Leo came to New York on business once or twice a year, he came for dinner. Sometimes he was with Oliver and sometimes he came alone, but he never stayed the night, even though there was plenty of room. Isaac, Simone, and Juliet always prepared a special meal—couscous or beef Stroganoff, the girls' favorite, and Leo always brought gifts and vodka, but both Leo and Isaac made sure not to drink too much, not to get to the point where they would start talking about Berlin and the apartment where they had been so happy together.

Only once, the summer after Simone's ninth birthday, did Simone and Juliet visit Leo and Oliver in California. Leo said he wanted Isaac to come along too, but Isaac knew that, though his presence would make things easier for everyone—he would play his usual ambassadorial role, be the good friend, the stable and responsible father—Leo needed to do this on his own. There was also a part of him that wanted the girls to be homesick, to miss him, their father. Thus he declined, explaining to Leo that he needed to devote the summer to getting started on his next book. It was to be his most important contribution to the field—an in-depth study of the reign of Catherine the Great and the westernization of Russia.

"Once the fall semester begins, there won't be much time for my own work," he explained.

"You could do it here," Leo suggested. "We could set up a study for you in one of the extra rooms."

"But I need to have access to the archives at the New York Public Library," Isaac said.

"There are libraries in California," Leo said.

"You know that isn't the issue," Isaac said.

"You're right. You're always right," Leo said, so it was decided.

But Simone and Juliet didn't want to go without Isaac. "We will write to each other like we did when I was in the Soviet Union and you stayed with Katya Ladijinskaya. Leo and Oliver's house is right on the beach. You'll fall asleep listening to the sound of the waves," Isaac told them.

"What if the waves keep us awake?" Simone asked.

"They won't," Isaac said.

"What if we get scared in the night?" Simone asked.

"Then you can call for Leo and Oliver," Isaac said.

"What if they won't come?"

"They will," Isaac said. "But you won't be afraid. You're never afraid in the night."

"But the night will be different there," Juliet said. "We won't understand it."

"You will learn to understand it. It won't be easy, but you have to learn to do difficult things by yourselves," Isaac said.

"We do difficult things by ourselves," Juliet said. "Yesterday I rode my bicycle to the store to buy yogurt and apples and I rode all the way home, uphill, holding on with just one hand because I had to carry the bag in the other. And we made you breakfast on your birthday. And we always do our homework all by ourselves."

"This is a different kind of difficult," Isaac said. "Leo misses you. All this time he has missed you." He paused, remembering Ulli's words: "I don't want them to be afraid to do what is right." "He needs your help."

"We'll try to help him," Simone said, "but if we are very afraid, can we come home?"

"You have nothing to fear but fear itself," Isaac said, which is what he told the girls on the rare occasion when they were afraid. Even though they didn't really understand what Roosevelt's words meant, he knew the words were still a comfort to them because they knew he was convinced of their truth. "It will be an adventure. Do you know of any girls your age who get to fly in an airplane all by themselves?"

"No," they said.

"There you have it. You'll be pioneers—the first young girls from Tenafly, New Jersey, to brave the skies solo."

"I get the window," Juliet said.

"You can take turns," he said, and he imagined them sitting on the airplane, looking out the window as the houses below them got smaller and smaller, until they broke through the clouds and all they could see was sky. What do you know about love, Leo? he thought. What do you know about love?

The Story of Lucas

LEO WATCHED SIMONE and Juliet walk through the gate at the Los Angeles airport holding hands, each with a Pan Am flight bag slung over her shoulder. Although there had always been a serious quality to the girls, especially Simone, this time they seemed more than serious, solemn, as if they were foreign dignitaries walking to the podium to give an important speech. Leo understood then that he was no longer their father, and he was filled not with sadness but with anger that he had been forced to make this decision, to choose Oliver over them. And so, while Leo stood there stiffly, his fists clenched, it was Oliver who ran to them, lifted Simone and Juliet into the air one by one, twirled them around until Leo was able to join them, to take his daughters into his arms and say, "Welcome, my children. Welcome to California."

They refused to let him and Oliver take the bags. "We practiced carrying them so we wouldn't be a burden," Simone explained. Leo and Oliver walked through the airport and to the car empty-handed, stopping every few feet to wait while Simone and Juliet adjusted their bags, avoiding the stares of the other passengers who, they were sure, were wondering why grown men were letting two small children carry such heavy bags all by themselves.

Each morning, by the time Leo and Oliver joined them at seven, the girls were already showered and dressed, lying on the living room floor reading or playing chess on the portable chessboard Isaac had bought them for the journey. They ate everything that was put before them, always said *please* and *thank you*, went to bed dutifully when they were told, and though they seemed to enjoy the outings Leo and Oliver had planned for them, they were perfectly content to spend the day reading, drawing, and writing in the leather-bound journals that Isaac had given them to document their trip. In fact, they wrote and drew so much that Leo had to buy them new journals after one week.

A week into their stay, Simone awoke just before dawn and snuck out through the back sliding doors onto the beach. Leo couldn't sleep when the girls were there, so he was up, sitting in the dark on the couch in the living room. He watched her tiptoe across the kitchen floor, strain to pull the door open, hesitate, and then walk out into the night. Leo didn't follow her. Instead he went out onto the deck to keep an eye on her, make sure she didn't walk too close to the water, which she didn't. The moon was full, so he could see her clearly. At one point she broke into a run, and he was afraid he would lose sight of her, but just when he thought he could no longer make out her figure, she stopped and turned around, and then she was running toward him, and he waved, though she could not see him, did not know he was watching her.

The following morning, she walked out into the predawn darkness again, and again Leo watched her. This time she did not run. She walked slowly, hands deep in her pockets. Once, she bent down to pick up something, a shell, Leo thought. She continued on and then abruptly she stopped.

From the deck Leo saw a man stumbling toward Simone, charging at her, it seemed, though later Simone told Leo that it seemed to her as if Lucas had fallen from the sky or emerged from the sand.

Leo jumped over the railing and down onto the beach. He ran toward Simone, but Simone was already running toward him, and he caught her, taking her up in his arms, but she wrestled free. "We have to do something. There's someone on the beach. He's hurt," she said.

After the ambulance had taken the boy away, Leo and Simone had to give their statements. "Don't be shy," the policeman said, and Simone said she wasn't shy at all and she proceeded to describe everything calmly and in great detail. The four of them drove to the hospital then, but when they arrived, they were told that children under twelve were not allowed in the hospital unless they were patients, so Simone and Juliet were going to have to wait in the car with Oliver while Leo went in for news.

"We could say that I'm twelve," Simone said. "I found him."

"That wouldn't be right," Leo said, and Simone accepted his decision, though later he wished she had put up more of a fight and that she had been there with him, waiting. She was good at being still. She would have told him not to go up to the nurse's station every five minutes to ask whether there was any news.

Finally the doctor appeared. "He was badly beaten, but he's going to be just fine. His face is completely unscathed. Usually they go for the face, the nose, the jaw," the doctor said, and it sounded to Leo as if the doctor was disappointed. "He shouldn't have been at that beach," the doctor added.

That beach, he had said, not *the* beach. Leo knew what he meant, understood, now, the disdain in the doctor's tone. Leo knew *that* beach, but how would the doctor know about it? Had he been there, not during the day—when it was just an ordinary public beach where families picnicked and children filled pails with sand and collected shells—but at night, when everything changed? Only once, soon after they moved into their house, had Leo and Oliver walked to that beach at night. It was a clear night, warm and still. The tide was low. After about a mile, the houses stopped, and that was when they saw them, the men—some standing alone, waiting, others together in the sand. Beyond the sound of the waves, they could hear moaning. After that they always walked in the other direction, even during the day.

"He can't be older than fifteen," Leo said. He had not meant to speak these words out loud, but there they were, waiting for a response, but the doctor just shook his head.

"You can go in and see him now." He paused. "If you like."

Leo sat with the boy, watching him sleep. He wondered whether he should go out to the car to tell Oliver and the girls that the boy was okay, but he didn't want the boy to be alone when he woke up.

After about half an hour Lucas opened his eyes. "Who are you?" he asked.

"I'm Leo. My daughter found you."

"I'm Lucas," the boy said.

"Your parents, they must be so worried."

"They don't care," Lucas said. "They hate me."

"The nurses will want to know who your parents are. They'll ask you questions."

"I won't answer," Lucas said.

"Is there someone else they could call?" Leo asked, because

he knew all too well that parents were not always what they were supposed to be.

"No one," Lucas said.

"You're too young to be on your own. How old are you?"

"Fifteen. Fifteen and two months," Lucas added, as if those two months made a difference. "I'm thirsty."

"Here," Leo said, pouring water from the pitcher into a cup and handing it to him.

"I'm still thirsty," Lucas said when the cup was empty.

"It's the painkillers," Leo said. "After my heart surgery I was thirsty for days."

"What was wrong with your heart?" Lucas asked.

"I had a faulty valve, but they put in a new one. I didn't even know there was something wrong until I joined the army. They told me it was just a matter of time before the valve would give out and I would die. If they hadn't come up with this new procedure, I would be dead by now. I was lucky. You were lucky too. The next time you might not be."

"You can never know how you're going to die. You could get hit by a car tomorrow."

"But it's not likely. You mustn't go back to the beach."

"I'm still thirsty."

Leo gave him more water. When he finished drinking, Lucas closed his eyes. "I'm tired now."

"Sleep, then," Leo said. "Sleep," he said again.

The next day, Leo and Oliver took the girls to the aquarium in San Diego, even though Simone said they shouldn't go, that it wasn't right to be looking at fish when Lucas was in the hospital.

"But he's going to be fine," Leo assured her, and Simone accepted going to the aquarium as she had accepted not entering the hospital. She marveled at the sharks and jellyfish, the huge, ugly bottom-feeders, and she bought postcards and a book about whales for Juliet with her own money even though Leo offered to pay for them.

That night, Simone and Juliet sat at the kitchen table writing out the postcards. "You're going to send them all to Isaac?" Leo asked, and both girls nodded without looking up from their task.

The next day the girls sat on the beach all morning drawing pictures for Lucas. All of Simone's drawings were of the ocean. She completed half a dozen studies of waves, both before and as they hit the shore, and then she did a series called *The Vastness of the Sky and Ocean*.

"The ocean will make him feel strong, like anything is possible," Simone said.

Juliet's pictures were all of gulls—seagulls standing alone and seagulls standing together, seagulls in the sky, seagulls swooping down toward the water.

That afternoon Leo took the pictures to the hospital, and Lucas looked at each one carefully, running his fingers across their waxy surfaces, breathing in the smell of crayon.

"Should I hang them up?" Leo asked. Simone had made him promise that he would ask.

"That would be nice," Lucas said.

"What did he say?" Simone asked as soon as Leo returned from the hospital.

"He's feeling better," Leo said. "They had him up walking for a short while today."

"I mean about the pictures," Simone said.

"Oh, he liked them. I hung them all over the room."

"Which one did he like best?" Juliet asked.

"He liked all of them," Leo said.

"But people always have favorites," Juliet said.

"Not necessarily," Simone said. "If they're all good, sometimes it's hard to choose. What will happen to him now?"

"He still won't tell anyone his last name or where he's from, so when he's released in a couple days, he'll be put in foster care."

"He won't be happy there," Simone said.

"There are some very nice foster parents," Leo said.

"But we found him. He will come back here. I know it," Simone said.

And he did. Leo found him several days later in the early morning, sitting on the beach in front of their house, smoking.

He was hungry when he arrived, and when he was finished eating the breakfast Simone and Oliver prepared for him, Leo and Oliver went out onto the deck, closed the sliding door, and talked for a long time while Simone and Lucas washed the dishes. When they finished washing the dishes, they sat down again at the table. Lucas put his head down and fell asleep right there, and Simone sat across from him until Leo and Oliver came back inside. They woke Lucas up and told him that he could stay until they figured out what to do.

"I won't be any trouble, sir," Lucas said.

"He can have my room," Simone offered. "I can sleep in Juliet's room."

Simone led Lucas to her room, to fresh sheets and a window looking out over the ocean. He wanted the curtains open even though it was midday and the sun was at its strongest. It would be like sleeping in the summer in Finland, she told him, like the white nights, and he laughed in the way that people laugh at jokes they don't understand, so she explained about the white nights and how in Finland in the summer they cover the windows with black paper so they can sleep, and Lucas said he would love to live where it was always light outside.

"But the flip side of it is that in the winter it's always dark."

"Then I would live somewhere else in the winter. I would migrate like the birds," he said, and later, after he disappeared, that is how Simone thought of him, as a migrating bird.

Lucas slept for twenty-four hours, and when he woke up, Simone brought him coffee and toast and strawberries sprinkled with sugar, which he ate slowly, savoring every bite as if it were a gourmet meal. Every so often he closed his eyes and murmured, "Delicious, thank you," and each time, Simone replied that it wasn't anything special, just breakfast.

When he finished eating, Lucas and Simone went for a walk on the beach. Simone showed him where she had found him. "Are you sure this was it?" Lucas asked, and Simone said that she was sure.

"How could I forget such a thing?" she said.

They sat down on the spot and looked out at the ocean. Lucas lit a cigarette and offered her a drag.

"I don't smoke," she said.

"But don't you want to try?" he asked.

She didn't want to, but she took a puff because she didn't want Lucas to think she was a Goody Two-shoes. She took a deep drag, pulled the smoke in, held it in her mouth, letting it out without coughing, though not coughing took tremendous concentration. She handed the cigarette back to Lucas.

"You're a natural," he said. "Usually people cough their guts out their first time. Are you sure you've never tried smoking before?"

"Never," Simone said.

"Want some more?" Lucas asked, holding the cigarette out to her.

"Okay," she said, and she took another drag.

Together they finished the cigarette, the only cigarette that Simone would ever smoke in her life.

"So Leo's your father?" Lucas asked, stamping the butt into the sand.

"Yes, but he's not our father anymore. Isaac is."

"Who's Isaac?"

"Our father, my parents' friend. They met in Berlin after the war. My mother's German, but we don't know her anymore."

"So she skipped town?"

"She left us with Isaac, our father. We love Isaac."

"But he's not your real father."

"He is," Simone said.

"So why doesn't Leo want you?"

"It's not that he doesn't want us. He knows that Isaac is better for us."

"That's bullshit," Lucas said. "So you don't miss Leo?"

"I hardly remember when he was our father. I was just four when he left," Simone said.

"But you can still want something to be different than it is. Don't you wish your parents hadn't left?"

"But then I wouldn't have Isaac, and they would not be happy. They had to leave us in order to be happy."

"Is that what you think?"

"That's what Isaac says," Simone said.

"Do you think Leo's happy now?"

"I hope he is," Simone said. "He has Oliver."

Lucas laughed.

"What's so funny?"

"Nothing," Lucas said, springing up and running. "Race you back to the house," he called over his shoulder, and Simone ran after him, ran as hard as she could, but just when she was catching up with him, she eased up, letting him reach the door first.

"I won," Lucas said.

"I wish you could come live with us, with Isaac," Simone said. "You could be our brother."

"That's the nicest thing anyone has said to me in a long time," Lucas said.

Three days after Lucas showed up at Leo and Oliver's house, it was time for Simone and Juliet to go home. Their flight left early, so they had to be up at what Leo kept calling "the crack of dawn." Lucas had promised her the night before that he would go with them to the airport, but when Simone went to awaken him, he mumbled something about not having slept all night, turned over to face the wall, and fell back asleep. "Poor Lucas," she said. She wasn't mad. He had bigger things to think about.

In the car on the way to the airport Simone had to focus all her attention on not crying. It was harder than smoking and not coughing, much harder, but she kept her eyes on the black asphalt of the road and repeated, "'Tyger! Tyger! burning bright, in the forest of the night, what immortal hand or eye could frame thy fearful symmetry?'" over and over in her head until they were there and she had to get out and they got their flight bags out of the trunk and Leo took their hands and they walked into the terminal.

"Take care of Lucas" was the last thing Simone said to Leo as he kissed her goodbye and told her to be good.

"We will," Leo said.

But she knew Lucas would be gone before they had a chance to take care of him.

"We were thinking you and Juliet should come again for Thanksgiving," Leo said.

"That would be lovely," Simone said, even though she didn't believe they would visit again, not because she didn't want to, but because they were no longer a family.

At the end of the trip the stewardess who accompanied them to where Isaac was waiting gave them both enamel Pan Am pins, telling Isaac as she affixed them to the girls' blouses that they were lovely and polite children. "Goodbye, girls," she called out as they walked away with Isaac, but they did not hear her, because Juliet was chattering away about her pin and how she had seen the Rocky Mountains from the plane and they were covered in snow even though it was summer and when would he take them to see real mountains close up?

Simone wanted to tell her to shut up, that mountains weren't important, but she didn't want to get into an argument when they had just gotten home and were all together again. Instead, she unfastened the Pan Am pin and pushed it deep into the crack of the car seat.

When the weather turned cool in the fall, Juliet transferred her Pan Am pin from her Windbreaker to her CPO jacket. In the winter she pinned it to the lapel of her ski jacket, and when spring came, she switched it back to the Windbreaker. She had flown in an airplane without her father, and when she grew up, she told herself, she would travel to every continent, even Antarctica, and she would see more mountains that were covered in snow in the summer.

The first week that Lucas lived with Leo and Oliver, they did not ask him questions. He was hungry all the time, so they prepared big meals, and he ate. He was polite and thanked them often for their hospitality. After every meal Lucas did the dishes, even though they had a dishwasher. He was always sleeping when they left for work in the morning. When they came home in the evening, they asked him how he had spent his day. "On the beach," he always said.

He had arrived empty-handed, so Oliver gave him a few pairs of pants and shirts to wear, and on the Saturday after they took the girls to the airport, they took him to buy clothes. "Pick out whatever you want. Don't worry about the price," they told him, but he looked at all the price tags and chose the least expensive items. "You need more than three shirts," they said.

He shook his head. "Three is plenty," he said. "Thank you. I'll pay you back for everything."

That Monday, Lucas was not there when they came home from work. But they heard him come in late, long after they had turned off the light, heard him tiptoeing up the stairs, shutting the door to his room gently so as not to wake them, but they had been awake, worrying about where he had gone.

The next evening, he stayed home, but they did not ask him where he had been the night before. They were afraid that if they asked him questions, if they tried to set rules, he would take off, and then what would become of him? Still, they knew that if he were to stay longer, they would have to do something. A fifteen-year-old boy could not just go wandering about at night. A fifteen-year-old boy could not spend his days sitting on the beach, watching the ocean, smoking.

On Wednesday night Lucas came home at four in the morning—drunk. Leo had to carry him up the stairs, take off his shoes, get him into bed. "Thank you," Lucas kept muttering. "Thank you, thank you."

The next day, Leo stayed home. Oliver didn't think it was a good idea. "You're getting too embroiled," he said.

"He needs guidance. He's like us. Don't you remember what it was like, how lonely, how frightening?"

"But he can't stay with us for good. It's not realistic. Eventually we'll have to tell the police. If someone finds out, we'll be in serious trouble."

"So what do you want to do, send him back out on the street, back to that beach?"

"I'm saying that we have to obey the law, Leo, go through the proper channels. What if his parents are looking for him, and they find him with us?"

"Follow the law? *We* are against the law, Oliver."

"That's why it's so dangerous."

"We have to do something," Leo said. "We can't just send him out there with no one to protect him."

"No, but we have to be careful."

"I'll call my lawyer. I'm sure there's a way."

"Even then, Leo. What if he runs off again? We can't get too attached."

"I know," Leo said, but he already was.

Lucas didn't get up until two that afternoon.

"I made coffee," Leo said when Lucas came downstairs.

"I thought you would be at work," Lucas said.

"Sit down," Leo said, setting the coffee on the kitchen table.

Lucas sat down, picked up the mug. "Thanks," he said.

"Where do you go?" Leo asked.

"Out," Lucas said.

"Why?" Leo asked.

"To make money," Lucas said.

"Not at the beach?" Leo said.

"Not at the beach. I'm never going there again."

"But Oliver and I can take care of you," Leo said. "We'd like you to stay. You could go to school. You have to go to school."

Lucas laughed. "You don't know anything about me," he said.

"I know you need a home," Leo said. "I know that if I had had a place to go when I was your age, someone to talk to who was like me, so many things would have been better."

Lucas did not reply, so Leo kept talking. He told Lucas about Bidor and how he had betrayed him.

"Why did you tell me this?" Lucas asked.

"Because I want you to know something about me," Leo said.

"I have no stories," Lucas said.

"Everyone has a story," Leo said, but he understood that if he pushed the boy to tell more, he would flee.

That night Lucas went out again, and this time he did not return. The next night, Leo and Oliver went to the cruises, looking for him. "He's so light you can carry him up the stairs in your arms," Leo said when anyone asked what he looked like.

"He could be anyone," one man said. "There are so many of them now."

They looked for Lucas every night for a month, until Oliver said that they had to stop. But Leo kept looking on his own, though he never told Oliver about it. On Thursday nights, when Oliver jammed with his jazz quintet, Leo went to one of the cruises, where he chose the youngest boy and took him out to dinner at a diner, telling him to order whatever he wanted. After dinner, he took the boy back to the cruise, gave him his card and a hundred-dollar bill, and asked him to call if he ever came across Lucas, but he never heard from any of them. Sometimes, late at night when Oliver was sleeping, Leo slipped out into the night and walked to the public beach where Lucas had been beaten. He didn't talk to anyone, didn't pass around his photo, hand out his card. He kept his distance, but he was sure that if Lucas were there in the darkness, he would find him.

Back in New Jersey, Simone filled three journals with a novel titled *The Story of Lucas*. The first volume was about his life before he ran away from home. His father was a drunk, like Huck's father. His mother ran off with another man, leaving him with his father the drunk, but after a few months she came back. Then she spent all her time crying about the man she had run off with, who had left her for another woman, until one day she found a new man and left Lucas alone again, though he had been alone all along. The second volume was about his journey to Los Angeles and how he wanted to be an actor, and the evil men who beat him up but didn't touch his face, and how Simone had found him. In the third volume he gets discovered by Hollywood, becomes a famous actor, and marries a famous actress who can't have children of her own, so they adopt twenty orphans and move to the mountains and build a house on the shores of a pristine lake that's so clear you can see the fish swimming and the rocks at the bottom.

What she didn't write about was Lucas's time with Leo and Oliver after she was gone, but at night, during those moments between wakefulness and sleep, she imagined the three of them walking along the beach, picking up shells. She thought of Lucas lying on the bed in her room when she visited Leo for the first and last time.

Then Leo called to tell them that Lucas was gone. She knew when Isaac got off the phone that something terrible had happened. Isaac made tea, brought it out to the living room. "Lucas has disappeared," he said.

"Maybe he'll come back," Juliet said, but Simone knew he wouldn't.

Later, after Isaac had tucked her in, assured her that Lucas was okay, that he knew how to take care of himself, she wondered whether he would have stayed if she had been there, but she didn't let herself think about that for too long. Instead, she called for Isaac, not too loudly so as not to wake her sister, but loudly enough so that he could hear.

"I won't ever run away," Simone said once he was there with her, sitting on the bed, stroking her brow.

"Neither will I," Isaac said.

On those nights Simone asked Isaac to type so that she could fall asleep to the sound of the typewriter. "Make it a long letter," Simone said. "It might take me some time to fall asleep."

"I will," Isaac said, kissing her good night.

On the day she finished *The Story of Lucas*, Simone decided it was time to learn how to type. She approached typing the way she did everything—with discipline and patience. She copied her favorite chapters from *A Wrinkle in Time* and typed her favorite poem, "The Tyger," one hundred times until she could do it perfectly, including the punctuation, without a single mistake. When she was able to type ten pages without errors, she felt she was ready to type out the final version of *The Story of Lucas*. She did it in one sitting, setting up at her father's typing table at dawn on a Saturday morning and working without a break until dinnertime. The next day, she proofread it and made corrections, though there were not many. When it was done, Isaac asked her what she had written. Isaac respected her project, had brought her lunch so that she could continue working. He knew she would show it to him when she was ready.

"It's a novel," she replied.

"Can I read it?" he asked.

"Not now," she said. "You have to be patient."

"I will be patient, then," Isaac said.

Simone placed both the typed and handwritten manuscripts in a box, upon which she wrote in thick Magic Marker: THE WRITING OF SIMONE BUCHOVSKY. She put the box in the right-hand corner of her closet, next to the shelf that contained Leo's gifts. After she finished *The Story of Lucas*, Simone did not add anything to the box until Mr. Modiano, her first patient, died. She wrote his story, *The Story of Mr. Modiano*, in five poems. After that she continued this tradition. When one of her patients died, she would memorialize the patient in a series of poems and put them in the box for safekeeping. *The Story of Lucas* would be the only work of prose in the box. Perhaps this was because prose was more suitable to honor the life of someone whose death had never been confirmed, who might be alive today, walking down a street, buying a pack of cigarettes, sleeping.

The Wedding

THE WEDDING TOOK place not too far from the Hotel Atlas, still within the walls of the old city, in the bride's family's palatial seventeenth-century home, which had an interior courtyard complete with fountains and magnificent tile work. Isaac and the musicians entered a large vestibule, where they added their shoes to the sea of footwear already accumulating. The musicians introduced him to the host, a plump, soft man with a prominent prayer bump on his forehead, who escorted Isaac personally to the grand room, where the wedding guests were seated on lavish cushions around brass tables piled high with pastries.

"Please," the man said, sweeping his hand in an arc through the air, indicating the vastness of his hospitality and goodwill. "I am most honored to have you as my guest." He clapped softly, and immediately a fez-wearing young man appeared and led Isaac to a table along the wall at which a group of young men, students at the university in Fez, were sitting. "Please," they said, sweeping their hands in the air above the table in the same manner as the host and making room for him to settle into the cushions.

Once seated on the floor, Isaac was surprised at how comfortable he was. He stretched his legs out in front of him and kept his back straight, like the *bufón* in the Velázquez painting, he thought, though, of course, there was nothing dwarflike about him.

The young men insisted that he eat pastries and drink tea, and Isaac ate heartily, trying all the choices, asking the young men about the ingredients. "I believe I taste a hint of cardamom and orange peel. Am I right?" he asked, chewing carefully, looking up to the ceiling as if he were tasting wine.

"We do not know about spices. We don't know how to cook," they told Isaac.

"That is a pity," Isaac said. "One cannot truly appreciate food unless one knows how to cook."

The young men laughed in that way young men laugh when they think they know more than they do. When the students learned that Isaac was American, they asked him quite earnestly about American politics and why Americans hated Muslims, why they couldn't understand that the terrorists who carried out the September 11 attacks were not real Muslims, and Isaac attempted to explain—the usual explanations about oil and fear, accompanied by reassurances that the majority of the American people did not agree with the government. His tone was that of a teacher—didactic yet patient—as if he were in a classroom, leaning on a lectern.

"Then why do they vote for people they don't agree with?" the young men asked.

"Many people don't vote, even when it's for president," Isaac explained.

"And why can't they vote?" they wanted to know.

"They can, but they don't believe in the system, so they don't vote."

"It is better to have a king," one of the students said.

"What if the king is bad?" Isaac asked.

"Then he will be deposed, *Insha'Allah*, and a better king will come to the throne."

"Like what happened to Idris I?" Isaac asked.

"Idris was a martyr. He died because he refused to turn his back on God. He was killed because of human greed."

"And why does God allow this greed?" Isaac asked.

"We must trust in God. We must trust in what he does," one of them said, and Isaac nodded in acknowledgment of what the young man had said.

The music grew louder, and the wedding guests, including their table companions, got up to dance, women in one group, men in another.

The young men stood up. "Come, let us dance," they said, and Isaac rocked to his feet and followed them to the center of the hall where the men were. "Like this," they said, raising their arms and shaking their shoulders, and Isaac raised his arms and shook his shoulders, closing his eyes, letting the music guide him, but he grew dizzy, so he opened his eyes, and there was Ulli sitting at a table of women on the other side of the room. The women did not make any attempts to pull Ulli into their conversation. She was looking into the distance, in the direction of the musicians.

Isaac walked toward her, moving with the current of the dancers, redirecting himself to take advantage of the flow. He had wanted to appear right in front of her, but instead he came up from the side, stood near her table for a moment, watching her before making his move.

"Ulli," he said, but she did not hear him because of the music. "Ulli," he said again, putting his hand on her shoulder.

She turned around then. "Isaac," she said. "What are you doing here?"

"I was invited by the musicians. I met them on the bus on the way back from the shrine of Moulay Idris."

The music was getting louder. "What?" Ulli said.

"I have been to the shrine of Moulay Idris," he said. "Inside," he added, sitting down on the floor next to her.

"I was worried," she said.

"You told me to go away."

"I know," Ulli said. There were circles under her eyes, and on her left cheek was a bruise the size of a coin.

"What happened?" Isaac asked.

"Nothing," Ulli said, covering the bruise with her hand. "So tell me, how did you get in to the shrine?"

"I just walked in," he said.

"Perhaps you are invisible," Ulli said.

Perhaps that is what you want, Isaac thought, but I am not invisible. I am here. "I thought for sure someone would stop me," he said.

"Maybe they decided you were a Muslim," she offered.

"Maybe they didn't want to have to scold an old man. It's quite something how much we can get away with at our age."

"I hate that," she said, "the pity. I would rather be pushed and shoved about like the rest of humanity."

"I guess people figure we've had our share of that," Isaac said. "Or maybe God was watching over me," he added, and for a moment she thought he meant it, but then he laughed. "You thought I was serious, didn't you?"

"Just for a moment," Ulli said.

"Well, a lot can change in forty years. I suppose we shouldn't assume that nothing has changed."

"You always said that the more things change, the more they stay the same," Ulli reminded him. "Do you still believe that?"

"I don't know whether I ever believed it. Like all aphorisms, it is true and false at the same time."

"What an Isaac thing to say," Ulli said.

"What do you mean?"

"I don't know. It's just something you would say." She put her hand to her cheek again, pressed on the bruise, felt her pulse in it, a throbbing and then a dull pain spreading into her jaw and throat.

"I'm sorry I sent you away. It's just that it's been so long, and it isn't easy. Isaac, I'm sorry."

He wanted to be angry, angry that she said she was sorry, angry about the girls, about her leaving him at the breakfast table, but all he felt was relief to be in her presence.

Four young men carried the bride and groom in on golden thrones, parading them around for all to see. The groom was not a young man. His suit, though obviously expensive and of good quality, might have fit him when he was twenty, but his thick thighs caused the fabric to pull at the crotch, and his belly strained against the jacket. The bride, who could not have been more than sixteen, sat frozen on her throne, looking straight ahead. She looked like someone with a gun held to her head.

Ulli knew the look. This was not her first Moroccan wedding, nor the first time she had been witness to the ceremony of an arranged marriage. She had seen the faces of fearful brides, makeup caked onto rigid faces, hands clasped nervously in laps, but she felt that this girl's fear was different. This girl knew she would not learn to love this man who was about to become her husband, knew that she would never want his touch, that she and her husband would not talk at night in the dark about their dreams of the future. No, this bride was sure about what was to come, like Renate as she took her first step toward the Russian soldiers. The bride sat tall on her throne, her hands calm in her lap. Ulli wanted more than anything else to close her eyes, but she forced herself to look. What would she have done if she had caught the bride's eye? Would she have smiled and waved at the girl the way she had waved at her daughters when she left them?

"Poor girl," Isaac said, but Ulli did not respond. He wanted to touch her, but he was afraid she would pull away.

The music resumed at an even more frenzied pace; the whooping of the wedding guests became warlike. Around and around they paraded the bride, whose expression never changed. The groom's golden throne passed so close to their table that Ulli felt a drop of his perspiration fall on her hand, like acid burning through her thinning skin. Her legs had fallen asleep, and she wanted to get up, stretch them, return them to life.

The servants brought food, covering the brass table with delicacies—a chicken, a plate of couscous with an entire leg of lamb, salads of all kinds, a grilled fish, pigeons, bread.

"Eat," said the women at their table, picking out the best pieces of lamb and chicken for Isaac and Ulli. "Eat, eat, eat," they said. Ulli wanted to explain that she didn't eat meat, but she looked over at the bride, who had been deposited next to her husband at the table of honor, and she imagined each morsel of food that the bride swallowed pushing its way into the tangled mess of her bowels. She imagined the groom's fingers, oily from the chicken, thick with the odor of fish, moving hungrily over the girl's rigid body, and Ulli picked up the chicken and lamb that was put before her and ate it all, washing it down with Sprite.

"I haven't drunk soda since I was in the army," Isaac said.

"And I have not eaten meat since I opened the hotel," Ulli said.

Finally, there was nothing left except the bones and a few crusts of bread. The men in fezzes took the platters away and brought more tea, as well as nuts and oranges, which the guests, sated now, ate with less urgency. The bride was lifted again, and when the young men carrying her reached the door, they paused, turned her around so that the wedding guests could see her one last time, and for a moment Ulli was sure that the bride was looking right at her.

"Where are they going?" Isaac asked.

"To the nuptial chamber," Ulli said. "The groom is already waiting there." She put her hands under her thighs so that Isaac would not see that she was trembling.

Ulli tried focusing on the music, but Renate's face kept pushing its way into her consciousness. Where had the Russian soldiers taken her when they left the apartment? Did it happen out in the cold, in the rubble of the bombed-out buildings, or did they take her to one of the apartments abandoned by their frightened neighbors? Ulli imagined an apartment like the one she had shared with Isaac and Leo, a comfortable sofa, Oriental rugs, perhaps a hungry little dog whimpering in the corner.

"Are you okay?" Isaac asked.

Ulli held her breath, trying to contain her dinner. "I'm just a little woozy," she said. She saw Renate lying there after it was over, the sound of their boots fading into the distance.

"You need some air," Isaac said, and he rose unsteadily from the floor, held out his hand, and pulled her up, and then she was standing, though she still could not feel her feet. "Come," Isaac said, taking her hand.

"The blind leading the blind," Ulli said, and they stumbled through the crowd of dancing guests and retrieved their shoes. Their host stopped them on their way out.

"You are not leaving?" he asked.

"Just going for some air," Isaac explained, and again their host called over one of the servants, who led them to the patio.

"Please," the servant said, pointing to a stone bench near one of the fountains. He stationed himself just a few feet away on the other side of the fountain. "Do not worry about us," Isaac called to him, and he smiled. He was not worried, he said, remaining in position.

Isaac put his arm around Ulli, pulled her in. She let her head rest on his shoulder for a moment, but she could feel the nausea building again, and she pulled away.

Isaac stood up, then sat down again, though not as close to her as he had been. "What do you want me to do?" he said.

Ulli did not answer, and Isaac thought that perhaps he had not spoken at all, that he had just imagined that he had spoken.

"I miss Leo," she said. "I miss everyone." She turned to him, and her upper lip was twitching the way Simone's lip trembled when she was trying not to cry.

Isaac took her hand. "It's okay," he said, and then she could not stop the tears, just as she had not been able to stop the soldiers, or stop Leo from leaving her, just as she could not keep Isaac from walking into the hotel, from taking her hand.

The Alley

Leo left the office at about eight. Right up until he got into the car, he was planning to go directly home. He was looking forward to a quiet evening with Oliver, but it had been more than a week since he had gone looking for Lucas, and he had a sense that this could be the night, that Lucas had finally returned. He could have telephoned Oliver to tell him he would be late, but he didn't like to lie, and Oliver still didn't know about his weekly searches, though he had been doing them for almost a year now. Leo followed his usual routine at the Hollywood cruise, showing the Polaroid of Lucas—the one Oliver had taken the day he showed up at their house—to the men waiting around for tricks. They looked at the photograph, shook their heads.

"Hey, let me see it again." A man he had never seen before came over and grabbed the photograph out of Leo's hand. There was something about him that made Leo wary. The real Hollywood hustlers kept up their looks. This guy had a paunch, and his fingernails were dirty.

"Nah, I thought he looked familiar, but the guy I was thinking about had dark hair," he said, returning the photograph to Leo.

Leo handed him his card. "If you see him, please give me a call."

"I sure will," the man said.

Leo started walking toward his car. "Hey, wait," the man said, running after him. "Maybe I have seen him."

Leo stopped. "Well, just give me a call if you see him again," he said.

"That's it?" the man asked.

Leo was suddenly tired. All he wanted was to go home. He wanted to have dinner with Oliver. Oliver would be waiting. He took out a hundred-dollar bill. "Here," he said, holding it out to the man.

The man grabbed the money the way he had grabbed the photograph.

"Hey," he said, suddenly joined by three other men. "I forgot to tell you something, you dirty faggot," he said.

Leo ran. He ran for a long time. He did not know he could run so fast or for so long. My heart, he kept thinking, but his heart was fine. "You can't escape," the men called from behind him, keeping up but letting him stay ahead. They were wearing him out, playing with him like cats play with their prey. Maybe, he thought, he could outrun them. He had his new heart now. Then they were upon him. He fell. They were dragging him now. Keep your head up, he said to himself, keep your head up. They let go, and he let his head drop to the ground.

"Just leave him there. He's learned his lesson," he heard one of the men say, and then they were upon him again with renewed fury, kicking him in the ribs, the head, the crotch. They lifted him up again; two of them held him while the others took turns punching him in the face. He could see into their mouths as they were screaming, but he could no longer hear. What if he could never hear again? What if he could never hear Oliver playing the clarinet or the waves crashing against the shore? He started crying, and they let him fall to the ground. One more kick, and then there was nothing.

A young man who wanted to be an actor found Leo later that night. He located a phone booth and called 911. For Oliver, the worst part was not that Leo's killers were never brought to justice or that the police had given up on the case so easily. Each time Oliver picked up his clarinet, he imagined Leo and a stranger in that dark alley near the cruise while he was home listening to "Begin the Beguine," waiting. He thought of that until eventually he stopped picking up the clarinet altogether.

"I couldn't go to the funeral," Ulli told Isaac. "I wanted to. I bought the plane ticket, but I couldn't share my grief with anyone—with Oliver. I couldn't face the girls, couldn't face you."

"I know," Isaac said. He had gone, had sat with the girls on the sidelines. "The eulogies went on for hours. They all loved him, talked about how good he was, how generous, how full of life."

"He was the only one of us who was happy," Ulli said.

"I was happy too. I had the girls."

"That is a different sort of happiness," Ulli said.

"You mean it's not love," Isaac said.

"I didn't say that," Ulli said, but they both knew that is what she meant.

"I really did buy the plane ticket," Ulli said.

"I understand," Isaac said, though he had been angry with her for not being there, for having to lie for Ulli yet again, having to tell the girls that her work was more important than a funeral.

"Do you ever hear from Oliver?" Ulli asked.

"No, but I know he died last year. His obituary was in *The New York Times*. It seems that after Leo was killed, he became active in the gay rights movement. He sold Leo's business and dedicated all the money to the cause. In the obituary it said that the last time he played the clarinet was at Leo's funeral."

"Leo would not have wanted that," Ulli said.

"No, he wouldn't have, but he would have understood that Oliver couldn't go on as before, that sometimes one has to give up what one loves in order to move forward." Isaac paused. He did not say that he understood why Ulli had given up the girls or that giving up the clarinet was in any way comparable.

"Leo made me believe that things could be simple and safe, like his stupid insurance policies, and then he just threw it all away to end up dead in some alley somewhere," Ulli said.

"Ulli, you can't blame Leo for what happened, and you were miserable with him, had been for a long while."

"That's because he was so far away, and I didn't know why, and he didn't have the courage to tell me."

"But he did. He did tell you."

Ulli was silent.

"I should have told you about Bidor," Isaac said.

"And why didn't you?"

"Because Leo was sure he was finished with all that, and what did I know about such things? I suppose I was angry too, angry with myself for not having the courage to tell you what I felt, angry because I was so afraid to lose you and Leo too. It was a trade-off. If I couldn't have you, I could always be near you, as long as you and Leo were together, but then look what happened. You left and have been away all this time." Isaac took Ulli in his arms, pushed her head to his chest, buried his face in her hair, breathed in the smell of her, his lungs reaching for her, for breath, but Ulli pulled away, sat up, her body rigid, frozen, as if the danger were right there in front of her, looking her in the eye.

"There's something else," Ulli said.

Isaac waited.

"Her name was Renate," Ulli began. "She was exactly the same age as me and had been working for our family for five years, since she was nineteen. She was from the country, like all maids were in those days. I didn't know much about her except that she had brothers who were soldiers on the Eastern Front. She had a boyfriend from her village. His name was Georg."

Renate was tall and bony, with big hands and feet, and so thin that one could see the veins in her forehead. In the evenings she retired to her small room next to the kitchen, where she made embroidered coverlets that she sold to make extra money. She always showed Ulli and her mother her handiwork before she brought the pieces to the shop to sell, and Ulli always made a point of admiring them—even though she wasn't really interested—because she knew Renate was proud of her skills.

Renate stayed with Ulli and her family until the end, until the Russians arrived.

They knew they were coming, so the night before the soldiers marched into their neighborhood, in order to keep herself from thinking about what was to come, Ulli typed. She typed faster than she had ever typed before, banging furiously on the keys, copying entire chapters from her old school textbooks. At one point her mother asked her to stop, but she couldn't, and her mother didn't ask again.

In the early morning before dawn, while their neighbors crouched trembling in the bomb shelters, waiting this time not for the sirens but for the sound of boots on the stairways, Ulli and Renate and her parents waited in the apartment. It was her father's idea. "The most obvious hiding place is sometimes the most difficult to find," he said. So they waited, listening to the shouting and the breaking windows. They watched through the tiniest slit in the curtains as the soldiers emerged from the bomb shelters, pulling women and children by their hair, the men walking in front, rifles pointed at their backs.

They heard them coming up the stairs, ringing doorbells, bashing in doors when there was no response. When their doorbell rang, Ulli's father went to answer it. "Hello," he said as the soldiers pushed past him into the living room, where Ulli, her mother, and Renate were sitting. They must have looked as if they were waiting for guests, Ulli thought later, because the soldiers started laughing hysterically. Her father laughed nervously too, thinking that this would assuage them, but one of the Russians punched him in the nose. He stood strong, so the soldier punched him again and then again, until he crumpled to the floor. The soldiers pushed Ulli, her mother, and Renate into the master bedroom and shut the door, leaving them alone to wait. They could hear them outside the door, could smell the cigarette smoke, while they trembled inside, each in a separate corner of the room.

After a while one of the soldiers opened the door and looked in, then left. The next time he opened the door, he put one finger up in the air. "One," he said in German. "One woman." They did not look at one another or move. He said it one last time, raising his rifle. He aimed it straight at Ulli. Renate stepped forward.

In the morning, the Russians cleaned up the broken glass and the chairs and tables that they had hurled through windows. Trucks arrived with potatoes and carrots, and the bravest of their neighbors, or the hungriest, emerged from their houses and lined up in the street to receive food. Ulli and her parents did not go out, but they watched all this from the window, from behind the curtains. In the evening Russian soldiers and German women strolled arm in arm as if nothing had happened. Days went by, but even when they were left with only two potatoes, they did not leave the apartment. After the potatoes were gone, they drank only water. Ulli's father believed that they should starve themselves together.

"In the beginning it will be terrible," he said, "but after a week or two, we will no longer feel hungry."

Ulli was ready to take on the challenge, ready to suffer, and for three days she was almost invigorated by her hunger, by the knowledge that soon her life would be over. She tried to keep a diary, but she couldn't bring herself to write about how she had let them take Renate away, so she gave up. There was, after all, nothing left to accomplish.

Ulli's mother preferred to keep moving, so she cleaned— scrubbed the floors, washed all the clothes and linens, even the clean clothes that were hanging in the closet. Her hands were permanently waterlogged, her fingertips fish-belly white and wrinkled. Ulli's father read the same newspaper over and over and tried to convince her mother not to work so hard.

"You will lose your strength," he said.

But to Ulli she said, "Your father is the strongest. Let him be the last one alive."

It turned out that Ulli's father was not the strongest, or perhaps he was, because aren't the strong the ones who want to live, who don't give up so easily? In any case, he could not take the hunger. On the fourth day without food, Ulli caught him eating paper, crumpling it into bite-size pieces, chewing slowly and looking straight ahead, as if he saw before him a vision of a holiday meal.

When Ulli told him that she was going to go out in the morning to find food, her father began to cry, at first softly and then harder, and she stood in the doorway, not knowing whether to comfort him or run.

"Leave me alone now," he said after a while, and she obeyed.

Ulli awoke the next morning to the smell of eggs frying and Mozart's Fortieth Symphony, her father's favorite. She thought at first that she was hallucinating, but it was too soon for hallucinations. When she emerged from her room, the table was set with the good dishes and silverware. The candles were lit. In addition to eggs, there was bread and carrots and cheese and sardines.

They devoured the food in minutes. After that, Ulli's father went out every morning to buy food. He found a place where the bread was not stale. He averted his eyes when he passed the Russian soldiers. Sometimes they said things to him, but he just kept walking. He would not let Ulli or her mother leave the apartment.

"Remember what happened to her," he said, unable to say Renate's name. So her mother cleaned and Ulli slept, and sometimes she found the energy to read a book. She ate and forgot what it had felt like to be hungry.

For eight weeks the Russians were there, but when peace was settled and the Allies drew the lines, Ulli's street fell just within the American Zone. The Russians departed, and Ulli and her parents were spared once again, spared the grim decades that were to come for their neighbors on the other side of the line.

The Americans threw chewing gum and chocolate from their trucks. Ulli and her parents ran out into the street with everyone else, and they clapped and waved and ate chocolate and chewed chewing gum, and her father started talking about selling typewriters to the Americans. It was then that Ulli began looking for Renate. For one week, she set forth every morning, walking until she no longer knew why she was walking.

"That's how I found the apartment. I was looking for Renate. Instead, I found you and Leo," Ulli said, allowing Isaac to hold her again.

"I almost told you, first during the Russian lessons and then later, when I left the girls. I wanted you to understand that I wasn't just running away from what happened with Leo. I wanted you to understand that I never felt that I could protect them, that they were not safe with me."

Isaac wanted to say that he had also felt that he could not protect them, that whenever the girls were out of his sight, he was always holding his breath and imagining the worst. Even when he was near them, when they were fast asleep in their rooms, he felt it. That is what it means to be a parent, he wanted to say, but she spoke first, saved him from being cruel.

"I never told anyone about Renate, not even Leo," she said, and Isaac realized that she had told him not because she wanted absolution or forgiveness, but to acknowledge his love for her.

"I'm sorry," he whispered.

"Please, Isaac," Ulli said.

Allahu Akbar. Allahu Akbar. Allahu Akbar. Allahu Akbar. The call to prayer surrounded them. It was as if they could feel the words brushing against their bodies. Their guardian took off his jacket, laid it on the ground before him, and kneeled. He raised his eyes to the heavens, which were beginning to take on a pinkish hue; then he bowed down, touching his forehead to the ground. When he finished his prayers, he stood up and came over to the bench.

He coughed; Ulli and Isaac did not respond. "Everyone has gone home," he said, and only then did they pull away from each other. Isaac stood up too quickly, which caused his head to spin so that he almost tipped over. Their guardian reached out to steady him, but he pushed him away.

"I'm fine," he said, righting himself.

"We are fine," Ulli said.

"Please, sit. I will call a taxi," their guardian said.

"No, we will walk," Ulli said, and Isaac took her hand.

"Yes, we will walk."

Sleep

"MAYBE IT WOULD be good for you to get away from the hotel for a while, rest. You have not rested in so long, Ulli, and I would like to see the desert again," Isaac said as they walked back through the old city to the hotel. "I haven't been in the desert since the war," he continued. "It's funny; I always thought I would take the girls, especially since they liked the heat. You could think of it as work. You will be my tour guide."

Ulli laughed. "We could go tomorrow, after we get some sleep. When I first started coming to Morocco, I used to go to Todra Gorge. It's all the way in the south, in Berber territory. There's a nice hotel there, a simple one. Abdoul will drive us."

"Don't you think a train would be better?"

"There are no trains, only buses," she explained.

"Then we can take the bus."

"We will be more comfortable with Abdoul. He knows the way."

"You are the Morocco specialist," he said, but she could tell he wanted to take the bus.

"No, let's go by bus. It will be an adventure," she said.

It was only once they were inside the hotel that Isaac realized how tired he was. Still, though they had said good night, rather than going to his room, he sat down in the lobby while Ulli checked in with the boy on night duty. He wanted to sit for a moment, use the inhaler before taking on the steps, listen to Ulli talking in Arabic in the other room. When Ulli came through the lobby on her way up to her room and found him sitting in the chair, he was thinking he would stay in Meknes for a while, learn Arabic. It would be good for his brain, keep him from losing his faculties.

"Isaac, I thought you had already gone up," she said.

"I was just thinking," Isaac said.

"You should get some sleep."

"And you?"

"I'm just going to check in with Abdoul before I retire, let him know that I'll try to sleep for a few hours," she said.

Isaac waited until Ulli was out of sight before climbing the stairs. He knew it would not be easy, and he didn't want her to see him struggling. Halfway up the stairs he had to sit down and use the inhaler again, and when he finally made it to his room, after taking off his shoes, he didn't have the energy to undress, so he lay down on his bed fully clothed. He was almost asleep when he heard footsteps in the hall. Ulli, he thought, and he got up, went to the door, opened it just a crack. He watched her walk down the corridor toward her room.

As soon as she was inside, he followed her. If someone had emerged from one of the other rooms, he might have lost his resolve.

He might have turned around and gone back to his room, but he met no one. He knocked. Ulli came to the door. She was still dressed.

"Isaac," she said. "Come in."

"I'm not disturbing you?" Isaac asked.

"No. Come," Ulli said, holding out her hand. He took it, and together they lay down on her bed, and Isaac closed his eyes and thought of nothing, and as the sun burned off the last of the early-morning clouds and the guests of the Hotel Atlas packed their daypacks and checked their guidebooks and stepped out into the day, Ulli and Isaac fell asleep.

Ulli awoke at around noon to the sound of Isaac's heavy breathing. She tried to sleep again, fall into the rhythm of his breaths, but they were getting more and more labored, his body shaking from the effort. "Isaac, are you all right?" she whispered, but he did not awaken, and after a while his breaths became less desperate, so she fell asleep again, but she awoke soon afterward with a start, for Isaac's breathing had taken on a terrible rattling. "Isaac," she said. "Isaac." He opened his eyes. "My inhaler. In my pocket," he managed to say before starting to cough. She helped him sit up, and he took a deep puff from the inhaler, then slumped down again from the effort. "Shake it," he said between coughs, holding it out to her. He took another puff, and then he fell back, and although the rattling and wheezing were even stronger than before, he fell asleep.

Ulli felt fear now, finally, not the distant fear she had felt when the man held the knife to her throat, not Renate's fear. Her fear. She could not lose Isaac now, when she had barely found him. Her whole body trembled, yet she felt calm.

She called Abdoul, and they stood over Isaac, listening to him breathe. Abdoul wanted to call a doctor, but the rattling had grown less violent and Isaac woke up and took a few puffs from the inhaler. Perhaps he would be fine. Perhaps all he needed was to sleep. She imagined the scene, the doctor arriving, Isaac annoyed at her for making such a fuss.

"Let's wait and see how he is later," Ulli said. "I'll be fine now," she told Abdoul, but he insisted on staying with her.

They sat together, watching Isaac, until the air began to cool again and the sun went down and it was night. Again the rattling grew more intense, and Isaac began to twitch and flail, though he did not wake up. Ulli placed a cloth soaked in cold water on his forehead to help stem the flow of sweat that was streaming down his face and into his eyes. She held his hand. For a while he seemed calmer, but then, suddenly, his eyes popped open. He stared into her eyes, as if he were communicating to her everything that he had not been able to tell her all these years. She did not look away. "You must go see the girls," he said. "You are the last one now."

"I will," she said.

"You promise?"

"I promise," she said, and he closed his eyes and slept.

In the morning Isaac's breathing was even more labored, and Ulli agreed to call a doctor. The doctor examined Isaac, shaking his head as he listened through the stethoscope. He pronounced Isaac's condition "very serious, very grave." Isaac's lungs were filled with fluid. His heart was weak.

They called an ambulance, and the paramedics tried to lift him from the bed, but he protested, his eyes taking on the glazed intensity of fury. Ulli believed that she saw in those furious eyes his final wish: to stay there, in that room, with her. So she told them all to leave, the doctor, the paramedics, even Abdoul.

"I will be waiting for your call," the doctor said.

Once the doctor was gone, however, Abdoul returned. "I will not bother you. If you need something, I will be here," he said gravely.

"If you insist," Ulli said, but she was relieved that she would not be entirely alone.

Ulli sat with Isaac through the long day, until it grew dark again and until long after the first call to prayer. Abdoul brought her tea and some bread and cheese, which she left untouched on the table. Isaac was tranquil for short periods, and during those peaceful interludes she recited all the poems she knew by heart in all the languages she had learned, beginning with Pushkin and ending, when the sun filled the room again with light, with "Dover Beach":

> Ah, love, let us be true
> To one another! for the world, which seems
> To lie before us like a land of dreams,
> So various, so beautiful, so new,
> Hath really neither joy, nor love, nor light,
> Nor certitude, nor peace, nor help for pain;
> And we are here as on a darkling plain
> Swept with confused alarms of struggle and flight,
> Where ignorant armies clash by night.

"You were the only one who remained true to all of us—to me, to Leo, to our daughters," she said, and she was sure he could hear her and sure that she saw something in his eyes, a glimmer of recognition, of forgiveness, though later she decided that this was one of those beliefs, like God and salvation, to which the living selfishly cling when the dying have already let go.

At dusk Isaac awoke, agitated, pulling at his hair and scratching his chest and arms and legs. Ulli could not bear to watch it, but she could not leave either, so she began pacing up and down the room. Abdoul took a small pipe containing *kif* out of his pocket, lit it, and held it out to her. "It will soothe him," he said.

"But won't it hurt his lungs?"

"The smoke is calming. It's not like tobacco," he explained.

Ulli tried holding the pipe to Isaac's lips, but he clenched his teeth and jerked his head.

"Let me try," Abdoul said. He knelt on the floor next to Isaac, humming a slow, deep melody until Isaac began to relax. He took a puff from the pipe, held it, leaning in until his mouth met Isaac's opened lips and he was able to blow the smoke directly into Isaac's mouth.

"You try," he said to Ulli, handing her the pipe. "Take some for yourself first," and she did, breathing in, holding the smoke deep in her lungs. Then she imitated Abdoul, pressing her lips to Isaac's, letting the smoke flow into his mouth.

"Again," he said, and after three more puffs, Isaac was calm.

They stayed with him, listening as the rattling got fainter and fainter, until it stopped completely and Isaac was gone.

Together Ulli and Abdoul washed the sweat from Isaac's body. When they were finished, she asked him to leave her alone. She sat next to Isaac, but she did not touch him, for he was no longer Isaac. This was simply his body, an object, like a branch or a chair. How stupid of me to think that at my age there can be anything but endings, she thought.

She went to Isaac's room to gather his things—his wallet and passport, pocket watch, address book. She got the toiletry bag from the bathroom, his clothes from the chair, and put everything into his backpack. It was his shoes that made her cry. They were sturdy walking shoes, almost new. He probably bought them just for this trip, she thought. She imagined him at the store, trying them on, walking around to make sure that the heel did not slip, that the toes were not too cramped. They were sitting neatly next to the door, waiting to be of service.

Abdoul had returned to her room when she came back with Isaac's backpack. "Let me help you, madame," he said, taking it from her, though it was not heavy, even with the shoes.

"Thank you, Abdoul. You have been very kind."

"Perhaps you can sleep, madame? You are looking tired," he said, but there was no time to sleep. She had to make arrangements for the body to be sent back to the United States, send Abdoul to the bank to bring back cash for all the bribes she knew she would have to pay to make things go smoothly, make the call, though that would have to wait until nighttime so that Simone would receive the news during the light of day and—Ulli knew this was the real reason—because she needed the quiet and solitude of night to face her.

At midnight Ulli told the boy on night duty to go home, assuring him that he would be paid his usual wages even if he left early. She sat for over an hour in front of the phone, listening to the buzzing from the fluorescent light in the entryway, trying to figure out how to identify herself when Simone answered. Was it better to go with a formal approach: *This is Ulli Schlemmer.* Or should she plunge in with a simple announcement: *This is your mother.* There was nothing in between. She tried to imagine how it would be when she walked through the gate at the airport and they were waiting for her. What if she didn't recognize them? What if they were standing there holding one of those signs with her name on it, the way taxi drivers do, or even worse, what if they ran up and embraced her? What if they cried?

Finally she just picked up the phone, dialed, and, in the end, "This is Ulli" was all she managed to say.

There was a silence on the other end, and then she heard Simone's voice. "I'm ready," Simone said.

Ulli explained what Simone already knew and said that she was making preparations to accompany the body to New Jersey. Of course Simone said it wasn't necessary. As long as she helped with the arrangements, they would manage on their side. He was going to be cremated. Those were his wishes. But Ulli insisted that she wanted to do it, and Simone agreed. "If that is what you think is best," she said kindly, the way, Ulli imagined, she spoke to her patients when they insisted on getting up without her help or said they did not need a bath. She said she and Juliet would pick her up at Newark. They agreed that Ulli would email the flight information once everything was arranged. All this took just five minutes. There were no more details to discuss, but they did not hang up.

"What did he say?" Simone finally asked. "At the end." And Ulli understood what she meant—that they should have been there with him, through the night and a day and then another night, listening to his last breaths, that Isaac's death was yet another thing she had taken from her daughters. The fluorescent lights flickered. The buzzing stopped. And then it began again.

Acknowledgments

Winter Kept Us Warm and the characters contained therein would never have made it beyond the borders of my mind and the memory of my laptop had it not been for the help and encouragement of the following people and organizations:

Thank you, Carolyn Kuebler, and the *New England Review* for setting the Buchovsky family free and sending them on their first journey into the world. Thank you, Nancy Zafris and the University of Georgia Press, for choosing my collection for the Flannery O'Connor Award for Short Fiction and, thus, breathing life into my diminished spirit. Thank you to my steadfast and true agent, Esmond Harmsworth, who stuck with me and this book until it could find its proper home. Thank you, Dan Smetanka, for taking on this project and for your brilliant and direct editorial guidance. Thank you to all the hardworking Counterpointians: Jennifer Kovitz, Alisha Gorder, Megan Fishmann, Sarah Baline, Wah-Ming Chang, Maxine Bartow, and Nicole Caputo. Thank you, Andy Allen, for the wonderful cover.

For giving me three and a half quiet and productive weeks of writing in Spain, the country where I first started writing in earnest decades ago, I thank the Fundación Valparaíso.

For her constant support and encouragement through childhood and adolescence and to this day, I thank my sister, Catherine Raeff. Thank you, also, to my friends around the world who have stood by my writing and to my students past and present who keep me "real" and hopeful about the future. Thank you to my parents for their stories, many of which were the seeds for this book.

Finally and always, I owe all of my accomplishments, literary and otherwise, to my wife, Lori Ostlund, my first reader, my editor, my muse, and, still, my harshest critic.

About the Author

ANNE RAEFF's short story collection, *The Jungle Around Us*, won the 2015 Flannery O'Connor Award for Short Fiction. The collection was a finalist for the California Book Award and named one of the 100 Best Books of 2016 by the *San Francisco Chronicle*. Her stories and essays have appeared in *New England Review*, *ZYZZYVA*, and *Guernica*, among other places. She lives in San Francisco with her wife and two cats.